Acclaim
America

"*American Static* is a have written it but Ton the mold for what the plastic copies."

—

"*American Static* grabs a dirty, dangerous tour of San Francisco. Tom Pitts serves up noir just the way you want it—dark, relentless, and inevitable."

—Rob Hart author of *South Village*

"*American Static* is a remarkable novel, a ride with brilliant twists and turns and a relentless momentum, racing to an ending both unavoidable and unexpected."

—Steve Weddle, author of *Country Hardball*

"*American Static* is a hot dose of pure adrenaline that will leave you gasping for breath and begging for more."

—Owen Laukkanen, author of *The Forgotten Girls*

Acclaim for *Hustle*

"Bold, honest and daring."

—Todd Robinson, author of *Rough Trade*

"...quick-paced and dark, sad and funny as hell, with a Thompson-esque cast of characters and echoes of Bukowski in its poetic sensitivity."

—Ro Cuzon, author of *Under the Dixie Moon*

"Unflinching and without apology."

—Joe Clifford, author of *December Boys*

AMERICAN STATIC

ALSO BY TOM PITTS

Knuckleball
Piggyback
Hustle

TOM PITTS

AMERICAN STATIC

DOWN & OUT
BOOKS

Down & Out Books
3959 Van Dyke Rd, Ste. 265
Lutz, FL 33558
www.DownAndOutBooks.com

The characters and events in this book are fictitious. Any similarity to real
persons, living or dead, is coincidental and not intended by the author.

Edited by Chris Rhatigan
Cover design by Eric Beetner

ISBN: 1-943402-84-1
ISBN-13: 978-1-943402-84-7

To my father,
who remains my greatest hero.

Be sober, be vigilant;
because your adversary the devil,
as a roaring lion, walketh about,
seeking whom he may devour.
—Peter 5:8:11

"We all grow up to be our fathers,
marrying the daughters of the
men we once despised."
—Micah Schnabel, "American Static"

CHAPTER ONE

It came as soon as he touched the flame to the end of his cigarette. Like a brick to the back of his head. The pain was searing, white-hot. For a split-second he thought he'd been struck with an aneurysm, but he saw his cigarette fly out in front of him and he knew that he'd been punched.

He crumpled toward the ground, powerless to the pain. The shock of it paralyzing his senses. He lay there confused, not knowing what was happening to him. "Gimme the bag, motherfucker."

Then a kick. A hard one, into his right kidney. Then another at the base of his spine.

"Give me the fuckin' bag."

The bag was a knapsack, a backpack tightly secured around his shoulders. He folded his arms into his chest and pulled himself into a fetal position. Whoever his attacker was, they circled round in front of him. He could see feet now, boots. Two more sloppy kicks to his stomach. He felt the bag being pulled from his back. Instinctively, his arms locked onto one another and held tight. There was a strong torque in his shoulders as the straps dug in, followed by the sound of the assailant's labored grunts. When they pulled the bag, his body moved with it, sliding across the gravel.

There were two of them, maybe more. One in front, kicking with those big black boots, and one behind, pulling at the bag. He held as still as he could, willing the attack to end through inaction. He waited for more blows. And they came. Kicks to his legs now, his lower back again, and to his head and face. He was sure they'd broken his nose. The pointed kicks turned to heeled stomps and, finally, he gave in. His arms let go as his mind flicked on and off in solids of white and black. He felt the bag being roughly yanked away.

He thought maybe he was unconscious, but he heard the crunch of boot steps on gravel departing. He lay warm in the sun, hot where the contusions throbbed, wet where blood trickled. In front of him he saw his cigarette, barely burning, a fine wisp of smoke curling up from its resting spot. He watched it, wanting it more than anything.

"What the hell's a matter with you, son?"

Steven opened his eyes. The first thing he saw was a pair of mirrored sunglasses. The sun reflected off them just right. It sent a piercing ray into his retinas. Fucking cops.

The man behind the sunglasses said, "Don't you know that smoking can be detrimental to your health?"

A set of near-perfect white teeth appeared below the sunglasses and out came a chuckle. Not a self-aggrandizing laugh, but a cool chuckle. Steven tried to focus and saw the man was wearing a dark brown leather jacket and jeans. Not a cop. Probably not, anyway. A hand came out and pulled Steven's forearm and he straightened himself up, the axis of the earth still pitching and tilting.

"Shit, son. They got you good, didn't they?"

Steven wasn't sure if he'd made a sound or just nodded.

"You gonna make it? You want me to call an ambulance...or a priest?" There went the laugh again. "You waitin' on the bus? Or just got off?"

"I got off to have a smoke. They took a ten-minute bathroom break. Thing hadn't stopped since Eureka. All I wanted was a smoke." Steven heard his own voice quiver.

The stranger reached into his leather jacket and pulled out a box of Marlboro red, flipped the top, and shook one out. "Here, kid. You look like you could use it."

Steven took the smoke and allowed the man to light it for him. The man squatted down on his haunches and Steven sat with his legs splayed out in front of him. They stayed still and quiet for a moment, Steven smoking and letting the air pass between them.

"Where were you headin'?"

"San Francisco." Steven's head throbbed and the knots on his forehead felt heavy and swollen.

"You know who it was that fucked you up?"

"I think it was two Mexican guys from the bus. Got on in Eureka."

"What'd they get?"

"My backpack. Everything. All I had was in there." Steven breathed out through his nose as the reality of what he was saying sunk in. "Fuck."

"You think they got back on the bus?"

Steven was sure they did. They'd been eyeballing him

since they got on up north. "I don't know."

"Did you see which way they went?"

Steven admitted, "No."

"Willits ain't too big a town." The man flicked a thumb behind him toward the 101, the only real artery running though the tiny burg. "Tell you what, get up, we'll take a quick cruise round. See if we see 'em." The stranger once again held out his hand. Steven took it. He pulled Steven to his feet. "If not, maybe we can catch up to that bus of yours."

Steven was sore and stiff from the beating and moved slow behind the man. "Where's your car?"

"Right there," the man said, pointing at a cherry red 1966 Mustang parked across the street.

"Nice ride."

"I'm just fuckin' with ya. My truck is over there." He swung his index finger to the right and pointed at a well-worn, gray Ford F-150. "Nineteen ninety-four. Nothing fancy, bare bones. But it gets the job done. Let's go."

First they headed south on the 101 as far as Brown's Gas Station, where the town began to thin out, then they looped around and drove north up the same stretch, all the way to Willits High School.

"See anything?"

"No," Steven said. The sad futility in his statement was hard to hide.

"What was in the bag?"

"I told you, everything. My money, my phone, my ID, even my bus ticket. *Everything.*"

"Everything, huh?"

The cynical tone in the man's voice made Steven think he didn't believe him. Steven said, "Yeah, everything. I don't know what I'm gonna do now. I'm fucked."

"Tell you what, why don't we grab some lunch. I'm buying. Then we'll figure out what to do."

"I thought we were gonna catch the Greyhound?"

"Trust me, we got time. You're hungry, aren't you?"

They drove directly to a spot on the southern edge of town, a diner. As they walked toward the front door, Steven wondered if it was one of those retro joints or just old. When they entered the dusty place, poorly lit and choked with greasy smoke, Steven decided it was just old. They sat in a vinyl booth with a scratched Formica table between them. The vinyl bench was worn and cracked and pinched Steven's ass when he sat down.

A waitress stood near the cash register calculating and recalculating a bill. She waved at the two as they took their seats. "I'll be right with y'all."

The man waved back. "Take your time, sweetheart." He removed his sunglasses, folded them, and took a menu from its cradle behind the napkin dispenser and dropped it on the table. "My name's Quinn, by the way."

Steven didn't answer right away. He wasn't sure if he was supposed to say pleased to meet you, or what. After a few seconds of the man staring at him with his cool blue eyes, he said, "Steven."

"What're ya havin', Steven?"

"I dunno. A cheeseburger, I guess." Steven looked out the window at the cars streaming by on Highway 101.

"Look, don't be so anxious. They're on a bus that stops every twenty minutes. We can catch 'em. We only need a schedule. You got a phone?"

"No, they took everything, I told you. No phone, no contacts."

"Right. Well, I do. We'll use mine."

Quinn pulled a flat black cell from his pocket and tapped the screen. "Let's see, Greyhound schedule. Where the fuck are we again? Willits, California?" He tapped in the letters, mumbling to himself.

Before he could complete the search, the waitress approached with two glasses of water and Quinn set the phone down to his right. "How're ya doing, sweetie? What's good here?"

The waitress blushed but managed to come back with, "Other than me?"

She chuckled and Quinn chuckled and she said, "The country-fried steak is good. Our gravy is the best in the county."

"You have any documentation to back that up?"

"Oh, sugar, you just get whatever you want, and we'll make sure it's the best."

Quinn ordered a cheeseburger for Steven and the country-fried steak for himself. "With the gravy on the side. I'm watchin' my figure," he said with a wink.

When the waitress had tottered back toward the kitchen, Steven said, "Friendly sort."

"What can I tell you, people love me."

They ate in silence. Steven was having a tough time chewing. His jaw hurt and every time he bit down sharp pains rocketed up his cheek into his eye socket. He swished water around in his cheeks to help aid the breakdown of the burger. He tasted blood in his mouth, but he forced back the nutrition, reminding himself he didn't know where his next meal would come from.

Quinn watched him while he ate, smiling at Steven while chewing his country-fried streak. Amused, but sizing him up, too. He picked up the small porcelain cup full of white gravy and poured a dollop over his steak. "How's your burger?"

"S'good." Steven nodded. He knew he was being scrutinized and stayed focused on his food.

"Gravy's excellent. Hard to find good gravy out of the South. You wanna dip your burger in?"

Steven shook his head.

There were a few more moments of silence. The only sounds were Quinn's cutlery and the hollow noises from the kitchen. Finally: "You better hurry up and finish if you wanna catch up to that bus."

They were back in the truck. The interior was bare except for a single roll of paper towels on the floorboard. No personal items, no tiny statue of a saint stuck to the dashboard. It was clean. Steven wondered if it had been rented.

Quinn started it up and put it in gear. The wheels spat gravel as he accelerated out of the diner's parking lot. As soon as they were traveling south on the 101, Quinn asked Steven if he wanted another cigarette.

"Sure," Steven said, taking one from the flip-top box. "You haven't smoked one yet. You keep these just for giving out?"

"Nah, I smoke 'em. I'm trying to cut back, though. I

usually don't have one 'til I've had a drink."

Their speed was increasing. From his vantage point, Steven watched the speedometer climb above eighty.

"But if it makes you feel any better, pop open the glove box."

Steven opened the box; inside was a pint-sized bottle of Jack Daniels sitting beside a chrome-plated .45.

"Pass that over. The bottle, not the gun."

Quinn took the bottle from Steven, unscrewed the cap with his teeth, and took a hardy swallow. He put the cap back on and passed Steven the bottle. "You wanna hit?"

Steven shook his head.

"Time for that cigarette," Quinn said.

The countryside flew by as they smoked. Steven peeked again at the speedometer. Ninety-five. He gripped the door handle with his right hand and fought the urge to brace himself on the dashboard with his left. He turned and looked at Quinn who looked relaxed, head tilted back, nodding his chin to a private beat that bumped on in his head. Steven couldn't decide if the man were deliberately trying to terrify him or just didn't give a shit.

After a few more miles, Quinn noticed Steven eyeing him and turned toward his passenger. "Shit, your eye is starting to swell real good. Look in the mirror. Hell of a knot on your forehead, too."

When Steven didn't check his bruises and kept his eyes glued to the road, Quinn added, "You said you wanted to catch 'em, right? You want me to slow down, just say so."

Steven finally gave in and put a hand on the dash.

Quinn took his foot off the gas and the truck slowed. As they decelerated around the next turn, they came up behind a Greyhound bus. Quinn got close enough to where they were engulfed in its shadow.

"Look familiar? We'll wait until the next stop."

"Then what?"

"Then I go see if they're on the bus."

"How?"

"What do you mean, how? I just walk on and take a look. But before I do, I need to ask you again, what was in the bag?"

Quinn saw Steven hesitate. The kid wasn't sure if he could trust him.

"Look, I don't want what's in it. I told you I'd help you. I need to know what I'm gettin' into though. You understand?"

"Smoke."

"Smoke? You mean weed?"

"Yeah."

"I figured. How much?"

"Three pounds." When Steven said it, Quinn didn't look surprised or impressed. He waited for a response.

"Not too much then."

"It is to *me*. That's all I had. It isn't paid for and there's people in the city waiting for it."

Quinn shrugged. "All right, all right."

They drafted the bus for about two miles before it pulled into a combination gas station, diner, and bus stop. The bus ground to a halt in a cloud of dust. It stood inert for a moment before it gave off a high wheeze of hydraulics as the front door opened. A few passengers disembarked. A mother with three young children, an elderly couple, and two young men. All of them appeared to be Hispanic.

Quinn nodded at the two men. "Is that them?"

Steven looked closely. "No. They were younger."

They waited another minute. No one else got off.

Quinn said, "Gimme that piece."

"What?"

"The gun. In the glove box. Let me have it; I'm going in to see if they're on board."

Steven opened the box. The gun felt heavy in his hand. He passed it over.

"How will you know it's them?"

"Easy. They'll have your backpack." Quinn opened the door and got out of the truck. He stuffed the gun in the small of his back, adjusted his jacket around it, and, without another word, walked toward the bus.

Steven watched him go, sauntering over like he was just another passenger. He watched him board the bus.

Inside the bus, Quinn walked down the aisle, looking from left to right. About two-thirds of the way back he saw two young Hispanic kids. The one closest to the window had a backpack clutched to his chest. They made eye contact. Quinn studied them for a moment, then winked. Both boys furrowed their brows. Quinn turned and walked off the bus.

Steven watched Quinn walk back empty-handed, giving his shoulders a small shrug. Before he got back in the truck, Quinn pulled the .45 from behind his back and handed it across the seat to Steven, telling him to return it to the glove box. With a grunt, he climbed back behind the wheel.

"They ain't on there."

"You sure?"

"Yeah, I'm sure. They're probably still in Willits, laying low and waiting for the next bus back north."

"Fuck."

"Sorry, kid. I did what I could. Now what do you want to do?"

Steven looked through the windshield at the bus. It was a good question. He had no idea. Without that backpack he was lost. No cell phone and no numbers to call anyone, he wasn't sure how to reach anybody without his phone contacts. He wasn't sure why this stranger had helped him. The man had a gun and a bottle of whiskey in the glove box of his truck, for Christ's sake. Steven knew trusting someone like this might be a mistake. But, he didn't want to get out of the truck either. Standing on the side of the highway, broke and alone, sounded even worse. Quinn didn't seem that bad, really. He kind of reminded Steven of his older brother. "I don't know."

"Tell you what," Quinn said, "I'll see that you get to the city. I've got to make a little stop, though. Keep me company, maybe you can give me a hand."

Far from home, pockets empty, no way of calling friends or family, Steven said, "Sure."

"All right, then. You ever been to wine country?" He didn't wait for an answer. "No? Napa Valley here we come."

CHAPTER TWO

"So tell me more about the drug running business."

They'd been on the highway heading south for only a few miles. The few remaining redwoods had dissipated and the hillsides were lush with green grass punctuated with clumps of oak and poplar trees.

Steven was looking at his contusions in the mirror behind the sun visor. He was caught off-guard by Quinn's direct question. "Huh?"

"Yeah, you know, the drug running business. You're a mule on the green highway. I saw a segment on the news at the motel the other night. You little fuckers are the scourge of Northern California."

"I don't know anything about that. I'm only trying to put together a few bucks with a friend."

"Amateur, huh? In on the ground floor of the next big thing? That's okay too, I guess. I didn't figure I had Pablo Escobar here in the truck with me. I only thought you might teach me something I don't know."

Steven didn't respond. He didn't know how to reply, not sure whether this guy was teasing or had turned on him.

"I'm always interested in how people make a living. 'Specially up here. Don't look like there's shit for money and even less opportunity. Fuckin' trailers and broke

down pickups. Looks like one big, sad country song."
When the comment failed to elicit a response, Quinn
said, "You know what I'm talking about. You're from
around here, right? Up north?"

"How do you know where I'm from?"

"Deductive reasoning, kid. You should try it some
time. If you were a little more tuned-in on that bus you
probably wouldn't a gotten bopped on the head back
there in Willits."

Steve looked up at his swollen forehead in the visor's
mirror.

Quinn said, "You know, you staring at that big ol'
lump ain't gonna make you feel any better. I wish I had
something to give you, but I don't. Why don't you take a
hit off that Jack in the glove box?"

Steven shook his head ever so slightly. "I'm not much
for whiskey."

"No? Then I will. Hand me that thing, will you?"

Steven did and Quinn unscrewed the cap with his
teeth once more, took a swallow, and handed the bottle
back to Steven. "Go ahead. It's medicinal. I won't tell
Mom and Dad."

Steven took a pull, winced at the burn, and placed the
cap back on the bottle. Then he flipped the visor back up
and steadied his gaze on the road.

"Let me guess, hippie parents, never kept the hard
stuff around but had no problem smoking dope in the
living room every night. Seemed loving, but permissive,
and ultimately didn't give a shit?"

Steven's voice rasped from the alcohol. "More deductive reasoning?"

Quinn laughed. "No, if you're from up here, then it's just playing the odds."

The road burned on south. The sparsely wooded areas had opened up and they drove through wide valleys. The green hills would only stay that way for a few months before they turned brown under the California sun. It was lush and cool and soon vineyards began to crop up, their vines young and sprouting, clinging to the acres of wire frame that stood in clean rows combed across the land.

Quinn finally turned off the 101 and got on Highway 128, a smaller road where the vegetation first clung to the edges of the asphalt, then it too opened up to the rolling hills filled with grapes. More and more grapes.

"Where're we heading?"

"A friend of mine's. He's gonna lend us his car. A little more stylish than this thing."

Steven fell silent again and watched the pastoral view. The road was smooth but the slightest jostle made his injuries flare up and he found himself pushing his back into the seat to absorb the shock. Although the sun was shining through the windshield, he grew cold as his body worked to push blood to all his throbbing bruises.

After a few more miles, just past the town of Calistoga, Quinn pulled the truck off the highway onto a smaller road. Their path remained paved, but gone were the painted lines on the sides or middle.

"I thought you said we were going to Napa?"

"Napa County. Not the town. Place we're headin' is a

little farther up the road here. You all right? Hanging in? You gotta piss or anything?"

Steven shook his head. He was hungry again, but, even if they had any food, his mouth hurt too much to eat. He wished he'd been able to finish the burger in Willits. He was thirsty too, but the only thing to drink in the truck was whiskey.

"This'll only take a few minutes. Then we'll be on our way."

"And you're still gonna take me to the city, right?"

"You bet."

The road wound away from the valley and soon Quinn pulled the truck onto a long thin asphalt drive-way. A white sign hung by the gate announcing *Oulilette Vineyards.* They passed a few workers tending the vines in the fields. Quinn rolled down his window and gave them a big open wave. They waved back.

They rolled up the drive to a Spanish-style villa. It was wide and low, white stucco with red clay tiles and a broad cement staircase curving up to its large oak doors. It reminded Steven of one of those old California Missions.

To the right of the house was a matching garage with four sets of double doors. Vehicles parked in front of every one. Most of them pickup trucks Steven assumed belonged to the workers. A couple of nice ones: a Mercedes, a BMW, some sort of sports car Steven didn't recognize. To the left was a tower at least three stories high. It was positioned to look out over the fields. It, too, matched the house and garage.

"Nice place, huh? Fucking pool in the back, hot tub, handball court and gym in the basement. This guy lives like a king."

"And he's a friend of yours?"

"A good friend." Quinn let the truck roll to a stop and pulled the emergency brake. "Open the box and hand me that .45, would you?"

Steven paused, looked at Quinn, trying to read him, wondering why he needed a gun to visit a friend—a *good* friend.

"Sorry, kid, but as many miles as we've traveled, I've barely gotten to know you. I don't leave guests in my truck with a loaded weapon. Bad etiquette."

Steven wasn't sure he knew what "etiquette" was. He opened the glove box and handed over the weapon.

Quinn said, "Help yourself to the whiskey, though. I'll be back in a few minutes."

Steven watched Quinn walk up to the large double oak front door and reach to the right to hit the bell. He heard the rich chime from where he sat. He could see the butt of the .45 sticking out of Quinn's pants at the small of his back. After a moment, the door swung open and Quinn went inside. He sat in silence, a light breeze floating up from the fields. He turned his head to see the workers toiling out there. They were busy, far away now, and ignored the truck.

"What brings you all the way out here?" the man said. He was portly and tanned from being out in the sun. He wore round spectacles and a white linen dress shirt.

"You knew I'd be stopping by."

"No, I didn't actually. I thought I was all done with Richard. I've steered clear of that bunch for years."

"Nice place you got here. You really bottle the shit or is this all for show?"

"What do you mean? Of course I bottle. The product is excellent. May I offer you a taste?"

"Of course. That'd be swell."

"Swell? Okay. Same old Quinn. Let me get you a glass."

The man walked toward the kitchen and Quinn followed. The kitchen was large and modern with an island in the middle that boasted eight burners and a grill. They were spotless and looked as though they'd never been used.

"This is a vintage from a few years back. Right amount of sun. Right amount of rain. I was extremely lucky that year." He reached up and took a crystal wine glass from a cupboard and set it on the counter in front of Quinn, then bent down and opened a large wine fridge built into the cupboard beside the dishwasher and selected a bottle.

As the man bent over, Quinn reached across the counter and plucked a large carving knife from a magnetic knife block sitting beside the cutting board.

The man straightened, turned, and saw Quinn with the knife.

"What's that for?"

Without hesitation or explanation, Quinn reached forward and slashed the right side of the man's neck. The man's eyes lit up behind his glasses. He dropped the bottle to the kitchen floor where it bounced without breaking. Both his hands went toward his neck. Blood was pulsing out, spurting between the man's fingers. He made a sound with his mouth that was really no sound at all.

"What a mess," Quinn said. "Let's stop that heart from pumpin' out all that blood." Quinn thrust forward and stuck the knife into the man's chest. As he pulled it back out, the man fell, first to his knees, then onto his back with his legs folded up underneath him.

Quinn checked himself for blood and didn't see any. He walked to the sink and grabbed a paper towel before turning on the faucet. Then, with some dish soap, he washed his hands and the knife. He dried his hands with the paper towel and let the knife clatter to the stainless steel basin. He tore off another paper towel and turned to walk out.

There was a long coat rack nailed to the wall by the front door, and next to it was a pegged board with several sets of keys. Quinn studied the keys without touching them before he selected a set.

With the towel, Quinn opened the front door and checked on Steven sitting in the truck. The boy sat with his head turned toward the fields. Quinn gave the doorbell a quick swipe and walked toward the truck.

"Beautiful, isn't it?"

The sound of Quinn's voice startled Steven. He turned and saw Quinn grinning at him through the open window, sunglasses back on.

"You know how to drive, right? I forgot that I told someone I'd lend him the truck after I stopped by here and picked up the car. Tell you what, why don't you follow me. I'm gonna head back into Calistoga and meet my friend at the golf course there. We can grab another bite and then be on our way. What'd you say?"

Steven said, "Sounds good."

Quinn walked back to the row of cars parked in front of the garage. He walked slowly down the line as though he were picking one out. Finally he stopped at a brown BMW coupe, opened the door, and got in. Quinn warmed the engine for almost a minute before pulling back and parking beside the truck. He left it running, got out, and returned to the truck window.

"Hey, what're you doing? Let's go. Slide over." He tossed Steven the key. One ring with one key.

Steven grabbed the steering wheel and used the leverage to pull himself across the seat and into the driver's position. He started the truck just in time to watch Quinn head down the driveway to the main road.

As they left, Quinn honked at the workers from the BMW and waved his arm out the window. The men in the field waved back.

They drove in tandem back into Calistoga. Quinn led the way through town to the St. Helena Golf Course. It was a small course that curved around the Calistoga Speedway. On Grant Street an entrance led into a parking lot that sat adjacent to an RV park. Quinn pulled the BMW in and pointed to a parking spot for Steven.

After Steven had parked, he rolled up the windows and ran over to the BMW. "What do I do with this?" he said, holding out the key.

"Hop in," Quinn said. "I'm starving."

Steven climbed into the passenger seat and they pulled out.

"The key?"

"I just asked you what you wanted me to do with it."
Steven again held the key out in his palm.

"Shit." Quinn pulled over by the side of the entrance
and said, "Be right back."

He took the key and jogged back to the truck.

Inside, Quinn wiped everything he could find. Steering
wheel, dashboard, radio. He emptied the ashtray into a
plastic bag and took the bottle of Jack from the glove
box. With a paper towel, he pulled forward the back rest
and pulled out a heavy black doctor's bag and set it on
the gravel outside the truck. After that, he locked and
shut the doors. He walked to either side and gave the
door handles a wipe, too.

When he was done, he tossed the plastic bag in a trash
can near the entrance and trotted back to the BMW.
Before he got in, he popped the trunk with the key fob
and dropped in the leather doctor's bag.

"I saw a place up here on the left that looked okay."
Quinn pulled the car back into the street. "Ain't much in
a burg like this, but I usually have a good sixth sense
when it comes to food." He turned his head and smiled
at Steven. "And a lot of other things."

CHAPTER THREE

"I'm here now. I'm standing in his kitchen, lookin' at him."

Maurice Tremblay was standing over Oulilette's body, talking on his cell phone. He was big, sturdy, and looked like a cop. Only he wasn't a cop. Not recently.

"I must've got here just after he left...No, they didn't see nothing. Bunch of fucking beaners, what'd you expect?" He listened to the phone. He felt like a cigarette, only he knew it'd be best to wait. It was a crime scene now and the less he did in there the better. He stepped back from the body to get a better viewing angle, careful not to step in any blood. "I gotta call the locals now, that's what...Yes, I have to. It's a fucking murder...We have to do the right thing here or it may come back to bite us, trust me...I dunno, I'll think of something." He looked down at Oulilette and the puddle of blood still growing around his body. The blood was thick, dark, but had not yet congealed. Oulilette's eyes remained open and had clouded slightly; they still held the look of surprise. Tremblay squinted at the opaque pupils as though they might tell him something. "C'mon, you knew he was coming...I don't know, but I can guess where he'll end up. He's going to try to get the girl."

Tremblay sighed. "I don't know. She wants to be found about as much as he does."

The conversation ended without another comment. Tremblay looked around the kitchen some more. He saw the knife in the sink, the empty glass on the counter, and the spilled bottle of white wine on the floor. He walked to the house phone and dialed 9-1-1.

Tremblay watched three squad cars file in, lights and sirens on. Probably going to be the biggest thing this town had seen in a while. He sat on the cement stairs smoking, waiting 'til all three had pulled up to the house before getting up.

"Are you the one that called?" The first officer looked to be in his twenties. Tremblay could see he was both nervous and excited.

The young patrolman walked toward Tremblay with his hand extended. When Tremblay didn't shake it, he asked, "Where's the body?"

Tremblay hooked a thumb behind him. "Kitchen."

The officer nodded. "Have you touched anything in there?"

"Phone."

The officer turned to his partner on the left. Same age, same mustache, same build, could have been his clone. "Peters, take this man's statement. I'm gonna have a look."

Peters sighed at being relegated to the role and took out his notepad. "All right. What's your name?"

As Tremblay told him, two more officers trotted up the cement stairs. Another pair stood near the patrol cars, facing the open and empty fields, as though it were their duty to keep back invisible crowds.

"How do you spell that?"

Tremblay spelled it out slowly.

"How did you end up out here today? Do you know the victim?"

"Yeah, I've known him for years. I had some personal business in Napa; I was gonna pick up a case of wine for my ex-wife. Try to appease the old hag. Figured I'd drop in on my old buddy and see how he was doing. Maybe get a deal on some vino."

The young policeman dutifully jotted down notes. "When is the last time you saw the victim?"

"Shit, I don't know. Years ago. I told you, he was an *old* friend, not a close one. How long you been on the job, Peters? Did I get that right? Peters?"

"Yes, that's right. If you don't mind, sir, I'll ask the questions."

"This's your first homicide, huh?"

Peters stopped writing and looked at Tremblay. Gave him his hard look.

"Take it down a notch, son," Tremblay said. "I'm ex-police. San Jose Police Department. The reason I mention it is: you haven't even asked what time it was I got here."

Peters relaxed a little, his tone softening as though he were now addressing a confidant. "To tell the truth, I don't think they've had one the entire time I've been with the force. This stuff doesn't happen too often up here."

"You mind if I smoke?" Tremblay shook one out of his pack before Peters answered him. The veteran cop acting cool and above it all. "San Jose, summertime, sometimes we'd get one, maybe two a week. Murder loves the heat. Mexican gangs mostly, but a one-eight-seven is a one-eight-seven, right?"

"We got the Mexican gangs up here, too. Plenty of 'em. But they're not shooting each other, far as we know."

"Hiding the bodies, huh? Using 'em for taco meat?" Tremblay laughed, but the young officer did not. Tremblay coughed, worked up a ball of phlegm, rocketed it into the grass a few feet away.

"What do you do now, Mr...." he glanced at his notepad again, "Tremblay, is it?"

"That's right. Now I'm in the private sector. Security, PI shit. Got to keep the bottle full, know what I mean?"

Peters nodded, but Tremblay could tell he didn't know what he meant. He would. One day.

The first cop that Tremblay had spoken to appeared at the entrance to the house. "Derek," he called to one of the officers on crowd control. "Get the yellow tape. This is the real deal. Goddamn. Peters, when you're done, have one of these guys stay with our friend here and come up and have a look at this. This is really something."

Quinn ordered a steak with a glass of red wine. Steven said he wasn't sure if he was hungry again, that he was still full from the last meal.

"That wasn't a meal, that was a snack," Quinn said, and told the waitress, "He'll have the bacon cheeseburger, medium rare, and a pint of Sierra Nevada."

When the waitress said she needed to see some ID from the young man, Quinn said, "Never mind. He'll have a coke, I'll take the Sierra."

While they waited for their plates, Quinn made comments on the décor: how they knew they were in an okay place because it had tablecloths. The drinks arrived and Quinn slid his beer across the table to Steven. His commentary continued. The weather, how all these green hills were going to be brown as camel humps in about a month. And the drinks, the wine was shit and did Steven like his beer. It was the Budweiser of micro-brew and gave you the farts, but it was still pretty good. Next round he'd get Steven an IPA.

During all this, Steven said next to nothing. After the food arrived, Quinn dug into his bloody steak and moaned with delight. Steven, still having trouble chewing, nibbled at his burger while his teeth ached.

"So you know a little about the marijuana business."

Steven nodded with his mouth full.

"How old're you, Steven?"

Still chewing, Steven said, "Twenty."

"No shit? Guess your ID wouldn't've helped much anyway. Goddamn, to be twenty again." Quinn paused to take a slow and thoughtful sip from his wine. "What do you know about the speed business?"

Steven didn't answer, but he arched his eyebrows as he swallowed his food.

"Speed. Meth. Crank. Go-fast. Whatever the hell you kids are calling it nowadays. You know anything about that stuff, Steven? Is it Steven or Steve?"

"It's fucked up. What else is there to know? I've done it; I don't really like it. I got an older brother that's wrecked his life over it. He was a good guy, we used to be close. Now he's gone, prison. I know it's hot, that you get more time behind speed than weed."

Quinn chewed and listened, studying Steven. The kid was showing what he knew, acting sage, but he was green. Quinn set down his knife and fork and took another slow sip of red wine.

"I was thinking maybe you could help me with something down in San Francisco. I need somebody young, somebody who's been around this shit before."

A thought had been stuck in Steven's mind ever since Quinn found him in the alley, so he finally came out and asked. "You a cop?"

Quinn laughed. That cool chuckle showing his white teeth. "No. I'm not a cop." He waved over the waitress and asked for an IPA. The server looked at the pint glass in front of the boy and gave Quinn a disapproving glare, but turned to go and fetch the beer anyway.

"Listen, I got a daughter about your age. Sweet kid. She's gone and gotten herself mixed up with some asshole in San Francisco. Some speed-freak fuck. She won't call; she doesn't have a fixed address. I need to find her. I thought you could maybe help me out."

"In San Francisco?"

"Yeah, that's what I said. In the city."

"That's why you wanted me along?"

"Honestly, I could use the help. You know, I help you; you help me. People been doing it for centuries."

Steven seemed to consider it for a moment. "I only need to get to the city. I can find my friend from there."

"Look, I'll get you there. You give me some help in finding my little girl, and I'll see to it you walk away with some scratch. Cash on the barrel. How's a grand sound? Not only would you be helping me, you'd be helping her. The real payoff would be karma, my friend. Nobody can have too much of that stacked up. What'd ya say?"

CHAPTER FOUR

Carl Bradley sat in front of his TV with the remote control in his hand. He thumbed the channels up, one after another. The curtains were drawn against the afternoon sun and the ceiling light was off. He reached the last channel and the screen flashed onto snowy static.

"Goddamn cable. Ain't a dang thing on," he said to his dog, a tired brown and white walker hound that didn't even lift his head at the sound of his master's voice.

Carl began to descend through the channels again. The phone rang. His cell. Not many people had that number. He was unaccustomed to the shrill ringtone. He let it ring.

It took about a minute after the ringing stopped before the home phone rang with its old-fashioned metallic bell.

"Jesus Christmas, what the hell is it now?"

He got up with a grunt and ambled over to the kitchen where the phone hung on a wall.

"Hello?" His throat was full of phlegm and he hoped it wasn't his daughter calling. She always felt the need to nag him about his smoking. He'd quit, but it didn't stop her from chiming in.

It wasn't his daughter. It was Patrolman Peters. He

recognized his voice immediately. The young officer was painfully polite.

"Yeah, this is Carl. How're ya doin', Peters?"

He kept the receiver to his ear while he patted his leg to summon the hound. The dog didn't move.

"You don't say? Well, I guess that *is* unusual...You talked to the help?...Perez can help you there; he can translate...Everybody still down there?...Sure, sure I can. All right, then. What's the address?"

He scratched the location down on a notepad fastened to the phone mount and hung up. He turned to the sleeping dog. "Boy, you're gonna have to watch that TV by yourself today."

He walked into the bedroom, entering it for the first time in weeks. Carl had taken to sleeping on the couch in front of the television. The bedroom air was musty and the stale smell of unwashed clothes hung in the air. Carl pulled open his dresser's top drawer and reached for his service revolver. Then he paused. No, I'm not a cop. Not anymore. I won't need this damn thing. I'm only a consultant here. Old habits die hard. He pushed the drawer shut. He sat down on the bed and pulled on his favorite pair of boots—his only pair of boots.

Carl moved quickly now, jacket on and toward his front door. It was hard not to feel a little excited. It was nice being called on for his expertise, nice being called on for anything. He hesitated at the door, his hand on the knob. He turned to his hound and said, "You might as well come, too, boy. Maybe you'll learn something."

* * *

29

Carl pulled slowly up the long driveway. The three squad cars still sat with their lights flashing in front of the villa. Something about the sight made Carl a bit melancholy and he savored the view. A crime scene.

He pulled his pickup in front of the house and rolled down the windows for the dog. The hound repositioned himself and sat his chin in the open space. Patrolman Peters stood on the steps of the house, a wide grin breaking on his face. Peters was one of Carl's last hires before leaving the department. It'd been a few years, but he still shared a unique bond with the young man. Peters had come in, full of enthusiasm, right when Carl was downshifting his career. Peters looked to Carl as a mentor in his first days as a policeman—a seasoned veteran to show him the subtleties of the job, the stuff that wasn't in the playbook—but Carl saw their relationship differently. Peters saved him from an irreversible slide into negativity. He'd become jaded, not with the job or the people of Calistoga, but with the department itself. The bureaucracy that buried him in the last decade of his job soured his outlook on life. His wife watched the burnout and urged him to speed up his retirement. It wasn't until she became sick that he finally pushed to leave. Too little, too late, in Carl's opinion. But something about Patrolman Peters had resurrected Carl's belief in being a police officer. Doing the right thing, protecting the community, fighting for what was right no matter the odds. What brought him to the job in the first place.

"Carl," Peters said. "Glad you could make it out." He tipped his head toward the dog. "Still got her, eh?"

"Him," corrected Carl.

"What's that?"

"Him. She is a *he*. And, yes, Buford is hanging in there, just like me." Carl arched his back and yawned. "What'd ya got for me?"

"Full-on homicide. The owner got it with a knife in the kitchen. Murder weapon is still in there. Killer left it in the sink. Washed it first, though. Not much in the way of evidence."

"Who found the body?"

"Fella named Tremblay. Ex-police outta San Jose."

"Where's he?"

"Cut him loose after we took his statement. Staying at the Holiday Inn Express. He ain't going nowhere, I told him if we needed him we'd call."

"Tremblay? Sounds familiar. You talk to the amigos?"

"Sanchez did. Said they didn't see nothing. Grey truck pulls in and then leaves ten minutes later trailing a BMW. Said Mr. Oulilette had all kinds of friends coming and going. They never took much notice. Ask me, they're telling the truth."

"They all still here?"

"Perez is still taking their statements. Fucking illegals are so tightlipped. They're afraid they might say something that'll get 'em deported."

"What time this thing happen?"

"Tremblay called us at one-forty-two."

Carl spat at the ground. "Mr. Oulilette smoke?"

"Excuse me?"

"See any ashtrays in the house? Smell like cigarettes in there?"

"No, why?"

Carl pointed with the toe of his boot toward two

cigarette butts sitting on top of the gravel. Fresh and uncrushed. "Think maybe our boy smokes Marlboro red?"

Peters said, "Shit, I didn't even see that."

"You might want to start treating this like an actual crime scene, Peters." Carl felt like having a cigarette himself. Two years he'd been wanting a cigarette. He took out a small tin of sugar-free mints and popped one into his mouth.

Peters called out to another officer to bag the butts in an evidence bag. "You want to go in and take a look?"

"You know I do."

Before they got into the BMW, Quinn tossed Steven the keys.

"I have the upmost confidence in you. I'll play co-pilot for a while."

Steven was excited to drive the car. He pulled out of the restaurant parking lot so quickly he didn't even see the waitress running out after them, angry, and waving the credit card slip in the air.

Steven had never driven anything so sporty and was surprised by the small car's power. He liked it, liked the feel of the polished wood steering wheel, liked the look of the modern dash. He forgot about his problems for the first time that day, enjoying the drive. He wasn't thinking about the cash he now owed his friends back home, or the guy waiting on him in San Francisco—or how he was flat broke, far from home, and cut off from his life. Even his pain receded a little. With Quinn pointing the way, they were back on the road south in no time.

They settled into the ride. Steven was starting to like the stranger, his endless rambling, his enthusiastic energy. Quinn kept the conversation one-sided, telling what he knew about the countryside, telling what he knew about wine. "I know how to open the bottle and pour," he said. How he thought global warming was bullshit. Stuff about unions and China, illegal immigration, and American-made as opposed to American-assembled. His take on the commonly recognized rules of etiquette: If I got an itch, I scratch it. I don't go checking to see if I got permission. On and on. Soon Steven tuned him out and just drove.

When Quinn realized his audience had grown bored, he started flipping back and forth between radio stations. He'd catch the news on AM and turn it back to a pop or country station, then fifteen minutes later, he'd flip back to hear the same news report.

"How old did you say your daughter was?" Steven asked.

"Hang on, I want to hear this." Quinn leaned in toward the radio. When the most recent news report turned to sports and weather, Quinn said, "She's nineteen. Sweet kid. At least I hope she still is."

"She lives with her mom?"

Quinn chuckled. "Hell no, her mom's been out of the picture forever. Lost in a bag of dope. Might as well be dead."

"Geez, I'm sorry. When's the last time you saw her?"

"Her mother?"

"No, your daughter."

"Almost two years ago."

"In the city?"

"No, she was in L.A. Culver City, actually. She was finishing out high school there. We were having trouble already, me and her. But, I figured, kids'll be kids. Bullshit. I shoulda known better."

Steven didn't say anything and kept his eyes straight ahead and on the road.

"You'll like her though. Pretty girl. Funny." Quinn paused a moment, then added, "Be a fuckin' shame if I lose her to drugs. What a waste."

Steven shifted in his seat. "I don't understand what it is you want *me* to do."

"Easy. We go to where she's at. You get in there, buying crank or whatever, chat her up and get her to walk outside. Go to the store for smokes, anything. I'll be waitin'; I'll talk some sense into her. That's it."

"How am I supposed to walk into some drug den where nobody knows me? They'll think I'm a cop or something."

"We'll worry about that when we get there," Quinn said. "You gotta piss? I gotta piss. Pull over next chance you get and we'll take a break."

Carl spent the afternoon mulling over what he'd seen. He started by heading over to Denny's and having a late breakfast. The food wasn't too good and the coffee was worse, but there was a cute little waitress who was always nice to him. Him and every other widower over sixty-five, he was sure. At least four other lonely old fools lined the counter getting unnecessary refills from the same girl.

He wasn't on the force anymore so he had to hightail it when the Sonoma County Sheriff's crime scene unit got to Oulilette's. It didn't bother him; he'd been around a few homicides during his thirty years on the job. When he saw the knife washed in the sink and the lack of bloody footprints, he knew the killer had been careful. He'd let the techs look for prints, but he doubted they'd find any. Peters and the police were still trying to locate next of kin; until then, there'd be no one who could tell them if there was anything missing from the house. It didn't feel like a robbery, though. What *did* bother him was Tremblay, the ex-cop. He'd heard that name before. He finished his meal and decided to call an old friend that used to be with the San Jose Police Department and check him out.

"Carl! How's it hanging, old man?"

"Old man? That's the pot calling the kettle black, Yuri. You've been out of the game for almost as long as I have."

"Loving it, too. Don't miss it a bit. What're you up to?"

"Me? I'm sitting beside my dog in a Denny's parking lot in Calistoga, trying not to look like the ol' curmudgeon I am."

"Listen, Carl, I heard about Barbra. I'm real sorry I didn't make it up to the services."

"That's okay, we had 'em without you anyway." He was tired of taking sympathy comments about his wife.

It'd been almost a year and Carl was doing his best to keep the memories at bay. "The reason I called is I got a question. You remember a guy on the force by the name of Tremblay?"

"Tremblay? Yeah, what a piece of work that one was. A real sleaze. Wonder how he ever ended up in law enforcement. He was working here late eighties, early nineties. They used to call him Terrible Tremblay or Tremblay the Terrible or some shit. I seem to recall some kind of trouble, something they couldn't quite pin on him. Probably had his hand in the cookie jar. Next thing you know he got a job with San Francisco. How he swung that with IA on his ass, I don't know. Last time I saw him must have been ninety-four."

Tremblay stood in his room at the Holiday Inn Express, wondering if he should stay the night. He knew in his gut Quinn would be heading straight to the Bay Area. He wanted to relax first, before the chase resumed. The air conditioning in the room churned. He wanted a drink. Or two. Or three.

He walked to the bed and unzipped a small overnight bag. He pulled out a thin laptop and sat on the bed, its mattress bending to his considerable weight. After the computer powered up, he brought up the browser and went to his favorite bookmark: Craigslist personals. He was thinking it might be tough to get laid in this little town. He was right. No amateurs working the Craigslist thing. He knew there was no strip in Calistoga. He figured he may as well head down to the hotel bar and try his luck there.

He set the laptop aside, stood back up, and checked himself in the mirror. He leaned in; saw his whiskers darkening his face. His hair was a bit greasy, but not too bad. No, he didn't need a shower, but he did need that drink. He said *Fuck it* to the mirror and headed down to the hotel bar.

The lounge was nearly empty, like he thought it would be. Subdued lighting, subdued atmosphere. Some shitty song whimpered in the background. Light rock hits from a lost decade. He hated that shit, too.

The bartender greeted him with a smile. "Good evening, sir. What can I get cha?"

"Dewar's, over."

"I'm sorry, sir. We don't have Dewar's. These're our whiskeys, right here." He swung his arm out, proudly displaying the three or four brands they carried.

"Never mind. Make it a Stoli tonic."

The bartender's smile squished inward and he squinted like he had gas. "Ewww, so sorry. Our top shelf is Grey Goose."

Tremblay was already feeling tired and he'd been in the bar less than a minute. The bartender was at least twenty years his junior. "Fine." He pulled back one of the high-backed bar stools and wedged himself between it and the bar. While the young man hurried and fixed his drink, Tremblay took a look around at the other patrons. All men. All sitting by themselves. Fucking Holiday Inn.

The bartender set the drink in front of him on a cardboard coaster. Tremblay took his own lime wedge from the open tray of drink garnishments and squeezed it in. He drained half the glass with one long, slow swallow. Little light on the vodka. He finished the short glass in two more slugs and waved the bartender over for one more.

He was halfway through his second when a woman walked in. The other customers all looked up from their laptops, their phones, or their coasters, whatever had been holding their attention up until then. She was blonde, tall, well-dressed by Holiday Inn standards. She walked straight to the bar and took a seat two stools away from Tremblay.

"What kind of red wine do you have?"

The bartender showed her what was already open, and, without looking at the label, she said that'd be fine. He poured her a glass and she slapped down a credit card. She took a good pull on the glass, smacked her lips, and let out a deep satisfied groan.

"Needed that one, huh?" Tremblay said.

"Excuse me?"

"The drink. You needed that one, eh?"

"I don't know what you mean," she said with a smile.

Tremblay wasn't sure if she was offended or flirting. He did notice that, once she smiled, she was not the same creature he saw walking into the bar. Her teeth were discolored and stained. Her eyes were bloodshot and cased by tired wrinkles. Her make-up was cheap and applied too thick, covering pockmarked and uneven skin. Tremblay decided right then that, if he was going to fuck her, he'd need a few more drinks. He preferred beautiful women, who didn't? But the ugly ones were more approachable if no less crazy. "You stayin' here at the hotel?"

She looked at him as though this was the stupidest

thing he could have asked. Tremblay decided her smile must be a snarl. He shrugged and went back to his drink, finishing it in one swig and holding his finger up to the bartender before he set his glass down.

After the bartender had poured him another, he tried again. "These places are all the same aren't they? Hotel lounges?"

The woman pulled a cell phone from her purse and pretended to turn her focus on it. She wasn't fooling anybody.

"Cunt," Tremblay said.

She looked up, eyebrows furrowed, and again said, "Excuse me?"

Tremblay said, "Cunt. As in: Stinking fucking cunt. Ugly cunt. Stupid cunt."

The woman got up, took her glass, and moved to an isolated table at the back of the room, leaving Tremblay alone with his drink.

CHAPTER FIVE

They were back on Highway 101 speeding toward the city. Steven still behind the wheel, Quinn riding shotgun. The windows were down and the music was up when Quinn noticed a highway patrol car behind them. He glanced from the sideview to the speedometer. "Slow down a little bit."

Steven turned the volume on the radio down. "Why?"

"There's a cop behind us. Take it down to seventy."

Steven did. The cop stayed where he was. Tight behind the BMW.

"This would probably be a good time to tell you," Quinn said. "This car may be hot."

"Hot? What'd you mean hot? As in stolen? I thought it was your friend's?"

"It is, we just don't always see eye to eye. It's a long story. Don't get pulled over. If that happens, I'm not sure what'll happen next. Focus on the road and see what he does."

Steven gripped the steering wheel. He didn't have any smoke with him, but he had no ID either. What the hell was he even doing in a car with this stranger? He didn't want to spend even a minute in jail. Never mind grand larceny and vehicle theft. He knew no phone numbers by heart that he could call for help. No one would know where he was. He would languish there, stuck. He must have been out of his mind getting in this car with Quinn, let alone behind the wheel. He began to feel a pressure in his chest. It was fear. He looked out of the corner of his eye at Quinn, who still appeared relaxed, even had a little smile curling up at the corners of his mouth. They rolled over the hills outside San Rafael, Steven working hard to control his speed. Not too fast, not too slow.

"Fuck," Steven said.

"Relax. Getting upset won't help. Odds are the car isn't in the system. Just drive and see what he does."

"What happens if he pulls us over?"

"Then I may have to kill him, so don't get pulled over."

Steven smirked. He thought Quinn was kidding, but the man's face didn't change. He had to be kidding.

As they approached the 580 junction, the traffic became muddied and the CHP car pulled off at an exit. Steven exhaled for the first time in minutes.

"That's that," Quinn said. "Now just get us to the city and I'll find us a nice motel on Lombard Street—on me. We won't be there 'til late. You can chill out and rest up while we figure out how to find our friends."

Steven kept his eyes on the freeway. It all seemed too easy. The car, the ride to the city. This man, a perfect stranger, willing to help him.

"What do you do again?"

"What d'you mean?"

"For a living. What do you do?"

Quinn smiled at Steven before saying, "I live in the moment, kid. It's a full-time job."

* * *

When he woke in the morning, Steven was alone in the motel room. He remembered driving across the Golden Gate Bridge shortly after sunset, how the glow of the city seemed both strange but familiar. He'd been to San Francisco many times during his life but never really knew his way around. Most of his visits to the city were with his parents when he was too young to explore. The strip of motels on Lombard greeted them when they came into town. Quinn chose the Francisco Bay Inn and paid for a double. He'd settled Steven in the room and went out to buy beer and whiskey. When he returned, they'd sat drinking and bullshitting until Quinn stood and said he'd be back in a little while. That had to have been before eleven o'clock. Steven, not accustomed to drinking so much, passed out on his bed with his clothes on and slept there through the night.

The sun was up now and beams of daylight streamed through the window. The TV was still playing and the bed beside his was still made. Steven went to the bathroom sink and guzzled as much water as he could. He wondered if he could get back to sleep, but decided to watch the local news instead. He flipped through the morning news broadcasts, both local and national. The stories were all the same. Puff pieces and interviews with celebrities pushing movies or books. Steven grew bored and dug through an ashtray for a butt long enough to smoke. After lighting one up, he felt nauseated and lightheaded. He stubbed it out and lay back on his bed and felt yesterday's bruises throb in time with his head.

He wondered about what he was doing there, in a

motel room paid for by a man he didn't know. He'd made it to the city, no reason he shouldn't strike out on his own now. He owed the stranger nothing. He'd agreed to help Quinn, but didn't promise anything. His mind drifted until he fluttered into sleep.

The door swung open.

Quinn said, "Rise and shine," in a bright voice that jarred Steven back to consciousness. "How're you feelin' there, bud? Shit, you were gettin' positively cross-eyed last night. You need to practice drinking liquor more often. All that weed has made you soft. Keep smoking that shit and you're gonna grow tits." He tossed a bag of donuts on the bed beside the boy. "Here. I brought you some breakfast."

Steven could see chocolate icing smeared onto the grease stains inside the bag. The thought of choking down a donut made him feel even worse. "No, thanks."

"Eat up, you're gonna need your energy. We got a lot of stuff to do today. It's already ten o'clock. Get your ass up, shower if you got to. Switched cars last night so you won't have to worry about that one being hot."

"You switched cars?"

"Yeah, got us a new one. Not as nice, but it runs fine. It'll get the job done."

"From another friend?"

"Your sarcasm would work better if you were standing up. Chop, chop, let's go."

As soon as Carl awoke he called Peters to tell him he ought to think about getting over to the Holiday Inn Express to have a chat with Mr. Tremblay. Why not bring him down to the station for a formal statement. He said he could meet Peters there about nine.

"Way ahead of you. I called down there this morning to make sure he hadn't checked out," Peters said. "I asked 'em to call me if he was on the move. Haven't heard a thing."

"That's fine. But let's not have the Holiday Inn employees do our police work for us, huh? Last I heard, they're still making minimum wage down there. Ain't no danger-pay in hotel management."

"You think this guy is dangerous, Carl? He have something to do with this Oulilette thing?"

"I don't know. I heard he hasn't always been a straight arrow, though. Let's make sure he's telling us everything he knows."

"You telling me everything *you* know?"

"Peters," Carl said. "That would take a lifetime."

Peters laughed and hung up.

Carl fixed himself a quick breakfast. Two eggs in a loose scramble scooped straight onto a piece of toast. The dishes were all dirty and piled in the sink, so toast would have to suffice for a plate. He ate standing up. He brushed off the crumbs on his chest and poured himself a second cup of coffee and thought about what he had to do next: call his old friend Bill Panzer down at SFPD. He had a bad feeling about this Tremblay character and knew calling Panzer was only going to cement that feeling. He sat down on the couch and wished he still smoked cigarettes.

Before he got up to make the call, the phone rang.

"Carl? It's me again." Peters' voice was quiet.

"I was just headin' out."

"He's gone. Tossed his key on the counter and walked out about twenty minutes ago."

"Shit."

Tremblay was well on his way to San Francisco in his rented Ford Focus. Radio off and windows down, he smoked cigarette after cigarette. He kept thinking about that woman last night. What a bitch. Some people just scream bitch as soon as they open their mouths. She was one of them. Shit, she was all of them. His hangover wasn't helping his mood. He was hungry and tired, but if he didn't get to the city soon, Richard would be all over his ass. He glanced at his cell phone plugged into the car charger. There was no blinking light informing him he had a message. He promised himself he would call that old son of a bitch as soon as he got to San Francisco. Until then, he'd leave the ringer off.

Tremblay clutched his jacket pocket. A wave of dread rushed through him. For a moment, he thought he'd forgotten his blow back at the hotel. He felt around in his pocket until he was sure he'd located the small plastic baggie. Relieved, he decided it was time for a short blast to help keep him driving. Numb that headache a little. He pulled off the highway and into a Starbucks Coffee. Cocaine and caffeine: the breakfast of champions.

Carl stood with his cell in his hand in the Holiday Inn Express lobby, waiting to be connected to Bill Panzer at the SFPD. Peters stood beside him, anxious as a pup. Bill came on the line and extended his late condolences for

Carl's wife. Carl got right to the point and asked what he knew about Tremblay.

"Maurice Tremblay? The French Connection?"

"Excuse me?"

"The French Connection. That's what we used to call him. He started in ninety-five or so and got in with narcotics. Fuck was dirty from the get-go. Most guys it takes a while before temptation wins 'em over. Not Tremblay. He came in with an agenda. Up to his armpits in shit within a year."

"What happened with him?"

"You don't remember? Shit, it musta been two thousand and two. His bullshit hit the fan big time. Big busts, dope disappearing. It was all over the papers. You get the news up there, don't you, Carl?"

"Refresh my memory."

"He got twisted up with some of our more greedy civic leaders. Turns out ol' Maurice had some mafia-type connections. The papers only covered the missing evidence angle, but he was suspected to be involved in some more shit. A city supervisor from the Sunset District went missing, a CEO from some big-money computer company turned up dead. The guy is bad news. I wouldn't be surprised if he turned up dead himself. Why you asking about Tremblay?"

"I guess he's what you'd call a person of interest in a homicide that occurred yesterday up here in Calistoga. You're ratcheting up the interest right now."

"You caught the case, Carl? I thought you were retired."

"I am. I'm helping out a friend. What else you know about this guy?"

"Well, SFPD dumped his sorry ass back in oh-four. He'd been fighting that shit for a couple years. He's lucky he didn't end up in jail. What happened to him after that, I don't know. You want me to ask around?"

"I'd appreciate that, Bill. Call me at this number if you hear anything worth repeating. Say hello to the missus for me."

When Carl hung up, Peters was looking at him excited. "What'd he say? He know him?"

"Yeah, he knows him. Or knew of him. And you shouldn't have let him slip through your fingers."

"He said that?"

"No, I'm saying it. We best be thinking on how we're going to find this man."

CHAPTER SIX

The new car was a drab late-model Nissan Sentra. Quinn unlocked the doors with the key fob as they approached. "What'd ya think?"

"What happened to the BMW?"

"I thought it was making you uncomfortable, so I dumped it. This one's a little more anonymous anyway."

They climbed in, Quinn in the driver's seat and Steven on the passenger side. The car wasn't clean this time. Garbage on the floor, CDs stuffed in the door pockets, and a layer of dust over everything. As Steven buckled his seatbelt, he noticed flecks of dark red in a fine pattern across the dash.

"Is that blood?"

"If it is, then I'm suggesting that it's not nice manners to ask."

Steven looked at Quinn to see if he was joking. There was that perfect white smile again.

"You know what? I think I'm going to be able to find my friend on my own. I'm pretty sure I know where to start. Maybe I should just cut from here and head out."

Quinn said, "Don't worry, no one's gonna be reporting this one as missing."

"Stolen," Steven said.

"Whatever." Quinn turned over the engine, buckled

his own belt, and pulled out of the parking lot.

"Where are we going?"

"You got any actual leads on how to find your friends?" asked Quinn.

"I just woke up; I haven't had time to think about it yet."

"No? Well, we'll work on my thing then. There's a guy that lives in the Lower Haight that might know who Teresa is shacked up with. Page Street, I think. I'll know it when I see it."

"Teresa. That's her name?"

"Yeah, didn't I mention it?"

"No, you didn't." Steven looked out the window as they scaled Gough Street up out of the Marina District. "Nice name."

"I didn't choose it."

They drove in silence with Quinn keeping beat on the steering wheel to some unheard music while he listened to a local news broadcast. Steven asked if he could smoke and Quinn said, "Sure, just put the butt right there." He pointed to a half-full beer can in the drink caddy.

The Lower Haight looked vaguely familiar to Steven. He wondered if this was the neighborhood his friend lived in. He kept his eyes peeled just in case.

Quinn found the house, then spent a few more minutes trying to find a parking spot. Getting frustrated, he pulled the Nissan into a driveway a couple of doors down from the house he'd pointed out as his friend's.

"You might as well come along on this one. Might be fun, who knows?"

Steven wasn't sure what that meant.

The two of them walked up to a three-story Victorian. It was painted asparagus green with a darker green on the trim. It looked nice, expensive.

"Is this his house?" Steven looked up at the tall building, impressed.

"Fuck, no. He rents a flat inside. This guy can't afford to own shit. Who knows how many apartments are in here."

A beautiful doorway was blocked by a wrought iron gate. There was a chrome box with four buttons by the right side. Quinn ran his finger down the names slotted beside each button. "What'd you know? It's Joe-Joe." He pressed the third button.

An intercom speaker crackled. "Hello?" The voice was infused with static.

Quinn pressed the buzzer again. The voice came back. "Hello?"

Quinn pressed the button three more times. When the voice came back this time, Quinn said, "UPS."

After a few moments, the heavy front door opened and a shirtless olive-skinned man appeared behind the gate. "What the fuck?"

"Aren't you going to invite us in, Joey?"

The man blanched. "Shit, Quinn. What are—when did you get into town?"

"Open up and I'll tell you all about it."

Joe-Joe, or Joey, or whoever he was, buzzed the gate. As soon as it opened, Quinn pushed it with his hand and started to walk in with Steven right behind him.

"Who's the kid?"

"He's my protégé."

"Protégé, huh?" The man grunted when he talked. He led them inside and down a hallway toward a kitchen. Sports memorabilia lined the walls. Mostly Niners stuff, but some Giants, too. Pennants and framed action shots and souvenirs from the games. They reached the kitchen and the man sat down first, planting himself heavy in an older chrome-plated kitchenette chair with a vinyl seat. Quinn took his own chair and sat down across from him. Steven stood by the kitchen doorway.

"What brings you back to town, Quinn? I thought we'd seen the last of you." His tone was conversational, but Steven could tell he was still spooked by seeing Quinn.

"I'm looking for Teresa."

"Can't help you there. Even if I'd seen her, she's a flake nowadays. Strung out. Who knows where she's at."

"You do," Quinn said. His voice was even and void of emotion.

The man chuckled. Fake and unconvincing. "What makes you think I'd know anything about where she is?"

"You always liked her. Richard asked you to keep an eye out before you ran into your troubles. I know you still do."

"No, man, not me. Her private school days are over. That girl is trouble."

"I'm trouble," Quinn said. "And I'm here. Now, why don't you tell me what you know."

"Quinn, really, I'd like to help—"

In one deft motion, Quinn reached across the table

and jabbed the man in the throat with his flattened hand. The man made a sound that was part swallow, part yelp. He teetered back in his chair, having trouble getting air back down his windpipe.

"You tell me what you know and I'll decide whether it's something I can use."

He grabbed the man's right wrist and twisted it inward. Both of their chairs fell back with a clatter. Quinn wrenched hard on the limb until the man was forced onto his knees.

"You know what the Marines call this? They call it 'makin' 'em pray.' It's what they use to convert zealots out there in Iraq." He kept twisting. "You prayin' yet?"

The man whimpered.

"You better be fuckin' prayin' to *me*. I'm your god right now, 'cause I'm the one deciding whether you live or die."

"I seen her. I seen her." The man could barely get the words out; the pain was so intense.

Quinn took his free hand, flat again, and jabbed the man in the sternum. A blast of wind coughed out of the man's mouth. "Spit it out, you piece of shit. Maybe I'll forgive you your transgressions."

Steven didn't know what to do. It all happened so fast he felt frozen, transfixed. He knew, on some level, he should run out of there. Get out of that flat and keep on going. But he couldn't move. He gripped the doorjamb and watched Quinn work.

Quinn applied more torque to the man's arm and there was a popping sound. The man began to wail. "C'mon, you fucker. You know me better than this. You know what I can do."

"I seen her around Powell Station. A few times," the man said between sobs. "Hanging out with the street kids there. Please. I don't know them. I don't know where she is. I swear."

Quinn took his flattened hand and curled it into a fist and punched the man hard in the right eye. The man fell back and Quinn let go of the arm. Quinn towered over him now, planting a foot on either side of his body.

"What else do you know?"

"Nothing, that's it, I swear to God."

"Steven," Quinn said. "Grab me a fork."

Steven was still frozen in the doorjamb, horrified at the scene unfolding in front of him. Quinn's request didn't register.

"Beside the sink. Get me a fork."

Steven saw Quinn glaring at him and he snapped out of it. He stepped toward the sink. Autopilot, moving on impulse without thought. He took a fork from the dish rack and handed it to Quinn. He couldn't guess why Quinn needed the fork. The whole time the man on the floor was whimpering, "No, no, no."

"Thank you," Quinn said before turning his attention back to the man on the floor. "You like to eat, you fat, hairy fuck?"

"No," the man pleaded. "Please, no."

Quinn ignored him, dropped to his knees, and stabbed the fork into Joe-Joe's bare stomach and plucked it back out. Four tiny holes began to bleed. "Stop crying, this ain't gonna kill you." He stuck the fork in again, then twice more, leaving it wagging near his belly button. Quinn stood.

Quinn, his voice calm once more, said to Steven, "You think he's lying?"

Steven couldn't speak. He only shook his head.

"You're lucky the kid likes you. I'm going to let you live your miserable life. If I find out you're lying, that you're somehow mixed up in this shit, you know I'll be back for a visit."

Quinn straightened up and went to the window sill above the sink. There was a small potted plant there that looked like it was dying. Quinn picked up its terracotta pot and dropped it on the man's head. It broke wide in a phalanx of dirt and shards of red clay.

"C'mon, let's go."

They hurried to the car and Steven got into the passenger seat. He knew he shouldn't have. Shouldn't have opened the door and climbed in, but he was scared. He wanted to get as far away from the fat man's apartment as possible.

Once Quinn was in the car, Steven asked, "Where are we going?"

"Powell Street Station, where else? See if we can find some kids down there who know something. But first I got some more sleeves to tug on." Quinn put the car in reverse and pulled backward onto Page Street.

"Aren't you worried about that guy?" Steven hooked a thumb back toward the building they were driving away from.

"Worried? What d'you mean? He ain't calling no cops, don't worry."

"Who was he?"

"Just some asshole who used to work for a guy I know. I thought he might know something, and I was right."

As they drove away from Page Street, Steven eyed the door handle, its lock, thinking maybe he should jump out. He should have run when he had the chance. Waves of fear kept him from grabbing the handle. He'd go with Quinn, he decided, but if he saw a chance to bolt, he would. He wasn't sure if Quinn would try to stop him. He guessed he would.

They spent the rest of the day visiting bars where Quinn thought he'd know the barkeep. At a few places the bartender asked Steven for ID and they had to leave. Other spots they didn't seem to care. After a couple of beers, Steven began to relax, even enjoy Quinn's company again. Steven got the impression Quinn wasn't only looking for information, he was trying to ingratiate himself back into San Francisco. It made him wonder why he'd stayed away so long. There was no denying the man's charisma. Steven felt bold when he was with him, too. Quinn laughed about sticking the fork in the fat man, and, eventually, Steven laughed along with him.

They hit several bars. Usually the staff had changed; sometimes even the name of the place had changed. Quinn would launch into a tale about how great the place *used* to be. At one point Steven asked, "How long has it been since you've been to San Francisco?"

Quinn said, "Too long."

After three or four bars and three or four drinks at each bar, Quinn said, "Fuck it. Let's go back to the motel and watch us some TV. We'll roust those little shits on Powell Street tomorrow."

* * *

"You didn't think we'd get outta here today, did you?" Peters was talking with Carl in the parking lot adjacent to the police station. They were surrounded by squad cars, a few black Crown Vics, and a smattering of Sonoma County Sheriff's cars. The light was beginning to wane. Peters' shift had ended a few hours ago. He stifled a yawn. "Even though it's you, I still got to clear a ride-along with the boss. Did you forget about the paperwork?"

"No, I did not forget about the paperwork. Son, let me tell you, sometimes I wake up in the middle of the night thinking about the damn paperwork. Nightmares that I'm stuck for eternity in front of a typewriter."

"Typewriter? Jesus, Carl, you really are gettin' old."

"You know what I mean. Typewriter, computer, whatever. Red tape is just that...red tape." Carl reached into his pocket and pulled out his tin of mints. He offered one to Peters and, when the younger man said no, he shook a few into his palm and popped them into his mouth. "In fact, I been looking up this character Tremblay on my own computer. Fair number of newspaper articles on him, but they all say pretty much the same thing."

"And what's that?"

"Mr. Maurice Tremblay—I figure him to be about fifty-seven, fifty-eight—dirty cop, missing evidence—both dope and cash—finally kicked off the force in oh-four." Carl rolled the mints over his tongue. "Now, I can read between the lines, and I can tell there's a lot more to this fella than what the papers saw fit to print."

"Like what?"

"Sumbitches like this are always in deeper than folks ever know or care to find out. Now he turns up on our front lawn with a dead body at his feet. No way he just happened by that winery. Stands to reason there's more to Mr. Oulilette than we know, too."

"Yeah, I've been having Perez dig in there. Hopefully he'll have some kind of news before we leave tomorrow."

"All right then, you'll pick me up at my place, what say around six?"

Peters smiled. "How about around nine? I'm a cop, not a farmer."

"We don't want to drag our feet here, son. If Tremblay ain't our boy, then he can take us right to him."

"I'll be there before nine," Peters said.

That night, after a modest supper of canned baked beans on toast, Carl sat on the couch before a picture of his deceased wife, Barbra. The hound was curled up beside him at the end of the couch. He held the picture in his hand. It was encased in an ornate silver frame that had a crack in its glass running diagonally across the photo. It was his favorite picture of her, taken when she was in her early forties. To Carl, she'd never changed since the photo was taken. She'd never gotten sick, never deteriorated.

"Sweetheart," he said. "I'm thinking on doing something foolish. Well, I'm not thinking on it," he corrected himself, "I'm goin' to go ahead and do it. I know I promised you when I was out I was out, but I just can't sit still here anymore. I been cooped up in this house too long. There's not much that could drag me away from retirement, away from you, but I think this is a good cause, a worthy cause." The hound lifted his head and put it back down again. "It's not just that, you know. I want to be of some use in this world. I'm not mistakin' this for anything it's not. I know I'm just an old fool, but I think I got a few more in me, honey. I'm not ready to hang up my hat just yet."

He sat the picture down on the coffee table in front of the couch. He lay back, adjusted the cushions into a pillow for his head, put his feet up on the dog, and drifted off to sleep in front of the muted television.

When Tremblay got into San Francisco he went straight to a motel. He considered calling an old friend or two but decided that he was better off alone. He'd start to focus on his prey tomorrow. Tonight he'd go out for a solitary drink and reacquaint himself with the city.

The Bay Bridge Motel was a dive, one that he'd visited many times before as a police officer. It'd been a few years since he'd seen the place and the staff had changed. The rooms, too, had been redone, upgraded. He tossed his small bag on the bed and walked out without even sitting down.

On foot South of Market, he discovered most of the bars he frequented had either disappeared or undergone drastic renovations. The people crowded into them were young and alien to him. Even 6th Street, the city's long-time skid row, was crawling with young, hip, well-to-do partiers. The sea of youth put him in a funk so he migrated toward the Tenderloin where there was sure to be bars more suited to his mood.

The faces of the derelicts on the street were more familiar to him. He thought he recognized a few of them, frozen in time. He stepped around carts and beggars, people doing drug deals on the open sidewalk. Some things never change.

He found himself at the Brown Jug, a joint swarming with barflies on the corner of Eddy and Hyde. It was the kind of place he never would have gone into for a drink in the past, but now seemed perfect for the solace he craved. He ordered a drink, didn't wait for it to be poured, and headed straight for the bathroom. The stall had no door and the front door had no lock, so he leaned up against it and dug his car key into his obligatory bag of cocaine and dug out a lump for each nostril. No one knocked or pushed on the door, so he did another two bumps before returning to the bar. His drink was waiting for him. He smiled when he saw the two stools on either side of his remained empty.

The bartender came back over and shouted over the jukebox, "Six dollars."

"Six bucks? For a shot 'n' water? You gotta be kiddin'."

"You said Maker's Mark, right?" The bartender's eyebrows furrowed. "It's six."

Tremblay screwed up his mouth and threw seven dollars down on the bar. The bartender scooped them up without saying thank you.

He turned around to survey the meager crowd. Scumbags most of them. They weren't drinking any six-dollar shots. The coke had woken him up after the drive and he was thinking he should be trying to find Quinn instead of sitting in a bar getting ripped off on drinks. Find Quinn or find the girl. One would eventually lead to the other. Richard wanted the girl safe and Quinn dead. If the timing was right, he could get them both at the same time. Problem was he had no idea how to find either of them. No idea where to even start.

He stepped out of the bar and onto the sidewalk. He fished in his jacket pocket for his pack of cigarettes and felt his phone vibrating. He took it out and looked at the caller ID. Richard.

"Hello...I've got it on now...I didn't see any missed calls."

The voice on the other end went on for a few moments.

"I'm here, looking around town...No, I haven't...I was thinking of going to see that fat fuck Joe-Joe first thing in the morning...Yeah, I remember. I won't bring it up, I want him to tell me *something* at least...Okay...I just told you I'm here, I'm on it. I'll call you back in the morning and let you know what I found out." He put a finger in his left ear to better hear the voice on the other end. He said, "I'm not losing steam. I'm on the fucking case."

The voice went on for a minute more before the line went dead. Tremblay pulled the phone from his ear and frowned at it. He said, "Asshole." But no one was listening.

CHAPTER SEVEN

"This is Peters."

They were on Interstate 80 pointing toward San Francisco when Peters answered his phone. Peters hadn't shown up at Carl's 'til nearly ten o'clock. He'd pulled into Carl's driveway in his green Acura, a smile on his face and ready for adventure. They stopped for lunch along the way in Vallejo and kept the talk light. Peters talked baseball to Carl and Carl, not being a fan, didn't say much at all. Finally, they'd gotten back on the road and were now bogged down in early afternoon traffic approaching the Bay.

After a few *okays* and *all rights*, Peters hit the end button and tossed the phone down between his legs.

"Was that Perez?"

"Yeah, sure was. Said he couldn't find out much about Oulilette. The guy popped up out of nowhere a few years back. Bought the winery and fixed it up and started doing business."

"He's legit?"

"As far as Perez can tell. No priors, no record at all. He owes money on the place, plenty of it. Owed, I guess you'd say. Probably took some cash to get it up and running, but everything else is on the books somewheres. Used to be Cavot Wines, remember?"

"Yeah, I remember. Old fella named Harrison used to have it. Retired to cancer as I recall. Poor bastard. Did Perez find out anything about Tremblay?"

"Didn't say, so I guess he's still lookin' into it. Maybe this is some kinda French mafia thing?"

"French mafia? Never heard of such a thing. Doesn't mean it don't exist, but I find that highly unlikely."

"Just thought 'cause of the names."

"I know what you're thinkin'. *I'm* thinkin' that if there ain't much paperwork on this Oulilette fella, chances are he used an alias to buy the place."

"That's what Perez said. He'll check that angle out, too." Peters added, "Hell of a name to choose."

"Sounds expensive though."

"Sure does. Good name for the wine business. People love to waste money on stuff they can't pronounce."

"There ain't no accounting for taste, I guess."

It was miles before they spoke again. The car was silent, no radio, only the sound of the wind whipping the windows.

"When'd you come out here, Carl?"

"Where? To San Francisco?"

"No, to California."

"Good Lord, seems like a couple of lifetimes ago. I left Oklahoma in sixty-four. Hell of a time to come to this state. Right before the sixties really took off."

"You with Barbra then?"

"Oh, hell no. She was a California girl, born and raised. Whenever I heard that Beach Boys song, I thought it was written just for her. Still do. Of course, I know it wasn't, but she was my California girl. Let's see, I met her up in Napa when I was twenty. We didn't marry 'til sixty-six. World was a different place then, let me tell you."

"I bet it was."

Peters looked at Carl gazing out the window and was sorry he'd brought up the subject. As they approached Berkeley, Interstate 80 straightened out and the lanes began to clog. They could see the San Francisco skyline across the bay, gray and cold.

"I know you dragged me along on this trip because you think that I'm smarter than you. It's not true. I'm only older."

"C'mon, you're a legend around the department. Nobody knows the job like you do."

"Nobody in Calistoga, you mean. And that ain't saying much." Carl paused and said, "I'm surprised you got Herrera to sign off on this."

"On what?"

"On this trip. On me going along."

"Oh, this ain't on the taxpayers tab. He said it didn't bother him none if I went off and chased my tail. I had to take a few personal days. You think he was gonna okay a weekend in San Francisco at the city's expense?"

"No, I guess I didn't. Doesn't surprise me either. He was never what you'd call a bold thinker." Carl looked out his window for a moment, then said, "You did tell him I was coming along, didn't you?"

"Hell, I'm footing the bill; it shouldn't matter who's coming along. Besides, he'll find out soon enough."

"I'm sure he will." Carl reached for his small tin of mints, popped the lid with his thumb, and shook two into his palm. "You gonna get some heat over this?"

"Heat? No. Maybe some teasing. We'll see what pans

out. It'd be nice to come back a hero." Brakes began to light up in front of them and Peters decelerated.

"Instead of a fool," Carl said.

"Right," Peters said. "Instead of a fool. How about your dog? She gonna be okay?"

"He? Don't let him hear you call him a girl. He may look passive, but he got feelings." Carl cleared his throat and flipped the mints over his tongue. "Buford'll be fine. Got a neighbor kid that'll come over. Feed him. Let him out. Buford don't like the city anyway. Too many freaks, not enough trees."

Quinn and Steven wandered the area around Powell Street Station looking for young people begging for change and sitting on the sidewalk. There were plenty to choose from. Along with the tourists lined up in a huge ellipse bordering the street car turn-around, there were street performers, hobos, cops, street vendors, and business people trying to make an early commute. Woven into the throngs were kids who sat with empty coffee cups in front of them, smoking cigarettes, looking dirty and as hopeless as they were.

"You want to make fifty bucks?" Quinn would ask them.

They'd eye him with suspicion, but their need and greed always got them to get up and talk.

"Okay, here's the deal: You can have fifty bucks or a punch in the face—or both."

Invariably they would choose the fifty and point to another street waif who maybe knew the elusive Teresa. Quinn would hand them a ten. If they complained, he'd tell them the punch in the face was still available and they'd quickly fade back into the crowds.

After several tries bracing the street kids, they stood smoking cigarettes on the corner of Eddy and Mason. A dirty kid in a heavily studded leather jacket and hair colored with what Steven guessed was spray paint walked up and asked if they were the guys giving out money to find a girl named Teresa.

"Why are you looking for her? You guys cops?"

"You know her?"

"Maybe."

"You seen cops handing out money before?"

"No."

"Well, I guess we're not cops then. I need to find her and if you know where she's at, I'll put fifty bucks in your hand right now. But if you're wrong, I'll come back tomorrow, the next day, the next week until I find you. You understand? This ain't free money."

"I know her."

"You think you do."

"I do, I know her."

"Describe her."

The kid did his best. His words jumbled and stuttered.

When Quinn was convinced it was the right Teresa, he said, "All right, that's her. What else do you know?"

"I think I know where she stays."

"Where?"

"I don't know the exact address, but I know the house. If you give me a hundred, I'll take you there."

Quinn shot a wink to Steven. "We've got a player." It was getting late and the wind had picked up, bringing the damp cold with it. Quinn and Steven were tired of bouncing between the runaways and tourists.

Quinn told the kid, "You're on. Let's go."

The three of them walked to the underground parking garage under Union Square. They piled into the Nissan, Quinn behind the wheel, the street kid in the passenger seat, and Steven in back. The kid asked them if they knew where the Mission was.

Quinn said, "Yeah, of course."

Before they got out of the parking garage, Quinn rolled down all four windows. The street kid stank. His musty body odor hung in the car even with the foggy air blowing in, a chemical tang layered with filth and mold. In back, Steven lit a cigarette to mask the stench. The kid was unaware of his offensive odor. He sat, smiling, enjoying the ride. Probably the first time he'd been in a car in months.

The Hall of Justice was a huge, gray slab. A full city block, still and unchanging. It was the way Carl remembered it. Always a beehive of activity in front, the building stood like the largest tombstone in the city. They'd added a new corkscrew-shaped jail on the backside, a McDonalds had sprung up on the corner, and the traffic was worse than it'd ever been, but the bold certainty of the Hall of Justice was there waiting for them.

They locked their guns in the trunk of Peters' car and kept their badges with them. They crossed Bryant Street and walked in between three news crews doing live remotes on the sidewalk and stairs.

"What's all the hubbub?" Peters asked.

"There's always some kind of somethin' happening

here. It's the big city. If there ain't no news, they'll make some."

They waited as the security line slowly moved toward the metal detectors. They passed their badges and keys to the officer on duty, but he didn't glance at them and handed both badges back when they passed though the detector's arch. Inside, the lobby was loud and chaotic. Footsteps and voices reverberated off the marble walls and floors. They made their way to the large back-lit directory. Carl extended his finger up to H—Homicide.

"Fourth floor, let's go." Carl pointed toward the elevator bank and Peters followed.

They found their way to Homicide on the fourth floor. Carl told the officer manning the front desk they were there to see Detective Panzer.

The clerk squinted back. "You're not reporters, are you?"

"No, sir, we are not."

"You better not be bullshitting or we'll ban you from the building for good." The clerk leaned back on his swivel chair. "Bill, you got company."

Bill Panzer stood up from a cubicle near the windows farthest from the door. He was heavier than Carl remembered, grayer, too. He figured he'd weathered the years pretty well considering how he must look to Bill.

"If it ain't the Calistoga Task Force." Panzer grinned and extended a hand first to Carl and then to Peters. "Call me Bill." Before the conversation could go any further, he said, "Let's go across the street and grab a coffee or somethin'. It's a crazy day in here."

The three exited the building the same way they came

in. Peters noticed four news crews now planted on the wide front steps.

"Big story today?" he asked Panzer.

"Found a body in the Marina district this morning. Right on the fucking sidewalk," shouted Panzer as they dodged traffic and skittered across Bryant Street. "TV news love that shit."

"Somebody important?" Carl asked.

They reached the sidewalk across from the Hall of Justice and stood under the awning of a bail bonds-man's. Both Carl and Bill were panting from their jag across the street.

"I don't know who the hell it is, or where he came from. But you leave a body on the sidewalk in a rich neighborhood at seven in the morning and the reporters will have a field day. We don't know any more than they do, as usual. Let's go into this place," Bill said, pointing to a café a few doors up the street. "The coffee's pretty good and the pastries are better."

They settled in at a round wood table by the window. They sipped their coffees out of paper cups. After the obligatory comments and compliments, Carl said, "What'd you find out about our friend Tremblay?"

"Ah yes, the French Connection." Panzer took a bite out of a large, round cheese croissant. "I talked with a few of the guys in vice and one guy in narcotics. Your boy doesn't have too many friends left on the force, I can tell you that."

"It'd be nice if we could speak to just one."

Panzer plied the plastic cover from his paper cup. "Well...there is one guy."

Carl leaned in, but didn't say anything.

"He's a younger guy from narcotics. You know how these narco guys are—cagey as fuck. He says he's still in touch with him. When I ask him why, he dodges, says Tremblay still has his ear to the ground. Comes in useful. I dunno whether they're in bed together or if Tremblay's feeding information, or what."

Peters cut in. "Does he know where to find him?"

"I think so, but he wouldn't say shit. I told him about you, Carl. Asked if maybe he'd sit down, have a word. Said to call him later tonight. He's on duty 'til eight."

"Set it up," Carl said.

CHAPTER EIGHT

"That's the place," the kid said. They were on Treat Street, a one block dead-end at the outer edge of the Mission District that sat above Precita Park. He pointed to an old Victorian in need of a paint job. The house was sandwiched between two nicer houses that looked as though they wanted to recoil from the gray shabby dump.

"You sure?" Quinn said.

The house had junk piled beside the front door. Bicycle parts, old TVs, big black rotting garbage bags with objects poking out their sides. The door to the place was covered in colorful stickers slapped on at odd angles, leafed over one another.

"Yeah, I'm sure."

Quinn scanned the street for parking. He spotted a space behind them and threw the Nissan into reverse. Once they were wedged in and Quinn was sure they still had a bead on the front door, he killed the engine.

"Now what?" Steven said.

Quinn reached over in front of the street kid and popped open the glove box. The kid's eyes went wide when he saw the chrome-plated .45 inside. Quinn took the gun out and, with his finger on the outside of the trigger guard, backhanded the kid in the face. The barrel of the gun connected nicely with the kid's forehead, but not too hard.

"Ouch. Shit, dude, what the fuck?"

Quinn bent his elbow and let the butt of the pistol come down on the side of the kid's head. The boy cried out.

"Is she in there?" Quinn said.

The kid held his head down near his knees. "I don't know if she is. I just know she stays there."

"Sit up."

The kid stayed down, still covering his head with his hands.

Quinn poked him in the ribs—hard—with the muzzle of the .45. "Sit up."

The kid sat up. "Dude, please."

"You want your money?"

The kid nodded. He was whimpering now, like a child.

"You want to wait here and see if she's in there? You want to sit with us a while and see what happens next?"

The kid didn't move. He wasn't sure how to answer.

"You sure this is the place?"

The kid nodded.

"You sure?" Quinn jabbed him again with the barrel of the gun. His top lip curled up, exposing a row of perfect white teeth.

"Dude, I'm sure."

"Stop calling me dude. It's annoying." Quinn pressed the barrel against the boy's cheek. He pushed until the boy's head connected with the glass of the passenger side window. "I got forty bucks for you, so you can leave and go get high or whatever the fuck you do. You're not going to say shit about this. If you get in the way of me rescuing this little girl, I'm going to come find you. You hearin' me?"

The kid tried to nod his head. The barrel dug into his face.

"Don't fucking move, this thing might go off."

Steven sat quiet and still in the back, afraid any movement on his part would also cause the gun to fire. The sight of the gun scared him, seeing Quinn's personality flip again scared him too, but there was an undeniable power there. It was hard to ignore. A thin smile appeared on Quinn's face.

"If you're smart, you'll go back to where we found you," Quinn said. "If she's here and I can get her and take her home, I'll come find you and give you the rest of your hundred. How's that sound?"

The sound that came from the kid's mouth was barely a breath. "Good."

"You'd like that, huh? Some extra dough? Get high for a day or two. Sounds nice." Quinn pulled the gun back. "Lemme see your wallet."

"What?"

"Your wallet, your ID."

The kid reached under himself and pulled his wallet from his back pocket and handed it to Quinn.

Quinn took it and flipped it open with his free hand. He thumbed out the ID. "California ID? You don't even have a real driver's license? No wonder you're on the fucking street. You should get your shit together." He paused to read the name on the card. "Phillip Cardasos."

The kid nodded silently.

"What do they call you, Phillip?"

"Why do they what?"

"*What.* What do they call you? On the street. You go by Phillip or Phil, or what?"

"Filthy."

"Filthy?" Quinn turned to look at Steven. "I couldn't imagine why." He poked the boy with the barrel of the gun once more. "Listen, Filthy, I'm going to hang on to the ID for a while, in case I got trouble finding you. You can get out now, go back downtown. And keep your fingers crossed that Teresa didn't move or disappear."

Quinn flipped the wallet onto the kid's lap. The kid picked it up and opened the car door and got out. He started walking straight down the sidewalk, away from the house, away from the car.

Quinn climbed out of the driver's side and called to him. "Hey, Filth, don't you want your forty bucks?" He held two twenties folded between his fingers.

The kid stopped, turned, seemed to debate it for a second, then scurried back to the car. He snatched the bills from Quinn's hand, turned again, and strode quickly away without saying anything.

When Quinn climbed back into his seat, he turned to Steven and gave him a broad white smile. "What about you? You're going to stay and help me, right?" He patted the seat beside him.

Teresa Alvarez didn't even notice the pale brown Nissan parked on the block. She and her friend, Paul, walked by quick and determined. She kept her hands together, right squeezing the left as she walked. She didn't see the young man's head leaning against the lightly fogged window, his mouth agape and his eyes fluttering deep in a dream state.

"He's gonna be home. He's always home. He doesn't go anywhere. He's got that bitch, Simone, running to the store for him, like, ten times a day."

"What the fuck does he need from the store?" Paul said. "The fucking guy never eats."

"Cigarettes and strawberry milk. He loves that shit. I think it's disgusting."

"Is he fucking Simone?"

"Probably. She shows up two weeks ago and hasn't left. He better not let me catch 'em. I hate her. She's probably diseased."

They made it to the front stoop of the peeling, grayed building. Paul pulled a small silver rectangle box from under his denim jacket. "You think he's gonna go for it?"

"Why not?" Teresa said. "He buys computer stuff all the time." She frowned at the inert box. "What is it again?"

"It's a hard drive. An external one. It's got, like, five hundred gigs or something. They're over a hundred bucks in the store; it's got to be worth fifty or something to him."

"Doesn't look like much."

"Looks are deceiving."

Quinn sat up straight in his seat and jabbed Steven in the shoulder. "Wake up, kid. That's her."

Steven pulled his head from the window and licked

his lips and teeth. His tongue was dry from sleeping with his mouth open. His neck was kinked and he had to pee. For a moment, he forgot where he was. He turned and saw Quinn, wide awake and excited.

"I'm thinking, fuck the original plan. Just go to her now and say her dad is in the car. Get her to come over here."

"Who's that she's with?"

"I got no idea. Doesn't matter, I'll take care of him. Go, go. Quick before she goes inside."

"I thought you wanted her to go inside. That was the plan."

"I changed my mind. This'll be easier. Don't worry, you'll still get paid."

Steven thought about the gun in the glove box. He thought again about the fork wagging in Joe-Joe's belly. He gave in with an almost imperceptible nod.

As they discussed their move, they watched the two young people on the stoop of the house discuss theirs.

Paul was pleading. "I can't go in. I still owe him money. You go, get whatever you can and meet me down at the park. I trust you."

"What am I supposed to tell him? He's gonna ask where I got it; I don't even know what *it* is." She took one step up. She stood a little taller than her friend now.

"I told you. It's an external hard drive. Just see what you can get and take it. I'll be at the park down the street."

Teresa practiced saying it. "An external hard drive." She took the silver box from her friend. "I don't know how long it's gonna take. You know how he is."

"Fuck. Do I ever." Paul thrust his hands in his pockets and started back down the street. Before he got twenty feet he turned and said, "*Don't* forget about me. I'll be waiting."

She waved him on, shushing him, and turned up the stairs.

Paul walked right past the Nissan, eyes straight ahead, lost in the daydream of hope, desire, and impatience.

"Now's the time. There she goes. Get out there before she gets inside. Go." Quinn reached across Steven and pulled his door handle.

"I don't think I should do this. I don't think I can do it."

Quinn said, his voice straight and low, "It's too late for all that. You *have* to."

Steven took a deep breath and got out of the car. The air felt cold because he'd just woken up. He stuffed his hands into his jacket pockets and pulled the coat tight around him. Her back was to the street and she stood still in front of the door. Steven didn't think she'd pushed the doorbell yet. He quickened his pace. Her hair was straight and uneven, hanging down her back. Red, but not a natural red. As he got closer, he could see the long brown roots at her skull before they shifted in color.

He reached the stoop and she still hadn't moved. "Excuse me."

She was motionless, lost in thought.

"Excuse me," he said again.

She turned. From where she stood, on the porch six steps above him, she looked statuesque. She was pale and the crimson hair increased her pallor. Bruise-colored purple bags hung underneath her eyes. She clasped a small silver box with both hands. She didn't say anything.

"Are you Teresa?"

The right side of her mouth twitched.

Steven started up the steps slowly.

"Whoa, whoa, whoa." She stepped back and held her palms up as though it would stop him. "Who the fuck are you?"

"Teresa? My name is Steven."

"I don't give a shit. How'd you know my name?" She looked past him and up the block, half-expecting reinforcements to be bounding up behind him.

"No, no, no, no. Hang on, let me explain. I'm not...I don't...look, sorry to creep up on you like this, but I was *asked* to speak to you." He reached the top of the stairs and was now close to her. She took another half-step back. Her face was pocked with blemishes and a curious red rash ringed her mouth. The two-tone hair was parted in the middle of her forehead and hung greasy and flat. She was tiny, frail-looking. He could see her eyes now, a strange combination of hazel and emerald encased in bloodshot white. They began to sparkle and shift.

"Hi." He tried to start over, but it sounded false and empty. He was nervous now. Not because he was accosting the girl, but because he was near her. He flustered. "I need to speak with you."

"Fuck off, weirdo. I don't know where you think you know me from. If this is Paul's—"

"I'm a friend of your dad's. He's been looking for you."

He waited for her eyes to light up. They didn't. Mistrust clouded them.

"Who are you?"

The front door opened.

"Teresa. Where the fuck you been?" An older guy, a little shorter than Steven, stood in the threshold to the house. The man was more stained and greasy than Teresa and he curled his lips as though he'd just tasted something bad. He looked up and down at Steven. "Who's your friend?"

Teresa shot Steven a look, a tight-faced scowl that told him to play along. Her desperation overcame any threat she felt from him. Her desire to score diluted any interest in why Steven was there. While the man looked Steven up and down, Teresa's lips quivered and fumbled with the answer to the question.

But before she could admit she didn't know who this stranger was, Steven held out his hand and said, "I'm Steven, a friend of Teresa's."

The guy didn't shake it. He looked down at the sidewalk like he expected there to be more visitors and said, "C'mon, c'mon, let's go. Get inside."

From the car, Quinn watched with excitement. A flash of pride shot through him. "That's my boy. Get in there." He removed the gun from the glove compartment and cradled it on his lap.

CHAPTER NINE

"I thought we were going to meet up somewhere we could eat." Peters was behind the wheel with Panzer beside him and Carl in the back as they plodded through the late afternoon traffic toward the Mission. "I really could have gone for a burrito or somethin'."

"I thought so, too," Panzer said. "I guess he doesn't want to meet inside. You want me to call him and see if he'll compromise and meet at a taco truck or something?"

Carl cleared his throat. "It's fine. If he doesn't want to be seen talking with us, then we respect that. Peters, you can wait an hour before you eat. I'll buy you a damn burrito."

"They got the best in the city on Twenty-fourth Street," Panzer said.

"Oh, I know. They ain't got 'em like that in Calistoga. Town fulla Mexicans and you can't get a decent burrito."

"Let's just try to stay focused on the job 'til we finish talking to this fella," Carl said.

"The job?" Panzer said. "Peters here told me you guys aren't even on the payroll for all this. It's personal time. Sounds a bit like a fishing expedition to me."

"We're on the job," Carl said. "We're just not getting

expenses down here. We're collecting evidence in an on-going homicide investigation."

"All right, all right." Panzer's tone receded. "I was just teasing," he lied. "But you may have to expense one of those burritos for me, too. I haven't eaten since lunch. Take a right here and go up about two more blocks, straight across Harrison and into the parking lot of the Best Buy."

Peters followed Panzer's directions and pulled into the lot. Best Buy was closing and the lot was emptying out. Panzer told him to drive through toward the alley in the back. "There he is."

An anonymous man with his head shrouded in a hoodie stood between two parked cars. They pulled up beside him. Carl opened his door and slid across the seat to make room.

The man climbed into the backseat and said, "Hey."

"Hey," Panzer said.

Peters chimed in, too. "Hey."

Carl stretched out his hand. "I'm Carl Bradley. I'm glad you could make time to meet with us. I really appreciate it."

The hooded man shook Carl's hand, but didn't offer his name. He looked Carl over. "Nice boots," he said.

Carl looked down at his well-worn cowboy boots, wondering if the stranger was teasing. "Thank you."

"I really don't have a lot of time, so if we could make this quick."

"Sure," Carl said. "I understand you have occasion to cross paths with Maurice Tremblay?"

"I do."

"Well, we'd like to speak with him. He's a witness of

sorts in a murder investigation up in Calistoga and we didn't finish up with his statement. We need to clear up a few things."

The man looked toward Panzer. Panzer faced forward and didn't turn around. "Bill, you didn't tell me they were looking to pull Tremblay in."

"We just want to talk with him," Carl said. "We're having a little trouble locating him."

"That's by design," the man said. "He doesn't want to be found."

Peters shifted in his seat and asked, "He's not involved in law enforcement anymore, right?"

The man laughed. "Not by a long shot."

"Well, what can you tell us?" Carl was getting impatient.

"Maurice was a half-ass bad guy, even when he was with the force. He rolled over drugs, information, whatever he determined was of value, to a few of the locals. Guys who could make use of that kind of thing. When they gave him the boot in oh-four, the tables turned. He started selling information the other way."

"He's an informant?"

"I guess you could say that. More like an informal informant. I don't know who else in the department is in touch with him. I only know what he tells me."

"Sounds convenient for him."

"It is. But the intel he gives has always been solid. You understand why I'm a bit reluctant to give him up."

"But you do know how to reach him."

"It depends. Usually he reaches out. He always uses a burner, so his number is always changing. After he calls,

I can reach him on the number—if there is a number—for only a day or two."

"You ever talk to him in person?"

"Sure, but only when *he* wants."

"Is he still living in San Francisco?"

"I don't think so. From what I gather, he's somewhere on the Peninsula. I know he's moved a few times in the last couple years. He's a slippery guy. He took what he learned from being a cop—a cop under scrutiny—and he applies it to his life now."

Peters asked, "What's he into?"

"Same as ever. Big money shit. Drugs mostly, but he knows a lot about what goes on. Big time bookies, union scale extortions. He's been tied to some heavyweights. Not officially, just word on the street stuff."

"Like who?" It was the first time Panzer spoke since saying hey.

"Miguel Diaz, Rollie Berg, most notably Richard Allen."

"I've heard of Diaz, don't know Berg," Panzer said. "Who's Richard Allen?"

"Maybe you know him as Ricardo Alvarez. He's a Mexican cartel guy, supposedly gone legit. The American face to the Mexican crime wave. He's a big shot in this town. Friendly with the local politicians, connected at City Hall. Nice on paper, but nasty in real life."

"And what's our Maurice do for Mr. Allen?" Carl asked.

"My guess is anything Mr. Allen wants."

From up front, Peters mumbled, "So much for the French Mafia."

"What the fuck is he talking about?"

"Nothing," Carl said, "he's just hungry. Listen, I need to talk to this man. How can I reach him?"

"You can't. But if he calls me, I'll call Panzer. Maybe we can set something up—*maybe*. But I'm telling you, I'm not looking to give up my source, or, more importantly, end up in the morgue."

"You scared of this guy?"

"Most definitely."

There was a moment of silence in the car before the man repeated that he had Panzer's number and Panzer had his. "By the way, my name is Pino." Then, without saying goodbye or goodnight, he opened the door, got out, and walked away.

Maurice Tremblay was on Page Street. He stood at the metal gate that barred him from Joe-Joe's apartment. He pressed the buzzer once. Then again. On the third try he kept his finger on the button. He heard the shrill buzz inside the apartment.

The inside door finally swung open.

"*What?*" Joe-Joe was standing behind the gate in shorts and a white T-shirt. There was a red puss-colored stain where the shirt stretched across his stomach.

Tremblay didn't greet him, he only said, "Let me in."

"Jesus, man, I didn't know it was you. Why didn't you call? I fuckin' wish you was here yesterday."

"Let me in." More terse this time.

Joe-Joe pressed a button inside his door and the front gate buzzed open. Tremblay pushed it open and pointed into Joe-Joe's apartment. "Inside."

Once they were inside Joe-Joe's kitchen, Tremblay sat

down at the table. "You know why I'm here?"

"I can fuckin' well guess." Joe-Joe pulled out the seat opposite. "You're lookin' for Quinn. You're a day late and a dollar short."

"He was here?"

"Fuck yeah he was here. How do you think I got this?" Joe-Joe pointed to the ugly stain on his shirt. "Fuckin' piece of shit stuck a fork in me. Like, four times."

"What did he want?"

"The girl."

"And what did you tell him?"

"I told him the truth. What was I supposed to do? He had a fork in my ribs. I told him that the girl's been hanging out around Powell Street with all them other druggie kids, you know."

Tremblay took a deep breath and let it out slowly through his nose. It made a hollow whistling sound. He rubbed his chin for a moment. "You mind if I do a rail?"

"Sure, man. Can I have some?"

"No."

Tremblay took out his baggie of blow and poured a little pile onto the Formica table. He plucked a business card from a cup full of cards in the middle of the table. He looked at it. Free cheesesteak with every ten purchases. The card had been stamped three times. He spread the coke out and chopped it with the edge of the card, combed it into two lines. He curled the card over onto itself and formed a short tube, bent over and sucked a line deep into each nostril. He pinched his nose with his fingers and waited.

Joe-Joe waited, too. Halfway hoping he'd change his mind about sharing.

After a minute, Tremblay said, "You think he's gonna be back?"

"I fuckin' hope not. If he does, you'll be the first to know. You got a number or something?"

"Yeah," Tremblay recited the number, his voice still tight from the lines. Joe-Joe scrawled it down on the backside of a Chinese take-out menu. Tremblay took out his phone and tapped in Joe-Joe's number as Joe-Joe read it off. He put his phone back in his pocket and pointed to Joe-Joe's belly. "Let's see the damage."

Joe-Joe carefully lifted his shirt. There were four sets of four-pointed puncture wounds close together on the bulb of his stomach.

"Shit, that looks infected. You should see somebody about that."

"No shit. A bit of numbing agent would help, too. If you know what I mean?"

Again Tremblay said, "No." He got up from the table. "If Quinn comes back, you call me. Before you even open the door, you call." Then he turned and walked out of the apartment alone.

The first thing Steven noticed was the man's bare legs. He was wearing olive green army fatigues ripped off at the knee. Below, his calves were bone-white with pocked sores in various stages of infection. The house was dark and it was tough for Steven to get a good look at the eruptions on the man's legs as they clamored behind him.

Teresa kept spinning her head back to Steven and sneering at him with her index finger pressed to her lips. He wasn't sure what she'd feared he'd say, but he intended on not saying anything at all.

The hallway was filled with debris. Dark green garbage bags piled on top of defeated cardboard boxes that left only a narrow margin for the three to get by. There were low-hanging chandeliers above their heads, but they held no bulbs. The only sign of any electricity was a far-off tinny guitar, someone playing badly through a small practice amp.

They reached the kitchen and passed right through. The smell of rotting food mixed with ammonia stung Steven's nostrils. The man led them into a back porch that had been glassed-in for years. The glass was covered with paper and foil, but it was the lightest spot they'd reached.

"Sit down," the man said, pointing to a huge wooden spool, the kind used to wrap industrial cable. It had been turned sideways and was covered with magazines, empty cartons of strawberry milk, and a large, round ashtray. And, Steven noted, an expensive digital scale.

The man sat down on an upturned plastic milk crate. Steven and Teresa did the same.

The man took a moment to light a cigarette, then said, "So, what's up?"

"I need some shit," Teresa said.

"That's all? You ain't been here for almost two days. I hope you brought some money back."

"Is Simone still here?"

He ignored the question. "Who's your friend?"

Steven gave his head a quarter-turn toward the direction they'd come, as if to remind their host he'd already introduced himself when he entered. "Steven," he said.

"I'm Raja." The man reached forward and pulled the ashtray toward him with one finger. "You a friend of Teresa's or a *friend* of Teresa's?"

"Just a friend."

The man, Raja, seemed to consider this. He studied Steven. He locked eyes with him while he took a long drag on his cigarette. "So, friend, what do you need?"

Teresa answered for him. "I got this hard drive. An external hard drive." The phrase sounded alien on her tongue. "It's supposed to be a good one." She set the metal rectangle on the table.

Raja broke his stare and looked down at the drive. "Lemme see." He examined it, flipped it over in his hands, looked closely at the plugs on the back, the specifications on the side. "What'd you want for it?"

"A hundred."

"You're dreaming."

"How about fifty?"

"Okay, but not in cash."

"No, not in cash."

Raja flipped the box over again in his hand before setting it down on the table. "I'll go a half-gram of dope and a half-gram of speed."

Teresa whimpered a little.

"Take it or leave it."

She glanced over at Steven. He wasn't sure if she was embarrassed by the transaction or using him to manipulate Raja. Then she said, "Well? You got anything to throw in?"

It took him a second to figure out what she meant

before he silently shook his head.

"Take it," she said to Raja.

The dealer rubbed his hands together and said, "All right. I was just getting ready to get well myself." He reached over to his left and flipped open a blue metal toolbox. Inside, on the top drawer that extended when the box was opened, were an assortment of baggies and a few sealed ten-packs of needles. The gulley of the box was stuffed with used syringes piled high and entangled like dangerous wooden matches.

Raja pulled a burned spoon and a ball of cotton from the top level and set it on the table. "You got your own shit?"

Steven looked to Teresa to answer before he realized that Raja was speaking to him. Steven shook his head, but Raja didn't notice because he was busy slicing off a wedge of black tar from a lump he'd unwrapped. He dropped it onto the scale. Steven looked at Teresa who barely moved an index finger, a signal to not worry.

"I need a new one. Steven here just smokes it."

Raja looked up from what he was doing with knitted eyebrows. "Really? Fuckin' waste." He took the piece from the scale and held it up with two fingers to examine it before passing it across to Teresa. He quickly carved off another piece and dropped it into his spoon without weighing it.

Steven watched as Raja added water and cooked the heroin with a disposable lighter. The acrid vinegar smell struck him where he sat. He looked over at Teresa; she had produced a spoon from nowhere and was going through the same ritual, although she'd broken her piece in half and left a portion sitting on the table, presumably for Steven. They both rolled tiny wads from the cotton ball and dropped them into the spoons. For a moment, Steven wondered if his brother had ever been into heroin, or just speed.

When they were both ready, Raja tore open the bag of new syringes, handed Teresa one and kept one for himself. They each carefully drew up the coffee-brown liquid into their needles.

Raja said, "I'll be right back." He got up and left the room without saying anything else.

When he'd gone, Teresa explained. "He's got trouble finding a vein so he goes in the bathroom. He can see better in there." She stood up and undid the top button on her jeans. "Plus he's a little shy."

She tugged down the back of her pants and stuck the needle into the topside of her right buttock. Slowly, she depressed the plunger.

Steven watched in amazement. She didn't flinch or whimper.

When she was finished, she sat back down. "What the hell happened to your face?"

Steven touched his forehead and ran his fingers over the protruding lump and didn't answer.

Teresa pointed to the wedge of heroin. "You don't really want me to find you some foil to smoke that with, right?"

"No," Steven said. "I don't want any. You keep it. I still need to talk to you about your dad. He's waiting outside."

"Bullshit." She smiled for the first time since they'd been in the house. Now that the junk was working its way through her system, she let down her guard a little, but only a little. "You're serious? I thought you were a friend of Paul's he sent in to keep an eye on me. How do you know my father?"

"I met him in Willits. He drove me down here. He's been searching for you."

"I doubt that."

"That I met him in Willits, or that he's looking for you?"

"Both." She eyed him for a moment, measuring his sincerity. "And you two get along, huh?"

"He's all right."

"You don't know my father."

"Maybe you're right, but he's outside now. Waiting for you."

Teresa got up from the table, her smile twisted into a disbelieving smirk. "Where?"

They left the makeshift porch and went back through the filthy kitchen and down the hall toward the front of the house. When they reached the front door, Steven put his hand on the knob and Teresa put her hand over his.

"Wait," she said. She stretched on her tiptoes and peered out the small frame of colored glass in the center of the door. "I don't see anybody."

"He's down the street a little. To the left. About five cars down."

He watched her from behind. Her T-shirt pulled away from her jeans as she stretched to look. Her skin was white as chalk. She was thin, rakish, beautiful. There was something gentle about her.

"I still don't see him. There's nobody there."

"Sure there is. He's right there in the car, sitting in the driver's seat."

She turned back from the portal; her eyes wide and scared. "That's not my dad."

Thoughts ricocheted through Steven's brain. He'd been duped. Used. He thought about the fork sticking out of the fat man's belly, wagging back and forth. He felt foolish. He'd brought something terrible with him into this girl's life.

She said, "I gotta go."

She skirted past him and ran back through the house to the porch room in back. There, she quickly began stuffing her things in her pockets. The small wedge of dope, the spoon, she grabbed the open bag of syringes and stuffed them into her boot at the inside of her right leg. "C'mon, c'mon" she said to herself. "He didn't give us the speed. Where's the fucking speed?"

She reached over to Raja's toolbox and flipped open the lid and grabbed a few of the plastic baggies inside and stuffed them into her pockets, too. She looked down at the box and grabbed the rest of them.

He stood watching her. She was near panicked, looking around the room for an escape. She peeled back the posters and foil on the windows, searching for one that wasn't painted shut.

"Isn't there another door to this place?" Steven asked.

She thrust a finger at him. "Look, I don't know who you are, or who that fucker outside is, but I ain't going with either of you no matter what."

Steven wanted to tell her he was trapped, tricked. He felt as scared of Quinn as she looked right now. "I don't know that guy. I mean, he found me. He fooled me. I'm afraid to go back out the front door. He's...he's fucking dangerous." Steven heard his own voice degenerating into a plea. "I don't know what to do. I don't know what to tell him. I thought he was your dad."

"There's no time for this shit. I got to go, *now*."

"What about your friend?"

"Fuck him." She threw her shoulder against a window frame. It creaked as the paint cracked apart and it separated from the wood. She looked down at the drop. It was only one floor up. Below was a cramped yard filled with the same debris that polluted the inside of the house.

"I'm gone," she said as she threw a leg over the windowsill. "You coming?"

He nodded, but she'd already dropped out the window.

CHAPTER TEN

Carl and Peters sat in a taqueria on 24th Street. Panzer had opted out of the meal but directed them to what he said were the best burritos in town. Carl shifted uncomfortably on the hard plastic benches. He peeled back the foil on his burrito and complimented the absent Panzer on a good choice.

"Hell, I could eat two of these things," Peters said. "I'm thinking of gettin' another one to go."

"I don't think I'll be able to finish mine, you can have it."

They ate in silence, dripping the bright green avocado salsa onto the open ends of the burritos and tempering their pace with tortilla chips. They moaned with exaggerated delight.

Finally, Carl sat down the stub of his burrito in the red plastic basket and said, "You heard from Perez?"

"Nope," Peters said with his mouth still full.

"Why don't we give him a call and see what he came up with during his hard day of investigation."

Peters agreed, wiped his hands with a paper napkin, and took out his cell.

"Perez? It's me, Peters. I'm down here with Carl enjoying the sights of the city and we was wondering what you come up with today." Peters listened to the phone for a moment. "Eatin' a *real* burrito, that's what."

Carl motioned with his hand for Peters to give him the phone.

"Perez? This is Carl Bradley. We're gonna be needing you to run point on this thing back home. I hope that's not too much trouble for you." Carl paused and listened, then cupped the phone with his hand and told Peters, "He says they found the gray truck."

Carl asked Perez if they found anything in the truck, anything at all. Perez told him, no, it'd been wiped clean. Carl sighed; he had a feeling that'd be the case. Then Perez mentioned a stolen credit card used at a restaurant not two blocks away.

"Why does that raise up your short hairs?" Carl asked.

Perez told him two men used the card. They'd bought a meal about an hour after the murder. There were, Perez reminded him, two men seen going into the Oulilette place and one a piece in the vehicles seen leaving.

"Well, might be something to that. I think it'd be in order to go down there and talk with the folks at the restaurant and see what they remember about these two."

Perez told Carl he was way ahead of him. He'd already gone down to see the waitress and taken a statement. He took down a vague description of the two men. One in his forties and one in his early twenties.

"Father and son?" Carl asked.

Perez said he had no idea, but it felt like a start. Policemen's intuition.

"She say if the older man had a gut on him?"

Perez said no. He was of average build. The waitress did say the older one was good-looking. "Movie star good looks" was what Perez had written down.

"It's not our boy Tremblay then," he said to Perez while he looked at Peters. "I guess we'd better be talking to the owner of that credit card."

Perez said he already had, sort of. He'd spoken to a woman in Clear Lake who said her husband had been missing for four days. She reported his credit card missing after the first two.

"That doesn't sound good. It even gets *my* short hairs standing up a little. Well, thank you, young man. I'll call back in the morning to see if we can't get somebody up there to talk with her in person." He thanked him once more, ended the call and handed Peters back his phone.

"What'd he say?" Peters said.

"He said you might as well enjoy your burrito, since he was the only one doing real police work today."

"He did not."

"No, but go ahead and enjoy it anyway."

When Tremblay returned to his motel room it was just as he left it. He'd bought his own bottle of Maker's Mark at a liquor store on 6th Street on the way back. He tossed the unopened bottle on the bed. No chaser. He could always hit the soda machine later if he wanted. Or drink tap water. He was drunk, tired, and had no energy to get undressed. He tossed his cell on the bureau before the vanity and stood looking at himself in the mirror. Same old Tremblay. The city had changed but he hadn't.

He rubbed his gut and decided he was hungry, but not enough to order in.

He leaned in toward the mirror. His eyes were bloodshot. His fleshy cheeks were red, too. Almost sunburned. After seeing Joe-Joe, he'd ended the day with a few drinks at a bar near Powell Street and wondered how he would find the girl. If the little bitch was strung out she probably wasn't spending a lot of time on the street. She was probably shacked up with some dealer. Giving it up in exchange for staying high. She was young and still a good-looking kid, though. Too young to be whoring, too old to be out there begging change with the runaways. He wouldn't mind a piece of her if he found her first. Richard would kill him, but there could be worse reasons to die. He smiled at his reflection in the mirror and picked up his cell and dialed.

"Pino? It's me."

Pino said, "Where you been, old timer?"

"Around. Listen, I need some help with something."

"You know how that works. I could use some help with something too."

"I'm looking for a girl."

"Who isn't?"

"I can give you a name to run, but I don't think it's gonna help much. I hear she's living a transient lifestyle. You want to meet up? Have a chat about this little bitch?"

"Sure. There's something I want to talk to you about, too."

"Good news or bad?"

"I'm thinking it's bad."

Tremblay took the diminishing baggie of cocaine from

his jacket pocket and held it up to the light. "Oh, and, Pino, maybe bring me a little something, I'm running low."

Quinn saw a shadow. A movement of some kind in the small, square opaque glass that served as a peep-hole in the front door of the house. Someone had been looking out. If his cover was blown, he may never get a chance to snatch the girl again. No way to tell if whoever it was saw him, but he was growing tired of waiting for Steven.

"Goddamn shame. I thought you were a good kid, too," he said to himself as he opened the car door.

He got out and walked directly to the house. The .45 in his hand at his side. He went up the front stairs and tried the door. Locked. He tried to peek around the sides of the building, but couldn't see anything. He sighed, stood back and kicked the front door right above the knob. It didn't budge. He tried again and felt the old jamb give a little. On the fourth try it gave way and broke open. The first thing that hit him was the musty funk from inside the place. The only sound was a far-off electric guitar. Sounded like someone was playing the tune-up blues. The uneven warble of the stretching strings went on as he entered the house.

He used his sleeve to open the first door on the right. Dirty mattress, piles of useless crap, mounds of clothes, three bicycles leaned on each other over a small pyramid of bike parts. The second door was padlocked from the outside. He moved on. On the left was another door. He tried the doorknob with his sleeve. Locked. A thin bar of light was glowing at the bottom of the door. A voice came from inside.

"Busy."

A man's voice. Not the girl; not the kid. Quinn knocked at the door.

"I'm fucking busy."

Quinn knocked harder.

"Get the fuck outta here. I'll be out when I'm out."

The voice was snide, serpentine. Quinn banged hard with the side of his fist.

"Who the fuck is it?"

He heard a clatter now, something metallic falling on linoleum, someone pulling on their pants. No flushing, though. He pointed his gun at eye-level and waited for the door to open.

When the door swung open a smallish man with a scruffy goatee and a sneer on his face snapped, "*What?*"

Quinn fired. He shot the man right in the forehead. A fine mist of blood bloomed behind the man's head and a rash of red splattered behind him on the bathroom wall. The man dropped to the floor and Quinn moved on.

The guitar had stopped. Quinn heard footsteps coming upstairs.

A voice saying, "What the fuck was that?"

Quinn turned his gun in the direction of the voice. A swinging door near the kitchen opened and a chubby, long-haired man in a black T-shirt appeared. He stopped as soon as he saw Quinn. He started to say something, but never got out a syllable. Quinn fired twice and listened to the body tumble backward down the stairs. Quinn could hear the empty static of the amplifier and no other noise. He guessed there was no one else downstairs. He'd have to check, though. First, he moved on through the kitchen.

"Fuckin' disgusting," he said to himself. The midday warmth had made the muggy stench almost unbearable. He moved to the back room, saw the drug paraphernalia strewn across the makeshift table, then saw the forced window. He looked out, looked down, and said, "Fuck."

CHAPTER ELEVEN

Steven scrambled to catch Teresa. They scurried down the graveled alley behind the house. He called to her, but she kept moving. At the end of the block sat Precita Park, a block-sized oval of green grass and trees. Several dogs fetched for their owners while a few hobos parked on the benches. She moved right through it without turning around. By the time they hit Caesar Chavez, she was forced to stop for traffic and he caught up.

"Hey," he said. "Slow down. What's going on? Who do you think that was?"

"It doesn't matter," she said between breaths. "I told you, you don't know my father. If someone came for me, it doesn't make a difference if he sent them or not, it's trouble."

"What kind of trouble?"

She looked him in the eye with all the sincerity she could muster. "*Bad* trouble."

Steven tried to take it all in, what it meant. "Are you in danger?"

"If you brought one of my father's friends to get me, then we're both fucked."

"I don't understand. Who is your father?"

"An asshole. *King* of the assholes." She looked behind them in the direction of the house, then turned and darted into the street between cars. Steven followed.

They zig-zagged through the back streets of the Mission District and worked their way toward 24th and Mission. The crowds and bustle there didn't calm either of them. Teresa looked impatiently up the street for the next bus and Steven looked for Quinn.

"You got any money?" Teresa said as the orange and white Muni bus wheezed to a halt.

Steven shook his head.

"Let's go." Teresa led him onto the bus through the back doors. There were several grunts and curses as they pushed through riders exiting. Once aboard, they moved farther back and found two seats across from each other and flopped down.

"Where're we going?" Steven asked.

Teresa, still breathing heavily, held her index finger to her lips and then shrugged her shoulders.

Steven watched her. A film of sweat glistened on her forehead. She looked better than she had at the house, as though the open air had pumped new life into her.

She looked back at him and said, "That fucking lump on your head looks terrible."

Before he left, Quinn went down the stairs into the cement basement. Like he'd suspected, there was no one there. The body of the overweight guitar player lay feet-up at the bottom of the stairs, the orange light on the amplifier glowed in the near dark. He stepped over the body and moved in the dim light of a bare bulb that hung suspended from the ceiling. Convinced there was no witness crouching in a corner, he went back upstairs.

He moved again from room to room and found them vacant. He kicked open the padlocked door, tearing the bracket from the face of the door. There, too, he found no one. A replica of the first room—dirty clothes, dissembled electronics, more bike parts, and melted wax candles on most of the open surfaces. He turned and left.

As he started the car, he thought about the young man Teresa was with. He'd shouted he'd be waiting in the park for Teresa. He didn't think the young man had seen him, but thought he might be useful. He turned the car around in the narrow street and rolled down the gentle slope to Precita Park.

He circled the small park once with his car. Streetlights now illuminated the park while the evening shade turned to night. No sign of Teresa's friend. He drove off. Police would be arriving soon and he wanted to be seen by as few people as possible. He started to weave through the nearby streets, guessing which way Steven and the girl went. No sign. He cursed himself for not shooting them both while they stood on the porch. He glanced at the digital clock on the dashboard. It'd been almost twenty minutes since he'd entered the house. They could be anywhere by now.

Teresa's plan was to stay on the bus. When it reached the end of the line, get on another bus. Stay on the buses all night. Maybe migrate toward the beach, Golden Gate Park, somewhere they could hide in true darkness.

"What'd he look like?"

Steven's thoughts were crowded with conflicting feelings. His guilt, his worrying about Teresa—a girl he didn't know—and his own dire circumstance. Teresa's question entered his mind like a distant ringing phone. "Who?"

"*Him.* The guy you brought to Raja's? The guy that's claiming to be my fucking father."

"I dunno. A regular guy, I guess. He was friendly, funny—at first." He told her about getting jacked in Willits, how Quinn found him, about trusting him, their ride down and the stolen car. He said he seemed okay when they drank at the motel. He thought Quinn was just a badass, like his brother. Then he told her about Joe-Joe and the fork.

"Joe-Joe? I know exactly who you're talking about. Piece of shit deserved more than a fork."

Steven wasn't sure what she meant by that, why she'd said it with such vehemence, so he continued with his story. He told her he feared Quinn after that. He didn't know why he kept going on with the search. He admitted he had nowhere else to go. "He made it sound like you were in danger. I thought I was doing the right thing."

"Even though you knew it was the wrong thing. In your gut, I mean. You knew he was bad."

Steven didn't answer.

"Who told you I'd be at Raja's?"

Steven described Filth, or Phil, or whoever he was. How Quinn had coerced him, then threatened him.

She looked out the bus's window and said, "Fuck."

The bus shook and rattled. They were nearly alone on it now as it reached the Financial District. The last of the nine-to-five crowd all moving in the opposite direction. They got off at Mission and Main and walked the block to Market Street. Steven asked if they should take the train out to the beach. Teresa said, no, it didn't make enough stops. They needed to be able to get off at a moment's notice.

"You really think he can track us down here?"

"You don't know my father's friends."

They migrated with the throngs of departing downtown workers onto an outbound bus. The Number 7 Haight Street. It was crowded, standing-room only. The two of them stood close together near the back of the bus, hanging on to the chrome pole for balance. Every time the driver hit the brakes, Teresa was bumped into Steven by the mass of riders that encompassed them. Every time their shoulders met, Steven felt a tingle of excitement. It'd been quite some time since he'd been in such close proximity to a female. Even longer since he'd had a girlfriend. Not since his first year in high school.

Teresa didn't seem to notice any chemistry. The riders had thinned out by the time the bus reached the Haight Ashbury, but there were still no spots for them to sit down. She told him, "A few more stops and we get off. We're going to head for the park."

Steven nodded, content for the moment to let her remain in charge. It was her city; he was lost. He'd given up trying to recognize his friend's house in a city that replicated the same look over and over. Wedding cake houses and Victorian flats.

They got off at the edge of Golden Gate Park. Homeless people and old hippies sat in circles under the lights at the park's entrance. A punk rock runaway dressed in rags called out to Teresa as they moved along the path into the darkness.

"Keep moving," Teresa said. "They're all scumbags here. She probably wants a cigarette or something."

The farther they went in, the darker and less populated it got. Teresa pointed right to a grove of tall trees that looked absolutely black.

"I can't see in here," Steven said.

"That's the idea. If you can't see out, they can't see in."

He stumbled on branches lying on the forest floor. "How far we gonna go in?"

"You scared?"

He couldn't see her face in the dark and he wasn't sure if she was teasing.

"I thought you said we were going to the beach. We're a long way from the beach, right?"

"The beach is too cold. Besides, the woods are infested with perverts down there. If you're gettin' tired, we can stop and rest."

Teresa used a Bic lighter to illuminate the woods around them. There was a large sawed-off stump a few feet ahead and they both sat down, back to back. Steven got out his cigarettes and offered Teresa one. They smoked in the dark, the orange glow from their cigarettes marking their place in the darkness.

CHAPTER TWELVE

Carl woke first. He wasn't used to sleeping anywhere but his couch, and his back was stiff and sore. He got up and used the small plastic one-cup coffee maker provided by the motel. Powdered creamer. He hated powdered creamer.

He stood at the window watching the morning traffic. He arched his back while he stood, hoping to relieve the pain. He thought about Barbra. She loved the city. She was always pestering him to go. The time was never right. Or the money. He should have taken her more often. He should have done a lot of things.

"What's the plan, early bird?"

Carl didn't notice Peters had woken up. He turned and looked at the younger man still in bed, rubbing his eyes.

"Get some real coffee," Carl said. "That's number one."

"Ten-four on that. Lemme shower and we can get out of here." Peters sat up and swung his legs over the edge of his bed. "You think we're going to hear from that Pino character?"

"I don't know. We can't sit around and wait for his call, though. That much I do know." Carl sipped at his coffee. "I thought maybe we'd see if we can visit this

Richard Allen fella. See what all the fuss is about."

"I'm game. Where do we find him?"

"Old school. Last known address."

"Old school, huh? I thought if you were from the old school you were too old to say old school."

"Hurry up with that shower, son. I still need to shave."

Carl finished his coffee while Peters took his shower. He was glad for the company. Glad to be distracted from thinking about Barbra. He had been dangerously close to slipping into a melancholy fog. As it had always been, thinking about a case brought him back to the present, kept him from dealing with his own life.

He readied himself, unplugged his cell phone from its charger, gathered what personal items lay on the night-stand, and took his service revolver from the drawer. His tried and true .38 policeman's special.

It felt good to be on the job again.

By now, Quinn was certain Teresa had told Steven he was not her father. He doubted Teresa would remember him. He didn't think they'd ever been formally intro-duced. She was kept away from her father's activities. With good reason, too. Her father's world was filled with people like Quinn.

Last night, Quinn had gone back to comb the Powell Street Station area, driven up to the Haight Ashbury, then back through the Fillmore. He eventually tired of the approach and decided to go back to the motel to sleep. He figured he had about another day before his latest credit card came up bad and he needed the rest.

There were still a few beers in the sink the boy didn't drink.

When he woke up he felt strong, ready, hungry. He went through the morning ritual he'd avoided when Steven was with him. He did push-ups, stretches, and dips on the furniture. Being alone in the room reminded him of why he was here, what he needed to accomplish. He pictured the girl, what she looked like now. The dyed red hair, the ragged clothes. She looked desperate and he knew, somehow, that would make her easier to find.

He took whatever he needed from the room. On the way past the front desk, the concierge asked if he was going to be staying another night. Quinn smiled and said, "Maybe two." He had no intention of returning. He was back on the hunt.

Tremblay waited for Pino in the parking lot of All Star Donuts at 5th and Harrison. He'd gone in to get a coffee, but was too queasy for early morning pastries. He watched as a patrol car pulled in and two young policemen walked into the shop. Cops and donuts. Textbook stereotype. Homeless people camping in the shop, hiding from the cool morning air. A couple of Asian kids talking and laughing with the man behind the counter. No Pino.

Tremblay picked up what was left of the bottle of Maker's Mark from its spot on the floorboards and uncapped his coffee to pour a hit in. He'd just unscrewed the cap on the bottle when there was a knock on his window. He rolled it down a crack.

"Don't you know that drinking and driving is illegal?"

"I'm only drinking and parking. Get in."

Pino walked around to the passenger side and climbed in.

"How you doing?"

"Terrible."

"Is that why they call you Terrible Tremblay?"

"Fuck you, Pino. It's too early for jokes. Did you manage to get what I asked for?"

"The info on the girl?"

"No, the other thing."

Pino smiled and pulled out a glassine baggie, fat with white powder, from inside his jacket. He dropped it into Tremblay's lap.

"Nice," Tremblay said. He set his bottle down and immediately opened the bag and stuck his finger in. He pulled out the finger with a little stook of white balanced on it. He stuck the finger in his nostril and sniffed hard.

"You're welcome," Pino said.

Tremblay didn't say anything. He repeated the same action with the other nostril and leaned his skull back against the headrest. "Not bad."

"San Francisco's finest from San Francisco's finest."

Tremblay decided not to pour the whiskey in his coffee, picked up the bottle and took a pull.

"Jesus, Tremblay. There're some fellow officers right there. Don't get yourself pinched."

"What'd you bring me on the girl?"

"Like I said on the phone, this is a two-way street."

Tremblay looked Pino in the eye for the first time. "I know it's a two-way street. You don't think I fucking know that? We don't have to be passing each other and waving every time we're on it either. I'm working on some intel for you, don't worry. Good stuff, too. But right now I need to find this little bitch. Now what can you tell me?"

Pino pursed his lips. "Same old Tremblay, huh? You might want to return your diploma to the charm school you bought it from." He took a postcard-sized picture from his pocket and held it out for Tremblay to see. "This her?"

Tremblay looked down at the photo of a greasy street waif. Not a mug shot, but not taken willingly either. The girl in the photo had stringy red hair that highlighted the blemishes on her face. She'd changed, sure, but no mistaking those eyes.

"That's her. She's got an arrest record?"

"Not really. This was taken by security at Macy's. She was held for shoplifting and let go. An officer who thought she might be involved in cashing some counterfeit checks got his hands on it."

"How'd you get it?"

"I know the guy. He was asking me about the check thing 'cause it's a drug addict's crime. There's been a rash of 'em. This was taken a few months ago."

"Can I keep this?" Without waiting for an answer, Tremblay said, "Thanks," and curled the photo just enough so he could fit it into the baggie of cocaine. He dug out another hit with the corner of the picture and stuck it up his nose. "Aaah, that's better."

"Take it easy with that shit, man. You're gonna give yourself a heart attack. You can't drink a bloody mary like everyone else with a hangover?"

Tremblay asked what else he had on the girl. Pino told him not much, but went on to list some known associates, possible hangouts. Reminded him that the methadone clinic might be a good place to check out, too.

"Who else got collared on the check thing?"

"A kid named Paul Testa, and a Wendy something, I don't remember her name. This Paul Testa gave up everyone involved, but it didn't do him any good. He still spent a week in county."

"Honor among thieves, but not junkies, huh? You got the particulars on him?"

"I do," Pino said. "They're in my phone, but first I want to talk to you about something. I got a visit from a couple of yokels from Calistoga. Said you're a person of interest in a murder happened up there? You know anything about that?"

"A visit? In person?"

"Yeah. Panzer put 'em on to me."

"Who's that?"

"Panzer? He's homicide."

"Is SFPD investigating a Calistoga murder?"

"No," Pino said, "I think Panzer and this old boy from Calistoga go way back is all. You know something about this or not?"

"I know I didn't do it and that's all *you* have to know. Now gimme what you got on the Testa kid. I got to get going."

Carl Bradley held Peters' iPhone in his hand while they navigated their way over Market Street to Portola and down into St. Francis Woods, an exclusive old-money neighborhood on the other side of Twin Peaks. Carl had called Panzer and caught him in a bad mood. The detective reluctantly gave them Richard Alvarez's address.

Just follow the blue dot, Peters told him as Carl looked from the map on the phone to the opulent area they descended into. They were both struck by the plush, well-kept hedges and gardens in front of the enormous single-dwelling houses.

"Jesus, who can afford to live here?" Peters asked.

"People who bought these places forty, fifty years ago, that's who."

The driveways were off the street and those that did have cars in them had nice ones: Mercedes, Bentleys, even a Rolls Royce. The area was quiet except for the occasional landscaping crew with mowers and leaf blowers. They found the address and noted three or four cars crowding its driveway, all behind an ornate wrought iron gate that fit in quite well with the house and the neighborhood.

"Here we are," Peters said. "Certainly looks like someone's home."

"Well, let's find out." Carl handed Peters back his phone and got out of the car. They wandered up to the sidewalk entrance. It was blocked by a gate that matched the driveway's. Carl didn't see a bell or an intercom. He did see a video camera near the top of the gate pointed right at them.

"What now?" Peters said.

"Can I help you?" A voice sounding like it was coming from an intercom speaker, but neither Carl nor Peters could see where the speaker was.

"Hello?"

"Can I help you?" the voice said again.

"My name is Carl Bradley and we're here to see Mr. Richard Allen."

"Do you have a warrant, or is this a service or a summons or other legal proceeding?" The voice sounded almost automated, modulated, like a robot.

Carl and Peters looked at one another. Carl hadn't mentioned being a cop.

"No, sir, we'd just like to speak to him."

"I'm sorry. Mr. Allen isn't in. You'll have to return at another time. If you'd like to leave a name or a number, I'll see to it that he gets it."

"Like I already mentioned, my name is Carl Bradley, and this here—"

The gate before them buzzed. Carl reached out and pushed it. Immediately they heard barking dogs. Three large Dobermans coming at them full speed, all teeth. Carl pulled the gate shut again.

"*Jesus*, look at them dogs," Peters said.

A thick man in a track suit appeared at the front door, arms crossed, smiling. Another, smaller man appeared behind him. The smaller man was dressed in an identical track suit of a different color. The smaller man whistled at the animals, then whistled again. He shouted something that couldn't be heard over the barking. After a few more shouts, the dogs obeyed and turned back toward the house. The first man in the track suit secured the Dobermans and the smaller one walked out to the gate.

"Can I help you gentlemen?"

He was small, thin, and sported a Clark Gable-style

mustache. Expensive-looking sunglasses covered his eyes and a modest gold chain hung around his neck.

"Are you Mr. Allen?"

"Let's start with who you are."

Carl told him. He omitted the fact that he was retired. He told the man he'd like to ask him a few questions about a fellow officer he was reported as being associated with, reassuring him this was not an official police visit. Trying to make it seem like they were searching for the whereabouts of one of their own.

"Only trying to get the rest of his statement in a police matter," Carl said.

The man took this all in without saying anything. He smiled and nodded, made dry smacking sounds with his lips, but did not open his gate. When Carl finished, he said, "If you came all the way over, you must already know I'm Richard Allen. You also must know I haven't seen Mr. Tremblay in quite some time. It's true that I know the man; he used to frequent my restaurants before his fall from grace. Legendary appetite." The man smiled to himself. "Somehow that relationship, a cook to a customer, was twisted into something more sinister."

Peters asked, "You're a cook, Mr. Allen?"

"I was being facetious. I'm a restaurateur. I own three here in the city, two in Marin, and two on the Peninsula. If you gentlemen like upscale Mexican, I'm happy to treat you both to an unforgettable culinary treat. If you feel like an early lunch, I can call my place on Geary and let them know you're coming."

"I'm still burping the burrito I ate last night," Peters said.

Allen's face didn't change, he only said, "I assure you this is quite different."

"When's the last time you saw Tremblay?" Carl asked.

"Honestly, I can't quite recall. I'm certain it's been years at this point. Why don't you tell me what this is really about? Do you think Maurice has done something?"

Carl realized that was the first time anyone had referred to Tremblay as Maurice. "No, sir, we don't. He just up and left before we could finish talkin' to him. I think maybe a few questions occurred to us after we'd spoken. No fault of his. We just want to get a better picture."

"Better picture of what?"

"I guess you could say he was a material witness at a crime scene."

"Being an ex-police officer, you'd think he'd be aware of how delicate that can be."

"You'd think so."

They stood for a moment more. Carl and Peters on the sidewalk and Richard behind the gate. Then Richard said, "If there's nothing more."

"If we could leave you a number, in case you think of a way to get in touch with him." He nudged Peters with his hand and Peters pulled out his wallet and slipped one of his cards through the gate.

Richard Allen took the card and said, very earnestly, "Of course, of course."

Peters and Carl returned to their car and Richard Allen returned to his house.

* * *

Inside, Allen stood before the large man. The man said, "How come you didn't let me deal with those cops?"

"Because subtlety and diplomacy are not your strong suits." Allen let the confusion settle on the man's face, then said, "I want you to call Quinn's attorney and find out how that motherfucker got released. Ask him why, in God's name, would he not inform me he was working on his case? Remind him of who pays his bills."

The morning sun crawled into the sky while Steven and Teresa were still asleep in the woods. The light shot through the treetops in long narrow shafts. They were curled together on top of the same stump they'd found in the dark. It was cold. Although the sun was up, its warmth barely filtered through the tall trees to the stump where they lay in the shadows.

Steven woke up first, happy to find Teresa cocooned in front of him. He leaned on one elbow and admired her. He noticed the soft nape of her neck, her ears that had holes for piercing, but no earrings. Then he saw a bluish spot near the front of her neck. A bruise spotted with tiny scabs. Teresa had been shooting up in her neck. Steven wondered why anyone would do that.

He lay back beside her and pressed his hips against her. She stirred.

She reached back and felt he was hard. She gave him a squeeze and he pushed a little closer. She wiggled her hips and adjusted so his dick was pushed directly on the crack of her ass. Steven draped an arm over her shoulder and pulled her close.

There was rustling of leaves, footsteps. Steven's stomach tightened. He shook Teresa then sat upright. The footsteps slowed, then stopped. Steven scanned the woods. Two vagrants had been tiptoeing up on them; they stood frozen, as though their stillness would camouflage their presence.

"What the fuck?" Steven said.

The two men didn't move. Then Teresa sat up. "*Fuck off!*" she bellowed. Loud enough that birds lit from the trees. Both the men turned and scurried away in the brush.

"Fuckin' assholes," she said.

"What did they want?"

"To go through our pockets. To fuck us in the ass. Who knows? Fuckin' scumbags. That's why I stayed up almost the whole night keeping watch."

"Sorry I passed out."

She smiled at him. A maternal warmth to the look made him feel good.

"That's all right. You musta been exhausted," she said. "Your forehead looks better."

He reached up and touched it. It was still sore, but he could feel the swelling had gone down. "I'm hungry," he said before remembering he was broke.

"Not me. I feel like shit. I got to get well before we do anything."

They tromped back the way they'd entered last night, easy navigating in the morning light. They left the patch of trees and walked toward a clearing where a public bathroom stood. It was cinderblock and yellow. Teresa said to wait and Steven did. Twenty minutes later she emerged with a soft smile on her face.

When Steven got close to her, he noticed that her facial muscles had slackened some, she didn't look as good as when she'd woken up. He tried to get a peek at her neck to see if there were new track marks there, but he couldn't tell.

"That's better," she said. Her voice was coarse and raspy. "Now we can eat."

Tremblay's cell phone vibrated. It was inches away from his face. Bent over the motel room's bureau inhaling a fat line of the coke, he saw, even from that angle, it was Richard. He stood up straight, pinched his nose and said, "Motherfucker."

When he answered, neither of them said hello.

Richard said, "How goes the search, old friend?"

"Just because I work for you doesn't mean we're friends."

"So surly in the morning, Maurice. You could use a lesson in positive thinking."

"I got a lead, I'm following it. What more can I say?"

"Well, you could tell me why two cops from Calistoga showed up at my front door asking questions about you."

"Calistoga, huh?"

"Yes. I thought you said you'd take care of that. Were you careful about what you told them?"

"What kind of question is that? Of course I was careful. I didn't tell 'em shit. That's probably why they're sniffing around."

"Right, but why would they be sniffing around *me*? One of the things you're supposed to be good at is making sure this kind of thing doesn't happen."

"What kind of thing? So they're following a lead too. They're not going to find anything."

"They better not find him before we do. And he better not find *her* before you do."

Tremblay recognized the tone. It was meant to intimidate, but Tremblay's job was intimidation. He wrote the book on it.

"No problem, *Ricardo*. I told you, I'm on it."

Richard told him to keep in touch. Tremblay set the phone down and began chopping up another line.

CHAPTER THIRTEEN

Quinn had no options. The dealer's house on Treat Street was out of the question, probably sealed up with yellow crime scene tape and crawling with cops. Any clues that may have been there were gone. He could call Ricardo Alvarez and make some threats, but that would be tipping his hand. Besides, they'd be empty threats until he found the girl. He'd taken a chance going in that house and gambled that Steven and Teresa wouldn't make it out. He lost and now they were lost, too.

She was strung out. He confirmed that much the moment he saw her. She looked like shit. All the money and private schools and nannies hadn't helped her one goddamn bit. It was clear that it was more than speed she was into. All that paraphernalia in the house on Treat Street, the needles, the spoons. He smiled knowing how much that would upset her old man. He knew, too, that junkies had to have their drugs, so *that* was where he'd have to lie in wait. Eventually, she'd come out of the woodwork for whatever she was hooked on. He'd killed off her main source, now he'd have to find her next source. In a town like this, the sources were endless.

There were two faces he could look for on the street. Other than Teresa and Steven's, that is. That scumbag, Filthy, who'd led him to the house on Treat, and that skinny fucker, Paul, who she walked up to the front door with. She'd left Paul waiting in the park for drugs or money. Paul would be looking for her, too.

Those scumbags had an advantage. They knew where she'd be going, where she'd try to cop her drugs. But if she already had drugs—if she took what she could from the dealer's—then where would they look?

Where the fuck do junkies socialize?

Two places: fucking donut shops and the goddamn methadone clinic. The first place he was going to look was the donut shop closest to the methadone clinic.

But before that he needed a new car, new credit cards, and cash. The Nissan had heat on it the moment he picked it up, and after last night's activity, it was too much. It had to go.

He drove to an automated car wash and rolled through. He opened his leather bag and pulled on a pair of gloves as the car was dragged though the suds and sprays. While the car dried, he methodically went through it, removing any kind of evidence—cigarette butts, receipts, wiping the fingerprints from the wheel and the dash. Then he pulled the car up beside the giant vacuums, pumped in four quarters, and sucked out any hair follicles that may have floated off his head. When he was sure the car was evidence free, he got behind the wheel and headed down to Union Square.

Quinn drove back to the same parking garage he and Steven were in the day before. Perfect. He thought about switching cars yesterday, but his methods would have spooked the boy. It was an ideal location: underground, secluded, limited video surveillance. He wound the car down several levels and found a spot. He backed in and waited.

He'd picked a corner of the garage with several empty spaces around him. Opportunity would show itself. He watched a couple park and leave. Two was hard to manage. A woman with her child returned to their car. No babies, too messy. After about ten more minutes, he saw the perfect target. A wealthy-looking white woman approached with bags in both hands. She struggled while she found her key fob and remotely unlocked the doors on a new white Mercedes.

Quinn unzipped the bag sitting on the seat beside him and took out his knife. The .45 was already in his lap. He waited until the woman was at the back of her trunk and setting her bags down. He got out of the Nissan.

He walked quickly toward her with sweeping, long strides. She placed her bags inside the trunk. When he was within a few feet, he said, "Excuse me."

"Oh," she said, high pitched and off balance. "You scared me."

Quinn held up the gun. Her eyes went wide.

"I'm robbing you," he said. "Get in the trunk."

She looked into the open trunk, at the bags she'd just placed there.

"It's okay, it's okay," she said, telling herself or Quinn. He wasn't really sure. "Take them, just take them."

"I don't want those. I want your money."

She held out her purse. He snatched it from her hand and stuck it under his arm.

"Get in."

"Please, please."

He poked her hard in the ribs with the barrel of the gun. "You'll be fine. Get in and wait five minutes, I'll be gone, then you can pull the release there, get yourself out and tell your friends about your exciting day." He shoved her a little. "Go on."

"Please," she said. "No."

For a moment, he thought he'd have to shoot her right there, but then she climbed in. She moved slowly so he gave her another shove. The Mercedes bounced a bit on its shocks when she hit the bottom of the trunk.

He leaned into the trunk, her purse in one hand, the .45 in the other.

"I want you to tell me your ATM PIN and then I'm going to shut this trunk." He lowered his voice, tried to reassure her. "You're gonna wait five full minutes, then you can pull the cord there and get some air. You're gonna be fine and all this will be over, okay?"

She nodded, quietly making little chirping sounds.

"Well," he said, "what is it?"

"Nine-two-two-nine."

"You wouldn't lie to me would you?"

She shook her head.

Quinn stuck the pistol in his belt at the small of his back and took the knife from his back pocket. He made a gentle shushing sound to the woman like he was comforting her, putting her to sleep, and stuck the knife deep in her heart. He heard the muted, meaty tear of ribcage cartilage. She let out a high-pitched wheeze. He pushed hard on the knife, driving it deeper between her ribs, then he twisted it to the right. Her eyes pleaded and iced over.

He tore open one of her shopping bags and pushed it

in front of her chest so the clothing inside would help absorb the blood, then wiped the blade back and forth on the clothes and returned it to his back pocket.

He shut the trunk, opened the driver's side door, and tossed in the purse. He walked back to the Nissan, took his bag from the passenger seat, locked the doors, and walked back to the white Mercedes. In the driver's seat, he examined the contents of the purse. Wallet, iPhone, make-up. The usual shit. It'd have to do. He opened the wallet. Four hundred and seventeen dollars. High roller. Then he found what he was looking for: the small time-stamp card to pay for the parking. He started the car and pulled out of the underground garage.

Tremblay wasn't sure where he should start. Looking for a junkie kid in this town was like searching for a needle in a haystack, or more like a needle in the gutter. Too many to count. Pino told him to check the usual spots, whatever that meant. He checked the rims of his nostrils for excess powder and headed out the door of his motel room.

He looked at his rented Ford Focus before climbing in. He knew the two cops from Calistoga were looking for him and probably knew the plates and make of the rental. If they were any good they did. He made a mental note to return the car and get another from a different agency as soon as he was done with his drive.

He decided to take a roll through the Tenderloin, maybe he'd get lucky. Maybe cruise by the methadone clinic. It was a spot all junkies ended up eventually. No clue as to whether the girl was a patient there. He could try to go in, flash his badge and get someone to check their records. It was the badge he'd kept from his days in San Jose—San Francisco demanded theirs back—but a badge was a badge. They were usually tightlipped about their clients when it came to law enforcement, but it'd work if he used just the right amount of abrasiveness.

He'd been told the girl was into methamphetamine, too. He didn't know where to look for those lost souls. Dumpsters? The psych ward? He'd stick with his plan, check out the clinic, and then call Richard Alvarez, or Allen, or whatever the fuck he was calling himself these days, and let him know he was in motion. Maybe the old man had some new information he could move on.

Nearing midday, the sky was clear and blue. The first time he'd seen blue sky since he'd been there. A film of sweat layered his forehead and he was sorry he left his jacket on when he belted in. He drove the car up 6th Street, through the gauntlet of winos and hobos, and entered the Tenderloin on Taylor. He knew where the methadone clinic was; he'd visited many times as an SFPD narcotics officer. Some of the staff might even recognize him. Hopefully as a cop and not the scandalous thief the papers had made him out to be.

He was lost in thought, thinking of the days before his reputation was sullied, when he realized he was a block from the clinic. He slowed down and looked for a place to park. There was a white Mercedes slowed down in front of him, clearly doing the same thing. Nothing so frustrating as having someone cherry-pick the parking spot that should be yours. When he reached the corner of Geary and Van Ness, the Mercedes turned right. So did Tremblay. Then the car in front of him turned down the alley way. Must be some rich bitch going to get her dose at the clinic. He'd have to wait for her to park before he'd find his own spot.

Tremblay squinted at the car, trying to get a look at the driver in the Mercedes' rearview. It wasn't a bitch; it was a man. And as the white car began to go round the block once more, it became apparent that he wasn't looking for parking, just crawling around the block. Tremblay hit his horn once and swerved around the guy. Just as he was about to pass and throw up his finger, he recognized the driver. *Quinn.* Right there beside him in the candy-ass Benz. Fucking Quinn, in the flesh.

Their eyes met for one quick second and Tremblay fought the urge to hit his brakes. He wasn't sure if Quinn recognized him too. He pulled into the bus stop on the corner and yanked the car over. He checked the rearview. Geary was a one way. Quinn would either have to pass him or park. He waited. The white Mercedes slowed then stopped, double-parked in front of the methadone clinic. Maybe Quinn was there to get the girl. Maybe it was Tremblay's lucky day. He'd get a bead on both of them.

The hazard lights on the Mercedes blinked on. He watched Quinn's head in the rearview. Same old Quinn, maybe a little older, a little more weathered, but he looked dapper behind the wheel of that car. It had to be stolen.

An orange and white Muni bus pulled up behind Quinn. It honked and waited a moment before pulling out around him. Tremblay watched as the bus maneuvered around the white car and pulled up beside the stop where he was parked. He was pinched in now, watching

Quinn behind him. The Mercedes suddenly pulled out and to the left, cutting off several other cars coming down Geary Street. Tremblay was still pinched in by the bus. He watched the light change and heard the quick squeal of Quinn's tires. By the time the bus had unloaded and pulled away, Quinn was on his way down Van Ness and the light was turning from yellow to red.

"Fuck it," Tremblay said. He shot into the intersection and forced his car from the far right side, across, and into a left turn. Oncoming traffic in both directions honked as he cut them off. People on the sidewalk pointed at the reckless driver. Tremblay kept his eyes straight ahead on the white Mercedes.

Quinn recognized Tremblay the moment the car pulled beside him. Terrible Tremblay. Sunken eyes on his fat face, hatred painted across his scowling mouth. No doubt about it, it was Tremblay. He looked just as surprised as Quinn felt.

He waited to see if old Maurice would get out of his car and try to plug him right there in the street. Of course he didn't; he had more to lose than Quinn.

Quinn turned on his hazards and watched as Tremblay pulled into a bus stop only fifty yards ahead of him. Quinn was tempted to get out of his car and go at Tremblay hand to hand, but, he reminded himself, he had a body in the trunk.

Then: salvation. A bus pulled up behind Quinn. The driver gave three angry honks and pulled around him. Quinn saw the driver give him a disgusted frown. Quinn smiled back. The bus pulled ahead to the stop and Quinn saw his chance.

He pulled into traffic. More horns honking. He hit Van Ness and pulled a hard left, starting toward Civic Center, weaving in and out of traffic, keeping an eye out for cops. A ticket now would mean the end of the game for him. Two blocks down he saw Tremblay's blue Ford coming behind him. Right on Turk, up Franklin, cut across to Gough. Tremblay was sticking right to him. Tremblay glared at him, saying something. Quinn kept moving.

Tremblay thumbed through his recent calls with his free hand and hit the one titled *R*.

"I got him."

"Who's this?" the voice on the line said.

"It's fuckin' Tremblay. Put him on the phone. I got this motherfucker."

"He's not here."

"Don't fuckin' lie to me," Tremblay shouted. "Put him on the phone, now."

The phone went quiet and Tremblay hit speaker and dropped the phone in his lap so he could keep both hands on the wheel.

After a minute, and a few more blocks, a voice came on and said, "Maurice?"

"Yeah. It's me. I got him. He's right fuckin' in front of me."

"That doesn't sound like you have him. That sounds like you see him. Are you sure it's him?"

"Yeah, I'm sure."

"Does he see you?"

"Goddamnit, yes. I'm chasing him up Franklin right now. Cocksucker's in a white Benz. You got a pen? The plate's two-D-H-C-four-five-seven. You got that?"

"What are you going to do, Maurice?"

"I'm gonna fuckin' kill him, that's what I'm gonna do."

"I assume that's just an expression. Watch what you say. Somebody might get the wrong idea. You may think we're on safe phones, but you never know. Call me later when you two have settled your differences."

The phone went dead. Tremblay threw it down on the passenger seat and it bounced onto the floorboards. Quinn taking rights and lefts, zig-zagging toward Pacific Heights. Finally he pulled a sharp left up a steep one way. Tremblay was about to follow, but he heard a honk behind him, the unique, powerful blast of a police horn. In his rearview he saw a patrol car, the driver shaking his head and holding up his index finger. "One way," the cop was saying. Tremblay shrugged as though it'd had been a terrible mistake he averted. Just another lost tourist in a rental car. The cop didn't light up or sound the siren, but the chase was over.

CHAPTER FOURTEEN

Steven and Teresa sat on the curb on Fulton Street at the edge of Golden Gate Park. The sky was clear, but the air blowing up from the beach was cold and bit right through Steven's denim jacket.

"What now?" asked Steven.

Teresa picked at some crusted mud on the edge of her boot. "I dunno."

Steven watched her pick for a moment and said, "You hungry?"

"No, not really."

She didn't lift her head.

"How far away are we from the beach?"

"'Bout twenty blocks. That way." She extended a finger toward the ocean. "It's not going to be any warmer there, though."

"I'm not cold."

"You look cold."

"I'm not," he said, even though he had his hands stuffed in his pockets and his denim jacket wrapped tight around him. "I'm hungry though."

"I thought you said you didn't have any money."

"I don't."

"You want a little speed? Just a puff? It'll warm you up and you won't be hungry, that's for sure."

"No. I don't know how you do that stuff."

"What? Speed? I don't do it all the time. I mean, I'm not a full-on tweaker. I just do it sometimes. It's okay. Just smoking it isn't too bad, not too intense."

"My brother got into speed. Smoking it. Turned him into a total asshole. Ended up in jail."

"For what?"

"Stealing copper wire out of abandoned houses. Dumbass had the shit on him too. Got possession and a charge for stealing or whatever they call it."

"Larceny."

"Huh?"

"Larceny. That's what it's called."

"Yeah, that. And some other stuff too. Some kind of special burglary. He's still locked up."

"You miss him?"

"Not really, he's an asshole," Steven said. The comment hung in the air unanswered, so he added, "I miss the person he used to be. He used to be cool. He used to let me hang out." His voice trailed off.

"Yeah. Fucking family. Never fails to let you down." Teresa looked up from her boot and smiled at Steven. She stood up off the curb and took his hand. He liked the way it felt in his, small and warm.

"C'mon," she said. "I still got a few bucks. Let's go get you something to eat."

Something to eat was two Homerun Pies from a liquor store. One cherry, one apple. Steven tore open the packaging and devoured them. He'd never tasted anything so delicious.

"These are fuckin' great," he said, wiping the crumbs from his mouth.

Teresa smiled at him in amazement. "You've never had a Homerun Pie? I used to live on these things."

"My parents would never buy this kind of stuff. They were strictly whole-food Nazis. If I wanted a snack, it was always granola or carrots or some shit like that."

"Ugh, sounds awful. Couldn't you just go to the corner store and get stuff yourself?"

"What corner store? We live in the middle of no-where. The only time I was in a store was when my dad drove to town to get supplies. There was never enough for anything extra. Or at least that's what he always said. They figured white sugar was worse than cocaine."

Teresa laughed and shook her head. "Hippies, huh? Livin' the dream."

"I guess. It always seemed normal to me. Most of the kids at school, their parents grew pot. It's what every-body does up there. Everybody but my mom and dad. Fuckin' idealists, I guess. Then I got into the weed thing on my own, sort of rebelling."

"It's not really rebelling if it's the same thing everyone around you is doing."

Steven nodded. She was right. He felt silly having said it.

Teresa said, "Sounds kinda nice, actually. Not like how I was brought up."

Steven watched her look off across the street to an empty space, expecting her to finish her thought. "How were you brought up?"

"Like livestock," she said.

He wasn't sure what she meant by that, so he didn't say anything at all.

"I'm sorry. I didn't mean to be so...so...ominous. It's just that my dad pretty much shipped me off the first chance he got. Montessori, then boarding schools. I saw more of the nanny than I did of him. Not that seeing his face would've made shit better. He's such an asshole."

"Yeah, you mentioned that. The king of assholes."

"What about your mom?"

"Shit, don't ask. She's not part of the equation, never has been. Dad told me she skipped when I was still a baby. Drugs. That's all he ever told me. Not even what kind of drugs. Maybe that's where I get it. You know, my appreciation for substances? Maybe it's genetic."

Steven thought about what Quinn had told him, that Teresa's mother was lost in a bag of dope. He wondered now if he'd been making it all up, or talking about the same woman.

"Don't get me wrong," Teresa said. "Life wasn't bad at my father's. It was just, I dunno, not me, I guess. When I saw my chance I took it." She paused a moment to see if he was paying attention. "By the time I finally left, I'm not sure he even noticed I was gone."

Quinn crested the hill of Pacific Heights. He kept checking the rearview but saw no sign of Tremblay. He had no idea why Tremblay had stopped following him, only that he was gone. So the old man had brought out Terrible Tremblay to try and stop him. He wasn't the best out there, but he certainly had balls. Nice that he sicced someone he knew on him. It'd be a pleasure to put that greasy piece of shit out of his misery.

Quinn thought about what seeing Tremblay meant. It meant that Alvarez knew he was here, on his home turf. It meant he probably knew why he was here. If Tremblay was on his ass, it also meant that he'd have to dump the car. They had the plates, the make, and the model. He'd have to find a new one quick or go it on foot. Quinn took a left on Post Street and rolled down toward the Tenderloin.

He reached the corner of Polk and Post and someone at the bus stop he recognized. He hit the button and rolled down the passenger window.

"Hey, Filthy. How're ya doin'?"

The scrawny kid's face went white with fear. Quinn could see he was deciding if it was safe to bolt. The kid nodded back with a nervous grin on his face.

"It's all right," Quinn said. "She was there. I found her, thank God. You were a big help. Sorry 'bout playin' rough like that. I was just so anxious to find my little girl."

Filthy Phil took a half-step toward the car, probably thinking about that fifty bucks.

Quinn leaned over. "I got a problem, though. She's not doing too well. She says she's sick, needs some shit. I'm here to help her, but I got to get her straight first. You know what I mean? I need to get her something. Think you could help me out with that? I'd pay you. You could get some extra for yourself."

That was all it took. Without another word, Filthy got into the car. "What do you need?"

"You know what I need, Phil. I need to get her well. I

need to keep her well 'til I can get her out of town. This city ain't no good for her."

Filth nodded. "Tell me about it. I can cop for you, but you gotta have cash."

"No problem," Quinn said.

They drove a few more blocks and when they were stuck at a red light, Quinn picked up the purse from where it lay between his legs on the floorboards. He opened the wallet with one hand and thumbed loose the ATM card. "Where's a Bank of America at?"

"Easy. Close," Filth said. "There's an ATM in front of Opera Plaza."

They drove in that direction and Quinn passed the young man the card. "It's her mother's," he said. "She wants her home more than I do. She's gonna shit when she sees what kind of condition she's in. I told her, though, we gotta do what we gotta do to get her outta here. Am I right?"

"Yeah," Filth said. "Definitely. She's got to *want* to go if she's gonna get clean. How much do you need?"

"As much as you can get. You can keep some, don't worry. I hope you don't mind going up to the ATM yourself, I'll stay in the car."

Filthy was shaking his head, he didn't mind.

"Let's see what you can get out of the bank. I trust you." Quinn was a block away from the ATM. "I'm gonna pull over here. There ain't no parking. You go to the machine and take a grand. If it won't let you do a grand try five hundred. If it still won't go, try three. The PIN is nine-two-two-nine."

Filth repeated the number back to himself and got out of the car. Quinn watched him hurry to the ATM. The boy's hunger for drugs overriding his common sense. The young man not asking why Mom wasn't here but her purse was, why hubby wouldn't know his wife's ATM limit. After a minute or two the boy came back, practically skipping, with a big smile on his dirty face.

He got back into the passenger seat. "I got five."

"Excellent," Quinn said with his hand out. "Where to?"

Filth handed him the bills and told him to take a right. He began pointing Quinn toward somewhere in the Western Addition. Filth was giving directions and telling Quinn about the deal they were about to make. How Quinn had to wait in the car, how the dealer was very paranoid about strangers, and how the dealer's wife was such a bitch. Quinn interrupted to ask if Teresa ever copped from this guy. Filthy said no, she didn't know this connection, and then he went on about the dealer's wife again. She'd be in a nod at the kitchen table all day, he said, only open her eyes to snipe at the dealer for doing business. What was her problem? It was the traffic that kept her high all day. What a bitch.

"You sure Teresa never gets her shit from this guy?"

"Yeah, I'm sure," Filthy said. "I never told her about him. You got to keep a connection to yourself as long as you can."

"You know anybody she cops from that we can go to?"

Filthy said no, but it was okay, the stuff was good.

Quinn pulled the car over in an open spot on the right.

"This is too far away," Filthy said. "We got to go a few more blocks. This is the projects, I ain't walkin' from here."

Quinn leaned forward and reached around to his left back pocket and pulled the knife. Filthy seemed confused, the danger didn't register.

"It's been my experience," Quinn said, "there's only one way to get off this shit."

Filth furrowed his brow, still confused.

Quinn lunged forward with his right hand and stabbed Filthy in the heart. The boy made a terrible inward sucking sound and tried to grab the knife before it went in any further. He sliced his fingers on the blade. Quinn figured he'd missed the heart, so he pulled the knife out and stabbed again. He was sure he'd hit the spot this time and he pushed and twisted the blade. The kid looked surprised, disappointed somehow that the deal fell through. He wouldn't be getting high today. What little fight remained left him. His features slackened a bit, and he was dead.

Quinn extracted the knife and wiped the blade on the kid's jacket. He wiped off the wallet, the car keys, and the purse with the edge of his shirt. He found the ATM card in the top pocket of the kid's jacket and wiped that off, too.

Quinn grabbed his bag of tools and got out of the car. He walked away in the direction they'd come, leaving the car, Filth's body, and the woman in the trunk, behind. He didn't care how it would look to the police, dead junkie in the front seat, dead woman in the trunk; they'd do their investigation, see Filth on the ATM camera, connect the dots and draw their own conclusions. They usually got shit wrong anyway.

Quinn walked away swinging the bag in his right hand, whistling a song he wasn't sure the name of, or when it'd popped into his head. He felt hungry again.

Carl and Peters sat in Peters' Acura South of Market. Carl was behind the wheel this time, giving Peters a chance to take in the scenery. Carl called Perez, who had nothing new to report. He'd heard nothing back on Oulilette, not even a hint of a motive. He was on his way to Clear Lake to take a statement from the woman whose husband went missing. There was no one else to go, so Perez was driving up himself.

The resources they could draw upon in San Francisco were limited, not without launching an official investigation with SFPD. Carl decided to call Bill Panzer and see what else they could find out about Richard Allen, the smooth-talking Mexican drug lord.

"Alleged," Peters said.

Carl was thumbing through the contacts on his phone. "What's that?"

"Alleged. Allen or Alvarez is an *alleged* drug lord. I thought there was no arrest record under his name."

"Under Allen's name. Panzer didn't really go into what they had on him as Alvarez." Carl found the number and hit the call button. "I can't help but think he's the key to this thing. Fella was too smooth. That kind of confidence breeds arrogance."

Panzer picked up on the other end. The strain of sirens whooped in the background.

"Bill, it's me Carl. I was wondering if we could press

you more on this Alvarez thing. We went and spoke to him and—"

"Shit, Carl, it's a helluva time. Things have gone nuts in this town since you've been here. I can't remember a time when we've had this many homicides back to back. Right after we spoke yesterday, there was a double reported in Bernal Heights, two gunshot victims, fuckin' mess. Then today we get two more stiffs in a car in the Western Addition. One in the front seat, one in the trunk. Both of 'em stabbed right in the heart. Damnedest thing."

Carl immediately thought of Oulilette and the fatal knife wound in his heart. "Lord, sounds like you got your hands full. You have any leads on these stabbings?"

"Drug shit. Isn't it always? The shootings too, some kind of dealer who let people shoot up in his house. Needles all over the place."

"Connected?"

"Nah, I doubt it. Still, that's a lot of business for me and the crew." Panzer barked some orders to someone securing the crime scene and then spoke back into the phone. "Listen, call me around six, I'll see if I can't pull a full sheet on this guy."

"Thank you, Bill. You get to work and I'll call you at six."

After he ended the call, Peters asked Carl what the commotion was all about. Carl told him his feeling about the stabbings.

"You think that's our guy?"

"If you mean Mr. Tremblay, no. I just don't think an ex-cop would be stabbing folks in the heart. Law en-

forcement officers, present or past, are too firearm ori-
entated."

Peters nodded, although he didn't really know what
to think.

Carl continued, "I can't help but get the feeling it's
connected, though, this M.O., too damn coincidental.
But we're missing something. A big piece. Maybe this
Tremblay didn't do Oulilette. I think we been leaning
that way 'cause we got no other way to lean. We'd better
leave him in that person of interest category and broaden
our sights."

"So what now?"

"Lunch, that's what."

Peters smiled. He was always ready for a meal.
"What'd you have in mind?"

"Mexican. Why don't we go out to one of these joints
that Alvarez owns, pick up our own tab and have a look
around?"

CHAPTER FIFTEEN

Tremblay pulled the Ford into a driveway. He was still breathing hard from the chase, the coke, and forty years of Marlboros. He pulled his pack, tugged one out with his teeth, and lit up. He put his head back on the headrest and blew smoke at the roof of the car. Fucking Quinn. He thought about the time they first met. How cocky he was. Quinn was a hired hand, just like him, but he acted like he was the only one on the block who knew his shit.

He'd seen Quinn around the restaurant a few times. Cocky motherfucker, always cracking jokes. Tremblay had thought he was one of Alvarez's new guys. In this kind of business it was never good to have a new guy around. Better you know someone your whole life— longer even. He told Alvarez that Quinn was some sort of cowboy, but Alvarez didn't want to hear it. It wasn't until he got stuck on a job with him that Tremblay found out how much a cowboy this Quinn was.

A crooked San Francisco politician had hired Alvarez to help take out some competition. Alvarez was embroiled in becoming a legitimate member of the business community. The target had gotten in the way of the plans he and his new politician friend were making. Hiring Alvarez to do the dirty work meant hiring

Tremblay and men like Quinn.

Tremblay had never been saddled with Quinn before and he was wary, even though Quinn's reputation had been solid. They went to the address they'd been given with one purpose: to stake it out and pick an opportune time to come back and do the job. They sat waiting and smoking and shooting the shit. No way was it going to happen that night, too many cars in the driveway, the target had company.

That's when Quinn said he had to piss and got out of the car. Tremblay warned him they could be compromised. Quinn said, "Fuck it then. Let's go take care of business," and walked up to the front door. Tremblay watched him ring the bell, pull his gun, and fire on the unlucky fool who'd answered the door. He sat helpless as Quinn went inside and slaughtered four people. They had to call Alvarez and tell him to send a whole team to clean up the mess. It was dangerous, foolish, and something Tremblay would never forget.

The backlash of that evening, the endless stories about the missing politician and his guests, went on for months. It almost got Tremblay put away and it kept him on the police radar forever. He hated that son of a bitch Quinn.

Tremblay picked up the phone and called Alvarez back.

When his lunk-headed bodyguard answered, he said, "Put Ricardo on," in an exaggerated accent, rolling out the r's in a long trill. He heard the bodyguard tell Alvarez that "the fat man" was on the line.

"Maurice? What happened? Do you have our friend beside you?"

"No," Tremblay said. "You got that plate number, right?"

"I do."

"Run it. Let's see whose Benz that is. I bet my life it's stolen and the owner hasn't called it in hot. Why? Because the owner is dead."

Alvarez didn't say anything. He hated phones. Even though he changed his number a couple times a week, he always assumed someone was listening. "Careful what you say. Someone may not realize you're joking."

"I think it's time we talked in person," Tremblay said.

"In person, huh? I thought you don't have any news for me?" Alvarez's accent was starting to come though. That only happened when he stifled his anger.

"I can be at your place in twenty minutes. We need to talk, *hombre a hombre.*"

"I think the expression you're looking for is *cara a cara.* Sounds less like a threat that way."

"Twenty minutes."

"No, Maurice. I don't want you coming here. Why don't we meet for lunch at my place on Geary?"

"I'm on my way. I'll wait for you there."

Teresa and Steven walked along 25th Avenue toward Geary. It was warming up now and Teresa took off her jacket. Steven was hit by the chemical musk of her humid body. It smelled good to him.

"You got any smokes left?" she said.

"Two."

"Two? Shit, why didn't you say anything while we

were at the store? Fuck, no smokes, no money. You ain't a cheap date, Steven."

It was the first time he'd heard her use his name. It sounded nice to him, flirtatious, playful. He smiled back, wanting to say something funny, witty, but he came up with nothing and just smiled. He felt like an idiot; he was probably blushing.

"Sorry. I'll get you back when I figure out how to find my friend."

"How hard can that be? Can't you send him a Facebook message or something?"

Steven reminded her that his parents were hippie zealots; they didn't even own a computer. And his friend, thinking he was a big-shot drug dealer, refused to have any social media accounts. "I think, in reality, he's just too stoned and lazy to open one up."

"Dude, you got no idea where he lives, where he works? You can't call him? You ain't gonna find him, not while we're hidin' out at least."

"I know. It's my only chance to get back home, though. I don't know anybody else here."

"You know me," she said.

"That's true."

She stopped on the sidewalk and turned to him. "And I don't think you understand, even with that fucker chasing us down. My father is a powerful guy with long fucking tentacles. If he wants us, he's gonna find us, and if he finds us, there's a good chance you'll wind up dead."

The word hung in the air between them. *Dead.* It sounded unreal to Steven, like a line from a movie.

"Why me? What did I do?"

"You're a loose end, an uncertainty. That's what he does. That's how he cleans up problems."

Steven felt a deep pit in his stomach. "I don't—I don't understand."

"I know you don't, that's what I'm trying to tell you," she said. "Gimme one of those smokes."

He brought out the pack and took the last two.

She pulled out her disposable lighter and lit his, then hers.

"I've been laying low forever now. I walked out on him. I hate that prick, but, if he wanted to find me, he could have. Now that someone else wants to find me, he'll want to find me too. That's how his mind works."

Steven drew deep on the cigarette and asked, "What's he do again? I mean, what's his job?"

"I told you, he's king of the assholes." She stared at him a second, waiting for that to sink in. "We're a block from Geary, let's get a bus toward downtown and I'll show you where he works."

"Is there a way we can talk to him? Go there and explain or whatever?"

Teresa didn't answer. She kept her head down and smoked. Her pace picked up a little. They reached Geary Boulevard right when the number 38 was pulling up, skipping the fare by once again entering through the back door as others were getting off.

"I got an idea," she said as they walked to the back of the bus. "There's only one guy I know that can reach out to my father, see what's going on. I hate him, but I think it's the only chance. At least the only one I can think of."

"You can't call your dad yourself?"

"No way," she said. "C'mon, I know where to go."

* * *

Carl pulled up to the address that Peters had found Googling high-end Mexican food on Geary. He pointed to the neon sign that sat dormant in the daylight. Todos Santos. They were trying to decide if they were at the right place when Peters punched Carl lightly on the arm.

"Look who it is," Peters said.

In front of the restaurant stood the large man who'd unleashed the Dobermans on them back at Alvarez's. He had his arms folded across his chest and was looking back and forth, up and down the street.

"Looks like he's got sentry duty," Carl said.

"You think Alvarez is in there?"

"Oh, I know he's in there," Carl said. "You want to go in now, or sit here a minute and see who else shows up?"

The man in front of the restaurant focused now in one direction. Then he gave a nod of his head to a passing car.

"Well, well, well. Look who's here." Carl pointed his finger at the rented Ford Focus passing under the Todos Santos sign. "There's the man of the hour right now." They watched as the car pulled into a spot only a few doors up and Maurice Tremblay hefted himself out and lumbered toward the big man at the front door. He barely acknowledged the man, but it was clear he knew him. The man opened the restaurant's front door for him and Tremblay slipped in.

"Let's sit for a minute. Then we'll go in and order us some of those fajitas. We'll see what's what."

* * *

As soon as he entered, Tremblay heard Alvarez's voice echoing from the office upstairs. He was yelling at someone. Tremblay passed through the restaurant and walked up the stairs.

"Listen, you motherfucker," Alvarez hissed into the phone. "I want to know why you didn't tell me you were working on this case. Yes, I found out he was being released, your boss told me about that. I want to know why a lawyer I'm fucking paying was working on this case for who knows how long and nobody tells me." Alvarez waved Tremblay in then sat down hard in his office chair.

"Listen to this shit," he said to Tremblay and hit speaker on the desk phone.

A small voice crackled out of the speaker. "I was instructed by the client not to inform anyone. I'm still bound by attorney-client privilege."

"But *I'm* your client, you fuck. I'm paying you and your whole fucking firm. You don't think this constitutes some conflict of interest? I'm the one that paid your fees in the first place on this case."

"I understand that, Mr. Allen. But my fees in this particular matter were paid for entirely by Mr. Quinn."

"Bullshit," barked Alvarez. "How is that possible? He was locked up; he had no money on the outside."

"He paid for my services with cash. Money that was delivered by courier."

"By courier? What fucking courier?"

"Sir, I'm bound—"

"You better stop with that bullshit right now. I want

to know how the fuck you got this motherfucker out of *la penta*."

Tremblay had to keep from smiling. The involuntary slip into his native tongue meant Alvarez was losing his famous control over his temper.

"It was a pretty simple case of *habeas corpus*, sir. Exonerated due to newly discovered exculpatory evidence. Well, no writ of *habeas corpus* is simple, but this one was at least clear cut. Once the new evidence was brought forth, it was only a matter—"

Alvarez hit the speaker button and ended the call. "Fucking lawyers," he said to Tremblay, then yelled downstairs to his bodyguard, "Manuel! Get on over to Weinstein's office and get that little *puto* that worked on Quinn's case. Bring his ass here, now."

The man downstairs said something in Spanish.

"Yes, right now!" Alvarez called back, then to Tremblay. "That shitheel thinks he's gonna unleash hell upon us and not pay? He's got another thing coming."

Alvarez had buried Quinn with a case of mistaken identity. Eight years before, one of Alvarez's men stabbed and killed a rival in his Fillmore Street restaurant, right at the bar, in front of a whole crowd of witnesses. Alvarez was there too, just a few feet away. It should have closed him down. It should have been the straw that broke the back of his illegal empire. The authorities would examine his whole operation with a great big magnifying glass, breaking apart what he'd built piece by piece. But what was a problem for most, Alvarez turned into an opportunity. He paid off witnesses to infuse their statements and set up Quinn for the crime. The only problem? The investigating officer discovered the security tape. Alvarez always kept a camera recording over the bar's cash register. That's when Alvarez reached out to the San Francisco DA and made sure the tape got lost. Relying on his memory alone, the homicide detective was only able to testify the man he'd seen on the tape was similar to Quinn in height and weight. It took some doing, a lot of bribes, but in the end three good things came out of it. He had a DA in his pocket, he made a lifelong friend out of the Honorable Judge Tanaka, and—most importantly—one of his biggest headaches and greatest liabilities was put away for at least twenty years. At least that's what he thought.

Tremblay sat quiet while Alvarez stared at his phone and breathed loudly through his nose.

Alvarez said, "Quinn had access to cash, plenty of it if he was paying Weinstein's fees. How do you think he pulled that off?"

"I dunno," Tremblay said. "Maybe he had some socked away. Maybe he was stacking it up with some bitch. Who knows?"

"No way, not that kind of cash. We made sure of that. There's a difference between making life in prison comfortable money and...getting yourself *out* of prison money. It's not just the lawyer; he had to pay for the evidence that got reintroduced, the whole investigation, bribes up and down the ladder."

"When we find him, I guess we can ask him."

Alvarez said quietly, almost to himself, "We should have hit him while he was inside. I don't know what I was thinking. Soon as he landed, we should have taken him out."

Tremblay said, "Why didn't you?"

"*You know why.* He was doing my time. If he wasn't inside, it was all going to come right back to me. I thought he had the ace. If he went down, he fixed it so it was all going to come out. Like a last will and testament. But as long as he was sitting there—still thinking he was going see daylight—we were all safe."

Manuel poked his head in the open office door.

"What do you want?" snapped Alvarez. "I thought I told you to get that *pinche* lawyer?"

Manuel started to say something in Spanish. Alvarez glared at him. "In English, please."

"It's those two cops, the ones that were at the house," Manuel said. "They're downstairs, right now. Ordering lunch."

Tremblay looked at Manuel, then to Alvarez. "What two cops?"

The place was empty. Wood tabletops, at least thirty by Carl's count, all of them set and waiting for customers. It was dark, lots of wood grains and black and white photos of old Mexico punctuated with antique brass ornaments hung between them. Carl nudged Peters and pointed to a picture of Alvarez and San Francisco Mayor Ronald Woo. They stood arm in arm, mugging for the camera in the same room where Peters and Carl now stood. In the picture, the restaurant looked lively and crowded. But there were no customers now. No warm inviting smells drifting in, no clatter from the kitchen.

"Looks like lunch ain't on the menu," Peters said.

The bodyguard they'd seen at Alvarez's house stood glaring at them. Then, a waiter who didn't look like a waiter sat them at a small round table in the middle of the room. He set some menus down, asked if they wanted anything to drink, then disappeared back into the kitchen. When Carl and Peters looked up, the body-guard had gone upstairs.

Before they could say anything to each other, there was Richard Alvarez, walking toward them with his arms spread in a great welcoming gesture. "Gentlemen, you've come to your senses and decided to have a decent lunch."

"Actually," Carl said. "We were hoping to bump into Mr. Tremblay here. You said he enjoys what you're cookin'."

Alvarez started in, "I thought I was clear when I told you at my home that—"

Tremblay stepped out from behind him. "That's all right, Richard. I'll talk to these fuckin' flatfoots." He walked toward the table. It was the first time Carl had seen Tremblay up close. He was overweight and looked like he hadn't slept. His voice was full of gravel as he poked out a stubby index finger at them. "What're you two yokels doing down here? Chasin' your tails? I told you what I know and what I saw at the winery. Why the fuck would you come down here botherin' my friends?"

"You're not that easy to get a hold of, Mr. Tremblay."

"I left a number with your boy here. Nobody called. Where I come from, that means we're done."

Carl looked at Peters, who looked confused.

Peters said, "You mean the Holiday Inn Express? We tried you there, you high-tailed it outta town first thing in the morning."

Tremblay's tone turned icy. "I'm sorry, was that illegal? Did you say *not* to leave town? Did you say you needed a further statement from me? I figured you dumbfucks could do your own police work without *me* helping you."

Carl cut in. "Now there's no call for—"

"No call for what? You two cowpokes got no idea where to look for the killer. No clues, no motive. You want a consultation from me? You can fuckin' well pay me a consulting fee. Otherwise, you can kiss my ass." Tremblay was practically spitting his words now, his face turning red and his eyes beginning to bulge. "Why don't you two scamper on back to wine country and set up a speed trap, leave the homicide investigations to someone who knows what the fuck they're doing."

"We only wanted to ask a few more questions," Peters said.

"Fuck your questions. You don't think I have friends left on the force? You're wrong. You don't think I can jam you guys up for conducting an investigation *way* outta your jurisdiction? You got no permission to be here, don't act like you're on official business, that's bullshit. You got no departmental backing. Homicides defer to Sonoma Sheriff's Department. That makes you two a couple of nosey citizens fucking with my good reputation."

Carl wondered how Tremblay could have known they were down here on their own. Was it his gut feeling, or had he called Calistoga to find out?

Peters stood up. "Your good reputation? We know–"

"Siddown shithead," Tremblay said. "You don't

know shit. If you did you'd be chasing the fuck who really did these murders."

"Murders?" Carl said.

Alvarez interrupted. "Gentlemen, please. Clearly tempers are rising and we don't want to get into some kind of confrontation here. Do we, Maurice?"

Tremblay took a step back, still breathing hard.

Alvarez continued, "If you would like to ask Mr. Tremblay a few more questions, to satisfy your curiosity, I'd be more than happy to let you use our dining room for a quick interview. Seems like it's going to be a slow lunch, we can lock the doors for a few minutes and let you conduct your business. But, beyond that, I think it'd be wise if you would go through proper legal channels if you feel the need to continue."

There was silent assent between the three.

"All right then, would anyone like a drink?"

Peters and Carl said no, but Tremblay said, "Maker's."

Quinn walked to Joe-Joe's. He stopped in the Lower Haight for a quick slice and headed over to Page Street. He almost rang the buzzer, but decided to ring a neighbor instead. The gate buzzed open and he slipped inside the foyer. Without knocking, he punched through a small pane of glass in Joe-Joe's front door and reached through to unlock the knob.

"Hello?" came a voice from down the hall.

Quinn let himself in, dropped his tool bag beside the front door, and walked straight to the bedroom. He flung open the door and saw Joe-Joe lying on his back, shirtless with his stomach bandaged. Quinn could tell by the sloppy job that Joe-Joe did it himself.

"Shit, man. It stinks in here. Can't you open a window?"

Joe-Joe grunted as he sat up. "Too afraid that somebody might break in. Fuck, Quinn, you couldn't knock?"

"Didn't think you'd make it to the door. Thought I'd let you rest."

"What'd you want, Quinn? I'm in fucking pain here and I don't need any more of your bullshit."

"I know you're in pain. I gave it to you, remember?" Quinn smiled at Joe-Joe as though he were expecting a laugh. "I need your car."

Joe-Joe shook his head. "No way. I'm not giving you my car. I need that thing. You're not dragging me into whatever shit you got going on."

Quinn stepped toward the bed. "But you're already in, Joe-Joe. You got in deep by trying to fuck that little girl. Everybody knows what you did, you scumbag. You owe a lifetime of favors trying to balance the karma for that one."

"I didn't do shit," Joe-Joe whined. His tone let Quinn know he'd sung this song many times before. "She was the one coming round here; she had a taste for the blow. Nothing ever happened, that's all bullshit. Alvarez just wanted to make me look bad. Besides, she wasn't that young."

Quinn reached out and poked two fingers into Joe-Joe's bandaged wound. "How's that coming along? Healing nicely?"

Joe-Joe winced. "Stop, fuck, that hurts."

Quinn pressed harder. "You seen our friend, Maurice, around? He come by for a visit?"

"I ain't seen nobody, I ain't talked to nobody. I'm just lying here. Stop, stop."

The doorbell rang.

"That's probably your neighbor wondering about the glass. You get up and tell 'em you forgot your keys, all right?"

The bell rang again.

Quinn slapped Joe-Joe. "Get up, fat boy."

With exaggerated difficulty and a moan, Joe-Joe got up and ambled toward the front door while the bell sounded a third time. Quinn stuck close behind him.

Joe-Joe looked out the door and didn't see his neighbor. He saw two young people standing on his stoop. Teresa and a young man right behind her.

Behind Joe-Joe, Quinn whispered, "Perfect."

CHAPTER SIXTEEN

Quinn pulled back along the wall toward the bedroom.

"Invite them in," he said as he slipped through the bedroom door.

Joe-Joe opened the door and said through the gate, "Well, look who it is. What're you doing here?" He tried to keep his tone sing-song, but he furrowed his eyebrows, shifting them from side to side. Trying to send a message.

"What's wrong with your eyes?" Teresa said.

Joe-Joe knew Quinn heard what she said. He was fucked now. He stopped the eye motions and said, "The sun. It's fuckin' bright out here. You two wanna come in for a minute?"

"Yeah, buzz us, Joe-Joe."

Joe-Joe hesitated. He knew it would be the end of Teresa, probably her friend too. Maybe he could beg for his own life, though. He buzzed the gate.

As Teresa and her friend came through the front door, Teresa patted Joe-Joe's stomach with her palm. "Ouch, buddy. That doesn't look too good. What happened?"

"Who's your friend?"

"This is Steven. He's from up north. He's a good guy."

"Hi," Steven said. Joe-Joe's eyes locked on him for a

moment and Steven looked right into the face of the man he'd watched Quinn assault and humiliate. If he'd known where Teresa was taking him, he never would have come along.

Without saying hello back, without acknowledging that he'd met him before, Joe-Joe said, "Is he like a boy-friend or what?"

"He's my friend, Joe-Joe. Now c'mon, I got something I need to ask you about."

"If you're lookin' for what I think you are, I ain't got nothin' here."

"No, it's something else," Teresa said. "I need you to make a phone call for me."

Inside the bedroom, Quinn listened as the three walked to the kitchen. As they passed the open bedroom door, Quinn inhaled deeply. He could almost smell her. His plan was coming together effortlessly. He listened to their footsteps creaking in the kitchen.

Teresa was saying, "I need you to call my dad."

Quinn imagined the look on Joe-Joe's face.

Joe-Joe said, "Why? Why now?"

"'Cause it's time. He's got some gnarly fucker out looking for me and I'm afraid he's gonna do something awful. I wanna talk some sense into him."

"You know who?"

"I didn't see him, but Steven did. Tell him Steven."

Steven spoke up, but didn't look up. "He said his name was Quinn."

Joe-Joe was silent, processing what he heard and what to say next. He took his phone from his front pocket and said, "Okay." He dialed, but instead of dialing Alvarez, he dialed Tremblay. "Guess who came to visit," he said.

"Yes and yes." And he hung up.

To Teresa he said, "He'll call me back in ten minutes. Siddown, relax."

Teresa didn't sit. She stood looking at Joe-Joe, studying his face. "You fucker. Let's go, Steven."

Steven didn't understand the look or the comment, but he was ready to follow Teresa as she stepped toward the hall.

Joe-Joe blocked the entrance to the kitchen with his considerable size. "Ten minutes," he said. "Just wait and see what he has to say." He spread his arms to touch both sides of the solid wall on either side of the entrance.

"Fuck you, Joe-Joe. That wasn't my father. Who'd you call?"

An arm reached from behind Joe-Joe's head, wrapped itself around his neck, and pulled him back.

From behind, Quinn punched him in the ribs and kidneys. His left forearm around his neck and his right punching and punching. "Yeah, Joe-Joe. Who the fuck you call?"

Joe-Joe tried to push Quinn backward and pin him against the hallway's wall, but Quinn was hitting him too hard. Joe-Joe began to fold.

"Let's go!" Teresa said. The two of them pushed past the tangled mess of Quinn and Joe-Joe. For one quick second Steven and Quinn's eyes met. Steven saw something he hadn't seen on the whole trip down. He saw his fate. Quinn's eyes were shining with bloodlust, pure hatred. Evil. Steven saw his own death. Teresa yanked on the sleeve of his jacket and said again, "Let's go!"

They tripped and stumbled to the front door while Joe-Joe and Quinn wrestled back near the kitchen.

Quinn was choking Joe-Joe and the big man was throwing all his weight behind him to slow Quinn down.

By the time Teresa and Steven had made it through the front door, Quinn said, "Damn," and changed his hold. He brought his left arm around Joe-Joe's face, got a grip, and twisted. Joe-Joe fell backward onto Quinn, who kept pulling to his left as hard as he could. Then he heard the crack. He kept pulling. There was another crack. Joe-Joe shook on top of him. Quinn could smell the shit in Joe-Joe's pants. He pushed the fat man off him.

He stood up and caught his breath for a moment, then squatted down and went through the dead man's pockets. He found the key fob for a Honda Accord and a wad of bills. He stood again, straddling the man. "Joe-Joe," he said, "you were a perverted piece of shit and a degenerate gambler and no one ever liked you." Then he kicked him in the face. He walked to the front door, wiped the knob—just in case—picked up his tool bag, and, with the scent of Teresa still in his nose, he was gone. Back on the hunt.

Peters and Carl ran through most of the questions they asked Tremblay the first time, at the winery. His answers hadn't changed. Carl wanted to ask about his relationship to the man calling himself Richard Allen but had no basis to lay the foundation. He knew it meant something, he just wasn't sure what. With Alvarez standing right beside the table, it was a tough subject to broach anyway.

Tremblay had calmed down after he got a few drinks in him. He recited his answers as though they'd been rehearsed, didn't miss a beat. He told Carl and Peters when and where he'd first met Oulilette, mentioning his ex-wife's love of wine. He promised that he knew nothing of Oulilette's business dealings and hinted that they were on the wrong trail. That there was a killer loose out there and they were focused on the wrong man.

Like any guilty party tries to do.

Carl felt as though they'd hit a brick wall with Tremblay, any real information would have to be uncovered on their own. Tremblay was calm and unfettered; he'd been through plenty of interviews, on both sides of the table. They were getting close to wrapping it up when Carl's cell phone rang.

He looked at the screen and saw it was Panzer.

"You'll have to excuse me for a moment. I got to take this."

Alvarez said, "Would you like to use my office?"

"No. Thank you," Carl said, and he walked to the front door with the cell still ringing in his hand. He stepped into the daylight and pressed the phone to his ear. "Bradley."

"Carl? It's Bill. I got a few questions about that case you're poking around in."

"Sure. What'd you need?"

"Well, seems we got us a witness on the Treat Street killings. Young man by the name of Paul Testa. Seems he was waiting for a friend of his to score some drugs at the house that got lit up. He was sitting up the street and thinks he saw the killer go in."

Carl said, "Okay."

"The killings today, the stabbings, we've got at least two residents who were looking out their windows and saw a white male leaving the scene. Almost identical in description."

Again Carl said, "Okay."

"You perked up when I mentioned the M.O. in today's homicides. What was it? What's got you twisted?"

"The knife in the heart. Oulilette, the fella back home, he got it in the heart too. That's a lot of killing in a short span of time. A lot of knife work."

"That's not all," Panzer said. "The guy they found on the sidewalk in the Marina, the first day you got in? Witnesses describe a similar man leaving that scene, too."

"What's the description?"

Inside the restaurant, Peters and Tremblay were at a bit of a standoff. Tremblay had less respect for Peters than he did for Carl, and his attitude turned sour once again. Peters was trying to get Tremblay to give more information on where he could be reached in the future when Tremblay's phone rang.

Tremblay eyed the screen. Local number. He answered without saying hello.

The voice on the line said, "Guess who came to visit?"

It was Joe-Joe.

"I don't have time for games," Tremblay said. "Is it the girl or that prick?"

Joe-Joe said, "Yes and yes."

"I'm on my way." Tremblay drained his glass of Maker's and said, "Interview's over. I got an emergency I got to take care of."

Alvarez said, "Maurice?" But Tremblay made no eye contact. He got up from the table and walked straight out the front door.

Peters, frustrated, asked Alvarez, "Maybe *you* know how to get a hold of this guy?"

Carl was pacing the sidewalk as he listened to Panzer recite the physical description of the suspected killer. He stuck a finger in his left ear to help blot out the traffic noise on Geary Street. No doubt, thought Carl, it sounds like the same guy who used the bad credit card in Calistoga. White male, mid-forties to early fifties, six feet, medium build, handsome. Movie star good looks, the waitress had told them.

"Get this," Panzer was saying. "Witness down on Turk today says he was whistling. Strolling away like he didn't have a care in the world. I'm thinking we might have a serial on our hands, some kind of psycho."

Carl turned toward Todos Santos and saw Tremblay rushing out the front door, moving as close to a run as a man in that shape could get.

"Dang it," he said into the phone, and started to follow. "Bill, I'm going to have to call you back."

He watched Tremblay heading for his Ford Focus, so Carl cut across the street to Peters' Acura. He stopped for a moment, clutching at his pockets, before realizing he still had the keys. No time to get Peters, he'd call him on the way and find out what happened inside, why Tremblay bolted.

In his rearview, he saw Tremblay waiting for a hole in traffic. Carl put the car in drive and pulled out. He had to make a U-turn on Geary where one was not allowed. He hoped no bored traffic cop was watching, waiting to stop him and slow him down. He yanked the car through the intersection, ignoring the honks and protests of other drivers, just in time to see Tremblay speed down Geary toward downtown.

Tremblay was moving fast, but not fast enough to attract attention. He was heading somewhere in a hurry, but not fleeing. He wasn't checking his rearview, looking over his shoulder, or making any evasive moves. Probably had no idea he was being followed. Carl gripped the wheel and focused on the bumper ahead of him. Tremblay hooked a right on red at Divisadero. Carl did the same.

Inside the restaurant, Peters smiled uncomfortably at Alvarez. Alvarez smiled back, cool and relaxed.

"Where'd your boy run off to?"

"He's not my boy," Alvarez said "He said he had a personal matter to attend to so I assume that's what he's doing. Would you like a bite while you wait for your partner?"

"He's not my partner," Peters said, adding, "And, no thanks. I'll just sit tight."

"I've already had the cook fix you up something. You

may as well eat it while it's hot. I'm sure your *friend* will be back in a moment."

A waiter appeared and placed a small dish of mango salsa and a large bowl of fresh guacamole beside a plate of warm tortilla chips. He told Peters his lunch would be out in a few more minutes.

Peters took a chip and scooped out a dollop of guacamole. It was delicious.

CHAPTER SEVENTEEN

Carl followed Tremblay on Divisadero until he saw the car go left on Page Street. He waited at the light, craning his neck, watching Tremblay's vehicle slow. He saw its brake lights and, when the blue Ford came to a stop, he made the same left and approached with caution. Carl watched Tremblay climb out of his driver's seat and run to the front gate of a Victorian that'd been converted into a small apartment building. The gate was swinging when Tremblay went in and he left it that way. Carl double-parked in front and hurried to the gate. He peered through an open door into the dark corridor. He couldn't see Tremblay or anything else. He'd forgotten his sidearm in the trunk of Peters' car so he went in without it. Slowly.

He saw the hulking shadow of Tremblay in front of him now, hands on his hips, motionless, with his head down. Carl stepped over the threshold and into the hallway of the apartment.

"Tremblay," he said.

No response.

He tried, "Maurice."

Tremblay grunted.

He stepped closer and now saw that Tremblay was standing over a body. A fat, shirtless man lay prone in the hall, his head twisted so far to the left that it was almost face down.

"Is he dead?" asked Carl.

Tremblay turned, as though he was hearing Carl for the first time. "What the fuck are you doing here?" Whatever amiability the Maker's Mark had poured into him was now gone. His words were clipped and snarling. "You fuckin' following me? You got some sort of cause? Some reason to suspect me of something?" He pointed down at the body before him. "There's your fuckin' killer at work...*again*. You want to stick your fat nose in? Here ya go, ready-made mystery. Solve this one, old man. Let me know how it works out for you."

"Who was he?"

"Fucking scumbag, that's who."

"I mean, who was he to you?"

"A nobody. His name is Joseph Prado. I'm sure you're gonna learn all about him."

"Why'd you take off from the restaurant? You flew down here. Somebody warn you this was gonna happen?"

Tremblay looked up and straight at Carl. "What're we, partners now? Do your own fuckin' police work."

"You wanna call this in?"

Tremblay sneered. "You're the fuckin' cop."

"I'm retired."

"That right? So'm I. Guess that makes two of us that have no business being here. You should clear out before you're a suspect too."

"Suspect? I'm a witness," Carl said. "I'm your alibi. I know you didn't do this."

"Nobody's going to think I did this, believe me."

They both stood for a moment, breathing and collecting their thoughts. Carl tried another approach. "Look, Maurice, it seems as though we're lookin' for the same fella. I just got word that this same fella may be involved in another homicide."

"No, you think? Just one?"

Carl ignored the sarcasm. "Is the guy who did this the same one who did Oulilette?"

Tremblay didn't answer.

Carl continued. "This is the second crime scene you wandered into just after it happened. I'd like to know what you're not telling us."

"I'm sure you would."

"Look, Tremblay, I'd like to cut the bull. We're both looking for the same thing here."

"We're *not* looking for the same thing. We may be looking for the same motherfucker, but we're not looking for the same thing." Tremblay turned and headed for the door.

"Where're you going?" Carl said. "You can't leave, you're a witness here."

Tremblay whirled around. "What're you gonna do? Arrest me?"

"What if I need to contact you?"

"I can't be contacted." Tremblay's eyes met Carl's for a moment. Something in Tremblay relented. "Okay, old man. I'll take your number. You got a card?"

Carl admitted, "No."

"A real professional, huh? All right," he said, pulling out his cell. "What's the number? If I got a reason to call you I will."

Carl recited his number and pulled his own cell from

his pocket, half-expecting it to ring with Tremblay's number. But it didn't. He watched Tremblay walk out the front door and then dialed 9-1-1.

By the time Quinn hit the sidewalk, Steven and Teresa were rounding the corner. He walked after them with a steady clip, swinging the tool bag at his side and hitting the lock button on Joe-Joe's key fob to see if the Honda was parked nearby. Hearing no honk from any of the parked cars on the block, he increased his pace. He reached the corner and saw them crossing Haight Street hand in hand.

Running after them would cause too much attention, so he walked. Long, quick strides. They weren't checking behind them, they kept moving forward, Teresa pulling on Steven's hand. As far as Quinn could tell, he hadn't been spotted. They were only trying to put some distance between them and Joe-Joe's. They crossed Waller and moved into Duboce Park. Quinn kept them in sight, waiting for the opportunity to move on them. He pocketed the car key and reached over to unzip the bag.

"Let's go." Teresa pulled at Steven's hand.

"Where?"

She didn't say, she only pulled harder and said, "Move. He's coming."

They crossed the street and kept moving through the park. "Don't look around," she said. "Just keep moving."

Steven followed, stumbling here and there. He knew

Quinn had a gun—that goddamn shiny cannon—and if he was behind them, he had a clear shot at both of them. Steven wondered how the frail and sickly Teresa was keeping her pace, forcing them on. Survival instinct. The danger was real and imminent, even out here on the streets in midday. He now knew what Quinn was capable of. He turned and looked behind him. He saw Quinn duck into a doorway. No doubt it was him, bag in hand, a half-block back.

Steven said, "Run."

Quinn followed them to 14th Street where they took a left. He'd just turned the corner when he saw the boy turn and glance back. He stepped sideways into an alcove, but he knew Steven had seen him.

He peeked back out and saw they were now running toward Market Street. Quinn followed suit. He'd gained a quarter-block on them by the time they hit the main thoroughfare. Trapped by the passing traffic, he saw them both look back, look at each other, and dart out into the street. He went right after them without missing a stride.

Taxis honked, cars braked, but nobody hit anyone. The two made it across the street only moments before Quinn jumped the curb. He was gaining on them, their pace starting to slow from exhaustion and fear. He got within a few feet and swung his bag at the side of Steven's head. It connected, solid and heavy. Steven went down.

Teresa paused, turning to look for Steven, and Quinn reached out with his left arm and wrapped it round her head, palming her face. He pulled her to his side, his strength no match for her puny frame. She squirmed, but was immobilized by the headlock. He punched her in the face with the fist that still clutched the bag.

From the ground, Steven cried, "No!"

Quinn looked down at Steven, towering over him with Teresa still clamped under his arm. "What's a matter with you, kid? I gave you a simple task. You run off with her? I told you I was here to help her. Now you've gone and made things worse for everyone."

Steven tried to get up and Quinn put a boot to his groin. "Stay down, kid."

Teresa was telling Steven to run. Quinn tightened his grip. "I liked you, Steven. You seem like a good kid, but you've upset the applecart. There's no turning back from here."

Teresa stomped on Quinn's foot and he struggled with her for a moment. He hit her again—closed-fisted in the face—and regained control. Steven used the opportunity to get himself up and run. Quinn was stuck; he couldn't pursue Steven and keep hold of Teresa. He let him go. He had the girl now, that's what was important.

With her head still under his arm, he told her to look into his bag. She did.

"I'm going to let go of your head now. We're going to walk together. You try anything and the barrel of that gun is going straight up your scrawny ass."

Teresa straightened up and curled a lip at Quinn. "I know who you are," she said. "I remember you."

"You do?" Quinn smiled. "Good. Then you know I'm not fucking around."

He pinched his thumb and index finger right above Teresa's elbow. She winced. He told her to get moving.

Carl trotted out behind Tremblay. He had his cell to his ear. 9-1-1 dispatch had put him on hold, their usual message repeating itself in Spanish, then Chinese. Carl hung up and redialed. The operator picked up this time and Carl reported the homicide. He gave the address and explained quickly that he was a police officer and could not remain at the scene. The operator pressed him for more information, telling Carl he must remain at the scene. Carl hung up.

Tremblay had already started his car by the time Carl reached him. Carl knocked on the window.

Tremblay powered down the window and, before Carl had a chance to speak, said, "No."

"Help me, please. I know there's still a shred of a police officer left in you. It never leaves us. You want to see justice done. Help us find this guy."

Maurice smiled. Half sneer. *"Fuuuucck you."*

"You want this guy out of the picture. Getting that done on your own could mean you going to jail. If we take him out, you can keep yourself in the clear. C'mon, Tremblay, do this the right way. Don't pull yourself farther into the muck."

Tremblay looked up. Carl could tell he'd hit a nerve.

Tremblay said, "I'll call you if I need any help." He rolled up his window and pulled into the street. Carl had to jump back to avoid getting his feet run over. He watched Tremblay's car turn the corner and called Peters.

The phone rang and rang. Sirens drowned out the ringing. He hung up and got into the Acura and drove back toward Todos Santos.

CHAPTER EIGHTEEN

Steven kept moving, out of breath and covered in a film of sweat. He was moving forward, but didn't know what direction. It didn't matter; he didn't know what direction he was supposed to go. Finally, he plunked down on a door step. He took a moment to look around, to realize he was lost. Beyond lost. He was alone again, broke, without a phone or a friend, lost in a city where he was now being hunted. He reached for his pack of cigarettes and flipped it open. It was empty.

He hung his head down, watching the feet of the few passersby stroll on. He felt beaten. He'd helped the predator find his prey, and now the girl was gone. The green light of Teresa's eyes flashed in his mind. He had no idea what Quinn had in store for her, he only knew whatever happened now would be his fault. He mulled over his options: call the police, go back to the house on Page Street, or wander the city streets hoping to find his friend. Forget it all and keep moving. Steven sighed and fought back an overwhelming urge to talk to his parents. He physically shook his head to rid himself of the idea. They would be no help, they never were.

An oblivious young man with headphones plugged into his ears flicked a long burning cigarette butt onto the sidewalk a few feet from Steven. Steven waited until the man had moved on, checked to see no one was watching, then picked the butt up and took the last long, deep haul.

Carl returned to Alvarez's restaurant, but when he tried to enter, found the doors locked. He knocked, then pounded on the glass. No response. A sick, sour feeling welled up in his stomach. He called Peters' cell again. No answer.

He thought about calling the police, have them bang on the door, but he wasn't convinced they'd have any better luck than he was having. He kept banging. He thought he saw a flicker of movement inside to his right. Nothing.

Carl's cell rang. He answered it without looking.

"Where the hell are you? You got me worried."

It was SFPD. 9-1-1 dispatch calling him back.

They wanted to know where he was, told him he needed to immediately return to the address of the homicide he'd just called in. Police were on the scene and they needed a statement from him. They'd be happy to send a cruiser to his location. Carl said that he'd be back there in less than ten minutes and hung up. He gave the door one last knock.

Richard Alvarez's diminutive frame appeared behind the glass. He made a production of pulling his key and opening the door, as though he had been wakened in the middle of the night.

"Yes, Mr...."

Carl didn't repeat his name. He said, "Where's my partner?"

Alvarez's eyebrows went up. "Oh, he left. He said something about going to find you. Didn't you see him?"

They locked eyes for a moment, Carl trying to gauge the truth, Alvarez throwing up a dead blank stare. Carl glanced over Alvarez's shoulder.

"You can come in if you like," Alvarez said. He swept his arm around behind him, showing an empty dining room.

Carl slowly shook his head. "No, there's somewhere I gotta be."

As Carl turned away from the door of Todos Santos, he heard Alvarez's cell ringing.

Steven summoned his strength and stood. He began to backtrack toward the house on Page Street. He had no reasoning; instinct drove him. There was no other place, he felt, Quinn would take her. At least he knew no other place. The bars they visited wouldn't work. There was the motel, The Franciscan Bay; he'd call them as soon as he could. No, it had to be Page Street; it was the closest on foot. He'd roll the dice and go there. He'd retrace his steps and hope that a better idea would spring forth. Besides, he had no other options.

As he walked he thought again about how he could reach out, to who he could reach out. Facebook, email, collect calls, he struggled to think of someone, somewhere he could go to for help. What would he tell them? He didn't even know Teresa's last name. Quinn could kill her and he'd never even know. He quickened his pace.

They'd fled so fast, traveling in a panic; it was hard

for him to find his way back. He moved up the streets toward the Lower Haight like it was déjà vu. He knew he was on the right track when he found Duboce Park. He kept moving.

By the time he reached Haight and Pierce, he knew the police were on the scene. He could sense it. One block up on Page and he saw the patrol cars, at least five of them. Several unmarked cars as well, Crown Vics and Tauruss, even two black SUVs. And the coroner's van.

He stood waiting at the corner, watching the SFPD personnel buzz around the door. He weighed his options, his conscience. Should he just walk in and announce he was a witness to whatever had gone on? What could he really tell them about Teresa? Would they hold him? Arrest him?

A car pulled up beside him and the driver's window powered down. An older man was alone behind the wheel. He, too, appeared to be gawking at the spectacle.

The man said, "How're ya doing, son?"

Steven looked at the old man, gave him a short nod, but didn't say anything.

"Hell of a thing," said the man in the car.

They were both quiet for a moment more, watching the police do their work, like any other curious onlookers. Then the man said, "My name is Carl. I'm looking for the guy that did this."

"Did what?" Steven said. He didn't even sound convincing to himself.

Carl smiled. "I think you know what he did, or at least have a pretty good idea."

"I don't—"

"Son, I saw the way you came up the street, saw the

caution you took. Tiptoeing like you're sneaking up on Santa Claus. I also saw the look on your face when you turned the corner. If you've got something to say, now's the time. Unburden yourself. Maybe we can put a stop to this before it goes any further."

Maybe it was the way the old man looked, the kindness in his eyes. Maybe it was the chance of actually stopping this, of saving Teresa from the madman, Quinn. Or maybe it was the way the man said unburden, but Steven, suddenly feeling more tired than he had in his whole life, walked around to the passenger side, opened the door, and got in.

"I might know something," he said.

Carl could tell the boy was shaken, nearly in shock. "Take your time, son. You're gonna be all right now. What's your name?"

The young man said his name was Steven and Carl introduced himself. When Carl told him where he was from, the kid followed by saying he was from the north, too. The north, that was how he put it. Carl asked him where, and the kid told him. Carl said he knew exactly where that was. Then the kid put his head on his knees, just folded up onto himself, and started to softly cry.

Carl stayed parked, a block up from the crime scene. He was supposed to go in and give a statement. Instead he sat with the boy. That's what he was, only a boy.

His phone rang and he checked the screen to see if it was Peters. 553 prefix—an SFPD number. He set the phone to vibrate. The kid began to talk.

Steven told Carl about getting robbed in Willits and

meeting Quinn. He told him about their ride to the city. Carl interrupted and asked if they'd stopped for lunch in Calistoga, but didn't ask about the winery, not yet.

Steven said, yes, they'd stopped for lunch, then moved on to the city. He told him about the motel, the search for Quinn's daughter. Then he told Carl about Teresa.

Carl asked if he knew where the house was located, the one where they went to look for Teresa. Steven said he didn't know where in the city it was, but the street was called Treat, and it was near a park. He knew that much. Carl pursed his lips.

Steven told him about what happened on Treat Street, the fear Teresa had of the man who'd claimed to be her father, how they jumped from a back window and ran. How they spent the night in Golden Gate Park. Steven didn't mention the drugs. Or how he felt about Teresa when they woke up together in the park.

Carl stayed quiet, letting the boy tell his tale, but his mind was racing, trying to piece together the puzzle. Big parts of the story were now falling into place. Big parts were still missing. What was it about this girl?

Every couple of minutes, as he listened to the boy talk, Carl's cell phone would vibrate. He'd glance down at it. More 553 numbers. The police up the block wondering where he was. He wouldn't be able to postpone that for much longer. The boy kept talking, really starting to let go. The story kept getting muddied. Carl didn't understand who this girl was or how it all related to Tremblay.

Then the phone vibrated with another number. Caller's name withheld. Carl held up an index finger to Steven and said, "I gotta take this."

It was Tremblay.

"You tell 'em I was there?"

Carl said, "I haven't talked to them yet."

"Bullshit."

"I was pulled away. I went to get my partner and he was gone. You know anything about that?"

There was a pause, then Tremblay said, "His name is Quinn. Quinn McFetridge. But he goes by Quinn."

Carl said, "I know. Who's Teresa?"

More silence on the other end. Carl could hear Tremblay breathing, the hot air whistling through his nose. Tremblay said, "We need to talk."

"Sure."

"No bullshit. You and me."

Carl said, "Okay."

"You really ain't been back there?"

"No. Are you with Alvarez?"

"No," Tremblay said.

"Where's Peters?"

"Your friend? I don't know."

Carl thought about what that meant. "Alvarez know you're talking to me?"

Tremblay said, "No. That's why we have to talk now. Meet me at the Cliff House. You know where that's at?"

Carl thought he did, but didn't know if he could put off giving a statement to the SFPD.

Tremblay said, "Sure you can. Cliff House. Fifteen minutes," and hung up.

Steven had listened to Carl's side of the conversation. He asked, "Was that him?" Fear rising up in his expression.

Carl told him, "No."

"Are we going to talk to the police now?" There was a resigned inevitability in Steven's voice.

Carl said, "No." He put the car in drive and pulled a quick U-turn, away from the clot of police vehicles, away from the crime scene.

Fifteen minutes later, Carl and Steven pulled up in front of the famous Cliff House. It was a tourist destination that sat on the edge of the Pacific Ocean, hanging off a sheer face of rock. Low and white on the street side, the ocean side opened up to three stories of glass-walled restaurant, boasting one of the most beautiful views the city afforded.

They spotted Tremblay immediately. He stood in front of the building and looked out of place among the fresh-faced tourists. He was the only one with a scowl on his face. Without saying anything, Tremblay pointed behind them, up the street, to a smaller coffee shop a hundred yards ahead of the Cliff House.

"I guess he wants to talk there," Carl said.

"You want me to come?" Steven asked.

"Oh yeah," Carl said. "I'm keeping you on a short leash."

Carl pulled the car into a spot. They got out and walked toward the impatient-looking Tremblay.

"You want us to go up there for a bite?" Carl said.

"Right here's fine." Tremblay pointed to a spot on a long stone wall that curved along the sidewalk, separating people from the edge of the cliff.

The three of them walked to the wall and stood facing the open air above the Pacific.

Tremblay said, "Who's the kid?"

"He's a friend of mine."

"Well, he ain't no friend of mine, so tell him to step off while we have our little chat."

Carl nodded to a spot farther up the wall and asked Steven to wait there. Steven moved beyond it, happy to be out of earshot.

Tremblay lit a cigarette. Carl reached for his mints.

After a moment, Carl said, "I'm here. Where's Peters?"

"Your partner? I dunno. Probably with Alvarez still. Call him and ask."

"I can't, that's why I'm here asking you."

Tremblay stared straight out past the wall at the Pacific Ocean. "If they don't got him, you'll probably hear from him. If they *do* got him, you'll definitely hear from them. They don't play, these guys. Watch what you tell your pals at SFPD."

"What is that?" Carl said. "A warning or a threat?"

Tremblay didn't answer. Instead, he pulled a photograph from his pocket. He handed it to Carl.

"There's your man. That's Quinn."

Carl looked at the picture. It was cropped from an original and blown up. It showed a man who had his arm around someone else who had been spliced out. The man was tan, good-looking, with almost blond hair. The man was also smiling. His eyes were blue and his teeth white and perfect. Movie star good looks.

"This is who did Oulilette?"

"Yep."

"*And* the fella we just saw down in that apartment?"

"You got it."

"And you know this, how?"

"Take my word for it. Why don't you talk to your friend in homicide? What's his name? Panzer? See if he's had any new business in the last few days. This guy Quinn don't go nowhere without leaving a body count."

"You already told me his name. Why bring me out here to hand me a photo? I could get his mug out of the system."

"To give you something you can't get from his record. Accurate information." Tremblay looked past Carl to make sure Steven couldn't hear what was being said. "Quinn's been one of Alvarez's boys for years. Hitting clean-up, know what I mean? He's good at it too, if not a little...overenthusiastic. He hooked up with Alvarez in Mexico some twenty years ago. I think Quinn was on the run down there, just a kid, hiding from something that never found him. They found each other, though. Richard brought him back and started using him. First string, see, 'cause he's an American. He could get close without spooking people. You only send a team of beaners after someone when you want to scare the shit out of 'em—let 'em know who they're dealing with. A guy like Quinn you send when you just want 'em dealt with."

Carl looked at the face in the photo. Smiling, handsome. Prince Charming.

"This guy moved up fast. Soon he was sitting at the grown-ups table. But he had no place there, no mind for it. The guy is a fucking psychopath."

Carl kept a straight face, but he was thinking, *it takes one to know one, huh?*

"So he's just been floating around the city, killing

people for Alvarez, and nobody touches him?"

"No," Tremblay said, "he's been in prison. Eight years. Homicide. He somehow managed to spring himself with some suppressed evidence and a very good lawyer. *Habeas corpus.* Free and clear. He's back to stir the pot. He wants revenge on Alvarez. I'm telling you, this thing goes deep. You're gonna find out how deep. He thinks the old man stuck him away on purpose. That he left him to rot in a cell 'til the end of time."

"Why's he think that?"

"Because it's true."

CHAPTER NINETEEN

"Where are we going?" Teresa asked.

Quinn didn't say anything. He had a pinch-hold on her right elbow and kept them both moving forward at a quick pace. She was panting, out of breath, but he was breathing normally.

"What do you want with me?"

"You're gonna help me settle some shit with the old man," Quinn said.

"Who? My father? When he finds out about this, he's going to kill you."

Quinn twisted her arm to guide her around a corner. "I'm counting on it."

They marched onward for two more blocks before Teresa said, "Can we at least stop for a smoke?"

Quinn considered this. He told her to reach into his jacket pocket and take out the pack. "Take two and light them both."

Teresa did as she was told and returned the pack to his jacket. She took one of the cigarettes and put it into his mouth.

"Not that I don't trust you, little girl, but I know you're smarter than people give you credit for. If I set this bag down and let go of you, maybe you'll make a break for it. If you did that, I'd have to shoot you. Then this little game would be over before it begins." He blew smoke out of the corner of his mouth. "Believe me when I tell you, it's your father that I'm after, not you."

"Is that supposed to make me feel better?"

"Yes, it is."

Richard Alvarez's voice was the first Peters heard.

"You comfortable, Officer?"

Peters sat quiet. He didn't know where he was. They'd stuck a gun under his chin and put two rice sacks over his head and zip-tied his hands behind his back. He still felt the gun poking into his jaw. Alvarez wasn't the one holding it, though. His voice was too far away.

He knew he was in a van. Had to be a van, he'd heard the metal side-door slide shut. From the tinny sound of Alvarez's voice, he guessed it was empty too. Except for whoever was holding the gun to his head. He heard that person's labored breathing. That meant two in the van's cargo area and one behind the wheel. They were moving through the city, weaving through the streets. He'd be able to tell if they got onto a freeway.

Alvarez's voice again. "You're going to be just fine, Mr. Peters. We're going somewhere for a...*debriefing.* Make sure we really understand what you are doing here, and, more importantly, make sure *you* understand what we are doing."

The vehicle bumped along farther. Peters heard the sounds of the city outside, but they were muffled. Even if he knew this city, there was no way to tell where they were taking him.

They had his wallet, his cell phone, his motel room

key. What he wasn't sure of, did they have Carl? Was he back at the restaurant? Did he leave and not return? Or had they already killed him?

The vehicle ground to a stop. Peters once again heard the roll of the side door. Someone exited, then silence. He still felt the gun barrel against his cheek. He wasn't alone. Including the driver, there were at least two others there with him.

Long minutes passed. Soon he heard voices outside the vehicle, muffled. It was hard to hear what was being said. Finally he made out one of the voices. "I'm not able to go with you, Mr. Allen. I've got appointments the rest of the day."

Peters heard Alvarez say something. He sounded angry, but was hissing his words, they were unintelligible. Someone else in the van was moving. The heavy-sounding door slid open again. There seemed to be a scuffle. Loud thumps on the metal floor. Someone was dragging something—or someone—inside.

"You can't do this. I can't leave here. People are expecting me—"

Then the heavy smack of something hitting flesh. The man with the voice was hit; Peters heard him grunt from the impact. A thud onto the vehicle's floor. The weight of a body. Unmistakable.

The side door rolled closed again.

Alvarez's voice now, "As you can see, we have a guest. I'd appreciate it if you'd keep your filthy hole shut. I don't want to upset our friend."

"But, Mr. Allen—"

Another thick smack. A kick, thought Peters.

"*Shut*," Alvarez said.

The engine turned over, the van pulled out. They were in motion again: Richard Alvarez, his men, and whoever the new hostage was. No more words were spoken. No directions given. Whoever was driving knew exactly where they were going.

Quinn and Teresa were deep in the Mission now, near 24th Street. Quinn saw Teresa trying to make eye contact with any of the cars that rolled by. It didn't work, none of them slowed, not one, none of them even looked back. It was as though they were invisible. If any of them did stop, what would they do? Quinn would deal with that when, and if, the time came. He wasn't worried about it. He'd have the upper hand. He always did.

They began to figure-eight through the short blocks near 24th, streets that were named after states. Teresa asked again where they were going.

"Just a little farther," Quinn said. His voice was pleasant, patient, as though they were out shopping. In a way, he was.

Up ahead a few houses a short, middle-aged woman was working her way up some marble stairs to her front door. A paper grocery bag hung from each arm. She lived in one of the endless Victorian-style homes sand-wiched together in the Mission, but this one seemed to be a single-dwelling.

Quinn slowed their pace. He timed it so he and Teresa arrived at the foot of the woman's stoop the moment she set her bags down and slid the key into the lock.

Quinn started up the stairs, still clamped onto Teresa's elbow.

"Do you need some help with those?" He was only a step from the front door.

The woman turned, startled. "No."

Quinn took another step.

The woman looked at him, then at Teresa. Her eyes lit up, she knew something was wrong. "No, thank you," she said, as emphatically as possible.

Quinn head-butted her.

She fell backward into her home. Quinn pushed Teresa in front of him and stepped inside, pulling the front door closed behind him.

The woman lay curled with her hands covering her face, saying, "Please, please, no."

Quinn kicked her in the crotch. "Get up, you old whore. Is there anyone else here?"

"No," she said, still on the carpet.

He kicked her again and dropped his heavy bag to the floor, relieved to have finally let go of that thing. "Good. I said get up."

The woman scrambled up.

Quinn cuffed Teresa in the back of the head. Not too hard. "Stand beside her."

She moved beside the terrified woman.

Quinn squatted down, reached into the bag, and pulled out his chrome-plated .45. He stood back up and held the gun in front of their faces.

"What's your name?"

The woman was too scared to answer, so Quinn repeated himself.

"Sofia," the woman said, softly.

"Sofia, this is Teresa. She's gonna open your front door and grab those groceries. If you move or make a sound, I'm gonna shoot you in the face. This is a .45 caliber. You know what that means?"

The woman shook her head.

"It means if I pull the trigger most of your face will go through the back of your head and end up on the wall behind you."

The woman whimpered.

"Are we clear on that, Sofia?"

She nodded her head.

"Cool. Me and Teresa are only going to be here for a few minutes, then we'll be on our way and you can get back to whatever the fuck you do. Okay?"

The woman nodded again.

"Teresa, grab them fucking groceries. Maybe Sofia here can fix us something to eat. All that hiking made me hungry."

Carl and Steven sat in the car. They hadn't moved. Carl hadn't even started the engine. He stared out at the ocean, apparently deep in thought. Steven sat quietly while the older man meditated. He was trying to digest all the man had told him. Carl seemed kind and trust-worthy, but none of what was happening made Steven feel any safer. His instincts were off—way off—and only seemed to be getting him deeper into a dangerous situation. How did he know that the man beside him really was a cop? He didn't. The silence in the car amped up Steven's anxiety. Teresa was missing. He was, from his own life, lost, and now he was getting further involved in something way beyond his control or com-prehension.

Finally, Steven asked, "Who was that guy?"

Carl eyed his phone, making sure it was still on, making sure he hadn't missed a call from Peters. "He was asking the same thing about you. You've never seen him, huh?"

Steven said no.

"His name is Maurice Tremblay. And who he is, I'm not one hundred percent sure. He was a cop, sort of. Apparently he's here to find your friend Teresa."

Steven looked confused. "Does he know Quinn?"

"Oh yeah, he sure does. Real well. He wants to help me find him. Only he wasn't much help. It seems everybody wants to find this girl, save her." Carl turned to Steven to gauge his reaction. "And you're the only one who's talked to her. Lately, anyway. Maybe you're the one that can help me find her before any of these characters do."

The way Carl said characters made Steven think of the worst thing a person could be. He didn't say animals, he didn't say killers, but the way he said characters made them sound even worse.

"What do we do now?" asked Steven.

"I don't know," Carl said. "But from what Mr. Tremblay told me about this Quinn, I'd say we better tread carefully. Let me think for a second. That Tremblay is a snake in the grass; I've got to decide how much of what he's feeding me is horse manure. I got a partner who has up and disappeared on me. First things first, I got to make sure he's all right."

Carl reached for his phone and it rang the second he touched it. It was Perez.

Perez's voice sounded small and far away. He said,

"We found our boy in Clear Lake."

"Is he still with us?"

"Nope," Perez said. "He's dead. Another homicide. His wife has already identified him. She did give us this tidbit of information, though. Her husband has a .45, chrome-plated. He kept it in the glove box of the truck, and, of course, it's missing. Strange thing is, he wasn't shot. We found him with—"

Carl cut him off. "Let me guess. Cause of death: A knife wound in the heart."

"How'd you know?"

"Some habits are hard to break, I guess."

Carl was ready to sever the connection, but Perez said, "There's more."

"What else?"

"I finally got word back on Oulilette. Found out his real name. It took a while because the change wasn't legal. He did a good job though, had some help, I'm sure."

"Don't keep me in suspense," Carl said.

"His real name was Julian Hyde. Ring any bells?"

"No. Who is he?"

"Julian Hyde used to be a San Francisco assistant district attorney. I looked into it; he took early retirement about eight years ago, then disappeared off the map. Oulilette's finance trail picks up about the same time."

Carl's eyes wandered back to the spot he and Tremblay had spoken. The crooked old cop was telling the truth. Alvarez had tried to bury Quinn and he used the DA's office to do it. Quinn was back for revenge and Julian Hyde was the first on his list.

* * *

Quinn stood while Teresa and Sofia sat at the small kitchen table.

"Who lives here with you, Sofia?"

"My husband," she said. "He's at work right now."

"Let's hope for both your sakes he doesn't come home early, eh?" Quinn said this with a smile. Sofia pursed her lips.

"Do I detect some kinda accent, you got there? You're not Mexican are you?"

"I'm Argentinian," Sofia said.

"Good, 'cause I've had enough Mexicans to last me a lifetime." Another laugh, then to Teresa, "How 'bout you, girl? You got enough Mexicans in your life?"

Teresa didn't say anything.

Quinn set his gun on the table and began to dig through Sofia's grocery bags, pulling out each item and examining it. "What the hell is this thing?"

Sofia said, "Papaya."

"Papaya, huh? They any good?" Without waiting for the answer he knew wasn't coming, Quinn bit into the fruit. A line of juice ran over his chin.

"How about these? Mangos, right? You know, you may find this hard to believe, but I've never tasted a mango. I heard once that they are the most eaten fruit in the world—*in the world*. The skin is tough, what do I do? Peel it?"

Sofia nodded her head.

Quinn bit open a flap of skin and pulled it back with his teeth then bit into the yellow flesh.

"Goddamn, that's good. What is that taste, it's almost

like, I dunno what. Perfume kinda. That's delicious."
More juice spilled down his chin. "Where I've been
living, you don't see many mangos. Or *any* mangos for
that matter."

Teresa said, "Where is that?"

Quinn smiled at Teresa, but kept his eyes locked on
her with an icy glare.

She swallowed. It was audible. Then she ventured
again, more quietly, "Where is it you've been living?"

Still with the smile clamped on his face, Quinn said,
"Oh, you and me are gonna have time later to catch up
on my personal history."

He went back to the bags, setting the items out on the
table. Cans of beans, a plastic container of hummus that
seemed to confuse him. Avocados, bananas, packaged
cold cuts, a loaf of whole grain bread, skinless boneless
frozen chicken breasts, coffee.

"Shit, Sofia, you eat pretty good. Think you can whip
us up a couple of sandwiches?"

She nodded and started to get up, but Quinn
motioned for her to stay seated. "I'll bring you what you
need. You can make 'em right there. Don't want you
reaching for the butcher knife when all you need is a
butter knife."

He pushed the bread toward her, along with the cold
cuts. In the refrigerator he found mayonnaise, pickles,
and a few other condiments he thought might work and
set them on the table. As Sofia began to busy herself, he
said, "Where is that butcher knife? Just so we don't have
any misunderstandings."

CHAPTER TWENTY

Peters felt the van, or whatever it was, pull off the city street into a driveway or parking lot. He heard Alvarez's voice say, "*Bag him.*" Then a struggle. Whoever the other hostage was, he was putting up a feeble resistance, pleading, saying, "Don't put a bag on my head, I'm claustrophobic." Peters heard a third man laugh, then a hearty slap. The side door slid open and Peters felt the cool rush of San Francisco air—if they were still in San Francisco. He guessed they were, but he couldn't know for sure.

He was led inside a building. Smells of clean carpet, flowery air freshener, and something else. Doors and hallways. Lots of poking and shoving, no words. They were on hard floor now. Tile or cement. The other smell, the one he couldn't identify, was stronger. He was pushed into a hard plastic chair and told to wait. Footsteps and the sound of shutting doors. He wondered if they'd left him alone. Then a voice, one he hadn't heard yet that afternoon, said, low and menacing, "I'm right fucking here, in front of you. I've got a gun pointing right at your forehead. You try to get up—try anything—I'm going to shoot you in the head. I'm going to love shooting you in the head. You're a cop and nothing would make me more happy and proud."

* * *

In the next room, Alvarez said, "Take off the sack."

Manuel yanked the rice sack from the man's head.

Alvarez said, "Counselor."

The pleading began. "Mr. Allen, I had no idea. Mr. McFetridge implied that if anyone were to know about his case, it would jeopardize its success. I was never given the impression that I was somehow colluding against you. I never would have continued if I thought it was going to be a problem." His voice squeaked with fear and sped up as he talked. "I assure you, I proceeded in good faith. I never had any intention of my work with Mr. McFetridge conflicting with your interests."

"Is that what you call this? A potential conflict of interest?" Alvarez stood in front of the man, arms folded, eyes unblinking. "What you say makes no sense to me."

"I assure you, sir—"

Manuel punched the attorney hard in the temple.

Alvarez continued, "I don't want to hear you say that again. Don't say 'I assure you' when you are lying to me. I know the evidence was bullshit, I know you bribed the court, so don't act like you're a good lawyer doing his best to see justice done. That is all bullshit. What I want to know is: how much? When did he pay you, how did he pay you, and how *much* did he pay you?"

The man was absolutely white now.

Alvarez continued, "The judge was Tanaka. We all know he can be bought, that wormy little fuck. That's how we sunk Quinn the first time. The DA held out the tape and the alibi and the judge turned his head. A hole in one, he should have never gotten out. You had Tanaka review tainted evidence? You know what that means?"

The man didn't move, didn't speak. He didn't dare.

"It means that you've now put a judge's life on the line. You think I can let this shit go? I pay a man to do a job, and some—" Alvarez's lip curled up in disgust, "— little shit outbids me? Gets the judge to undo what *I* paid him to do? I don't know what kind of business you think we're in, Counselor, but this kind of thing cannot happen. It *cannot*."

The room was silent. The young lawyer seemed to be weighing the seriousness of his captors. Quietly calculating odds.

Alvarez took a single step toward the attorney and said in a near whisper, "Start talking."

The young man took a deep breath. "You have to understand, I am *bound* by attorney-client privilege. What Mr. McFetridge entrusted me to do—"

Manuel hit him with a solid punch square in the solar plexus. A huge blast of hot air expelled from the man as he doubled over. A sick, wheezing inhalation followed while he tried sucking air back into his lungs.

"What I understand is: you broke the law. You did it at the behest of Quinn McFetridge. You did it, as far as I am concerned, on my dime. You have now endangered the lives of others, most pointedly, I must say, your own. If you do not start telling me what I want, no, what I *need* to know, we are first going to torture you and then we are going to kill you. Do you understand?"

He was still doubled over, still trying to suck air back in.

"You have a girlfriend, yes?"

The man couldn't answer. The single blow from Manuel had completely incapacitated him.

Alvarez turned to a third man seated behind them. This third man sat before a small table with a laptop and a cell phone sitting in front of him. Compared to Manuel, this man was small and thin. He wore wire rimmed glasses pinched on his narrow nose.

"Gutiérrez? What's the girl's name?"

Quietly, without lifting his head, Gutiérrez said, "Sally."

"Sally? Really? How absolutely boring. Sally, ugh." He asked the lawyer, who still had his head down between his knees, "Is that her name? Sally?"

He found the strength to sit up. He didn't recognize the third man, but he did recognize his laptop and cell phone sitting in front of him. His chin moved a little. Yes, that was her name.

"She's got a young daughter too, yes? A seven-year-old I'm told?"

Another small nod.

"She's not yours, I know, but you have to have some feelings for the child—even though you are a lawyer." Alvarez paused to snicker at his own joke. "We'll kill them both. Maybe we'll keep you alive long enough to learn that we keep our promises, maybe not."

The young attorney threw up all over his expensive-looking shoes.

Teresa said, "I have to go to the bathroom."

She sat at the table beside the shaky Sofia, who was

overcoming her fear just enough to be able to wipe mayonnaise on bread.

"You can wait a minute," Quinn said.

"No, I really have to go. Right now."

Quinn looked at Teresa. This was the boldest she'd
acted all afternoon. He measured the determination in
her eyes. This was the drugs talking. Quinn picked up
the .45 and asked Sofia where the shitter was and then,
gun in hand, took two steps back toward the hallway.
He peeked into the bathroom. One small window above
the tub that looked like it'd never been opened. Quinn
weighed the risk. She wasn't looking to escape, he
thought, only to get high.

"All right," he said. "But leave the door open in
there."

She crinkled her eyebrows as if this request were too
much.

"I know what you're going in there for. No need to be
shy. Just leave the door open and we won't have any
problems."

Teresa sneered. Like a teenager being sent to her
room, she marched directly toward the bathroom.

Quinn waited several minutes until he heard the water
in the bathroom running and then told Sofia to get up.

She looked terrified. "What about your sandwich?"

Quinn switched the .45 to his left hand and picked up
the large knife he'd set on the kitchen counter. "You can
finish it in a couple of minutes. I need to ask you something and I don't want the girl to hear. Step into the bedroom, please." He pointed to an adjoining room with
the tip of the butcher knife. "Get in there. This won't
take but a minute."

She shifted in her chair and started to get up, but then sat back down.

"C'mon," he said. "We haven't hurt you so far. Everything's gonna be okay."

He could see it in her eyes as she rose from the table. She thought she was about to be raped. Trembling, she backed into the room, her eyes jumping from the knife to Quinn's white smile.

"It's okay. Step in there with me. I'm not going to hurt you. Don't worry. Look, I'm setting the gun down." He set the pistol on the Formica counter top that stretched nearest to the bedroom door. "See? You're gonna be fine."

Sofia got up from the table and circled wide toward the room. She didn't want to turn her back on Quinn. As soon as Sofia stepped backward over the threshold, Quinn lunged forward with the knife. She was ready for him. Her hands flew up, deflecting the thrust of the knife. The blade sliced her palm but missed its target: her heart.

He stepped back with the knife. She began to cry out. With one sweeping motion, Quinn leaned in and drew the blade across her throat, slashing it deep. Her cries now became something else, something animal. Pathetic. She fell to her knees and Quinn, with an underhand swing, took aim again at her chest. This time he struck her right where he needed. She fell backward, knife still wedged in her ribcage. Her heart had stopped; she was dead.

Quinn stood above her, breathing hard from the intensity. He'd almost blown it. The kill was nearly fumbled. Too much noise, too much struggle.

When he turned, Teresa was standing in the kitchen doorway, staring into the bedroom, gaping at Sofia's body on the floor. It was a mess. Throat slashed, limbs askew, the black-handled butcher knife still sticking straight up.

"What...what...what did you do?"

Quinn stepped into the doorjamb, obscuring Teresa's view, reached over to the counter and picked up his gun. "Sit down," he said. "She was never gonna make it anyway. Besides, you got some phone calls to make. I didn't want her thinkin' we were running up her bill." Quinn nodded at Teresa's left sleeve rolled up above her elbow. "You finish your business in there?"

Teresa sat down on the same chair she sat in before going to the bathroom. She looked shattered, shocked. The reality of the situation was breaking through her newly applied medication. She looked like she was about to be sick.

"Get a hold of yourself, girl. Don't go all rubbery on me. We still got some chores to do."

"What about..." She cupped her forehead with her hands. "What about her husband?"

Quinn laughed. "There is no husband. You kidding? She was just trying to make me think twice about killing her. You think a woman who has a husband buys shit like this?" He pointed his gun at the groceries spread across the table. "No steak? No beer? She's alone in the world. Or at least she was."

CHAPTER TWENTY-ONE

Alvarez and his two henchmen waited for the man to finish his dry-heaves. When he was done, Manuel yanked him by his hair back into an upright position.

Alvarez said, "While you were wallowing in self-pity, we found out a couple of things. Gutiérrez, tell him."

Gutiérrez said, "The girl goes to Montessori on Pacific. Expensive. Mr. Wallace here has several bank accounts. He cashes his checks at Wells Fargo. He's got two savings accounts with Bank of America, but his real treasure is out of the country. In an Austrian account. Can't tell how much is in that one, but there's only one reason people have those accounts."

"Austrian? Smart," Alvarez said. "People put too much faith in those Swiss accounts. You want to keep a secret from the government, you got to use an Austrian account, eh, Mr. Wallace? How much is in there?"

The man looked at Alvarez like he didn't understand the question. Manuel took a step toward him and he said, "A little over half a million."

"Five hundred thousand dollars? After Judge Tanaka's cut? Not bad. Where do you think some piece of shit sitting in a prison cell got that kind of money?"

The man's voice was raspy, sullen. "I don't know."

"How did he get it to you?"

"A transfer, I got the account numbers from a guy he sent by the office."

"Ooh, how very cloak and dagger. Just like in the movies, eh? Who was this guy?"

"Seth Friedlander. He's a reporter for the *Chronicle*."

"A reporter?" Alvarez's words choked in his mouth. He was not prepared for such a surprise. "Why would a reporter be running errands for a murderer?"

Wallace said, "I don't know. Quinn had a deal with him. Some kind of big story he promised. Seth told me his career was going to be made. He'd break the story, write the book, be famous. He wanted to be the next Bob Woodward, I guess. I dunno. I thought he was full of shit because he wouldn't tell me what the story was. The guy seemed coked up a lot or something. He started coming to the office, stinking like alcohol, asking when I was getting Quinn out."

Alvarez turned to Gutiérrez and said something in Spanish.

Gutiérrez said, "We got emails. Plenty of them. Last one was in January. Gimme a second to read through these."

Alvarez said to Manuel, "*Mierda*, where the fuck is Tremblay? Call him and tell him we got someone else to grab now."

Tremblay was sitting in his car on 30th Avenue in the Richmond District with a new bottle of Maker's Mark between his legs and his baggie of cocaine in his hand. He scooped a key-load into each nostril, inhaling deeply. He pinched his nose and leaned back against the headrest. His phone began ringing. One of Alvarez's numbers. He let it ring.

He worried he'd said too much to the old cop. Was his plan going to work? He tried going over exactly what he'd said, but his mind was cluttered. He wasn't sure if he told him too much—or not enough. How much was too much? He took a pull off the Maker's. He wasn't sure if he even had a plan. He only knew that he hated Richard Alvarez, hated Quinn. He'd be happy when they were both dead.

The phone stopped ringing. It lay quiet for a moment and started ringing again.

"What do you mean you don't know the number?"

Quinn sat across from Teresa at the dead woman's kitchen table. He was eating the rest of the sandwich she'd made him. He took big, voracious bites.

Teresa had her head in her hands and elbows on the table. "I mean I don't know it. I forgot it. I don't call him, not ever."

"You better reach in that pocket fulla drugs you got and find one that makes you remember, kid. I need to make that call. That's why we're here."

"What am I supposed to tell him?" Her voice was cracking now, breaking with emotion. She began to hyperventilate.

"Don't worry, I'll tell you what to say. Calm down and catch your breath. Jesus."

Quinn leaned back in his chair and looked at the girl. Fucked up, on drugs. What a mess. She looked so small, so pale. Alvarez sure did a shitty job raising her. He reached in his pocket for his cigarettes and offered Teresa one. "Relax and think. Go to the phone and just start dialing. It'll come to you."

She took the cigarette. Her hand was shaking badly. She looked like she had palsy.

Quinn said, "Tell you what. Why don't you go back into that bathroom, calm yourself down a little with whatever you got in your bag of tricks, then we'll talk about making this phone call."

She nodded.

He smiled his most reassuring smile and said, "Go on, now. Time's a wastin'." It was true. He didn't want Sofia's body to get too cold.

Peters sat listening. At first there was almost no sound. Then he could make out the faintest conversation. He was sure he heard Alvarez's voice. Then everything went quiet again. This gave him an opportunity to focus on his other senses. With the bag still on his head, he could only do one thing: try to figure out what that strange smell was. It reminded him of something. Trying to separate the scent of his own breath, the strong façade of flowered air freshener, he was left with that chemical. What chemical? It was almost a burning scent. He felt it in his nose. The memory finally floated up: high school. Biology class.

The smell was formaldehyde. Embalming fluids. He was sitting in some kind of makeshift morgue. Or a funeral home.

His stomach sank. The possibilities rushed to him. The ease of body disposal. The probability there were already bodies all around him. The man owned restaurants. Panzer didn't say anything about funeral homes. His sinking stomach told him he'd most likely never leave this room.

A squeak of footsteps sounded on the floor and the rice sack was pulled from his head. The shock of florescent light hit his eyes. He blinked and squinted and took in his surroundings.

The man who had taken his hood said nothing. He walked away into an adjoining room and shut the door behind him.

After a minute, the door opened again and Alvarez walked out.

"Officer Peters. Still with us, are you?"

"Where am I? Where's Carl?"

"You're deep in the bowels of McGovern's funeral parlor. So deep that the only way out is to get shit out. As for your partner, who knows? I was just going to call him and ask. Maybe you'd like to speak to him? You two have a spot picked out to meet up in case either of you get lost?"

The man who'd first left the room walked back in and whispered something in Alvarez's ear. Alvarez said something back in Spanish. The man disappeared back out of the room. Alvarez kept his eyes locked on Peters. There was a gunshot. The flat slap sound of a 9mm. It echoed high and quick throughout the space. The corners of Alvarez's mouth curled upward.

A minute later, the other man, and the bodyguard Peters had seen at Alvarez's home, and later at the restaurant, came in carrying a body. The big bodyguard supported the body underneath by wedging his forearms into the armpits and the smaller man struggled with the feet. They laid the dead man out on the floor, flat on his back, right beside Peters. It was for him. They were showing what they could do.

The man stretched out on the tile beside him was young, white, and well-dressed. He was also very dead. His eyes were wide, a meaty round bullet-hole right square in the middle of his forehead. It bled some, not as much as the exit wound in the back of his head now making a small puddle on the floor. Peters now smelled gunpowder along with the formaldehyde.

"You know who this is?" Alvarez said.

Peters shook his head.

The two men moved out of sight behind Peters. He couldn't turn in the chair, but he felt them back there.

"This is a lawyer. A fucking good one, apparently. Or at least he was, 'til he couldn't follow my simple instructions. Goddamn lawyers always think they know better than you do. There's only one thing that I hate more than a lawyer, Officer Peters, and that's a cop."

There were more footsteps behind Peters, some furniture scraping the floor. Manuel, the bodyguard, appeared at his side with a black ballpeen hammer in his hand.

"First we gonna find out what you know," Alvarez said. "Then, you gonna make a little call for us."

Carl was on the phone trying to explain to Bill Panzer why he couldn't come in for a statement. He'd been circling a few blocks aimlessly and he was now pulled over to give the call his full attention. He told Panzer he still hadn't heard from Peters and he was beginning to worry. Beginning? Hell, he was seriously worried, he said. He told him about seeing Tremblay at the scene, but didn't tell him about their second meeting.

Steven sat in his seat across from him. Silent, watching. Carl didn't mention Steven to Panzer and he didn't mention Teresa either. He wondered what the old man was up to.

Panzer was saying, "That's all well and good, Carl. But we need to make it official. We need to get this all in a statement. You know how this works. I don't understand why you can't come in here. You're stalling. I'm sure Peters is fine. Shit, if you'd pick up your phone when it rang you probably would've heard from him by now. I'm still at the scene, but if you'd like, we can meet at the Hall of Justice. Either way is fine with me, but we got to see you right away."

Carl said okay, he'd be there soon, and broke the connection. He stared at the phone screen, willing it to ring.

Quietly, he said, "C'mon, Peters. Where the hell are you?"

The phone rang.

It surprised Carl and his hand twitched on the first ring. He read the caller ID and read it again. It was Peters. He hit the answer button.

"Carl? It's me."

"Where the hell have you been?" Carl said. "And where the hell are you? I was getting ready to send out the dogs."

"I'm okay. After you left I followed the big guy that was with Alvarez. He tore outta the place. I lost him though. I'm not far from there. I'm at Anza and Blake. Come pick me up."

It was Peters' voice, but his cadence was halted. His speech was robot-like, unnatural.

"Followed him? What for? Why haven't you called?"

"Have you talked to anybody?"

It was a strange question for Peters to ask.

"What do you mean, have I talked to anybody? Are you all right?"

Peters only said, "The battery on my cell is dying. Just come and get me. Anza and Blake. We'll talk then. I'll be waiting."

Carl started to ask him something else but the call went dead. He stared at the screen. *Call ended.* He didn't know what to think. He was relieved to hear Peters' voice, but something didn't sound right. Peters didn't have the goofy upbeat tone he usually had—always had—no matter what the circumstance. He also didn't sound like he was outside. For a guy standing on a city street corner, it was deadly silent in the background.

Carl broke his gaze at the phone screen and looked up at Steven. The boy sensed something was wrong, clearly the call they were waiting for didn't go as Carl had hoped.

"You know where Anza Street is?"

"Sounds kinda familiar," Steven said, hoping to be helpful. "But, not really...no. You got a map, though. Right in your phone."

Carl nodded and reached into his jacket pocket for his mints. He popped the tin with his thumb and shook a couple into his palm.

Steven asked, "What are those things?"
"Just mints. You want one?"

CHAPTER TWENTY-TWO

Alvarez was back on the phone with Manuel. He paced back and forth in front of Peters who still sat tied to the chair.

"Are you sure you see no other cops?"

Manuel was sure. He was at Anza and Blake. He'd been planted near the corner watching even before they'd forced Peters to make the call.

"What do you mean, he's got a kid with him? Are you sure it's not another cop?"

Manuel was sure.

"How old's this kid? You mean like a toddler, or what?"

Manuel described the young man sitting in the car next to Carl.

Alvarez said, "What the fuck? You keep an eye on 'em. Stay close and keep me updated."

Alvarez heard the other line ringing. Holding the phone away from his head he saw the screen ID: *Home*. He had an elaborate system of forwarding calls so they could not be traced. He couldn't tell where the call was coming from, only that it was forwarded from home. Very few people on earth had his home number. He told Manuel, "I gotta go."

* * *

Quinn sat across from Teresa with a big grin on his face. He could hear the phone ringing in her hand while she held it to her ear. It was their fourth try. The previous three had all ended either with a wrong number or a frustrating recording telling them the line was no longer in service. He had no doubt Teresa was trying to get the right number. Why wouldn't she? Her life depended on it.

It must have rung a dozen times. No message was picking up.

Then someone answered. Quinn heard a male voice say hello. His smile broke into a toothy grin.

Teresa went right into the routine they'd rehearsed. "Dad, it's me. I'm in trouble."

She told Alvarez she'd been abducted. She didn't know where she was. She was scared. Where was the guy? He was taking a shit. She spoke in a hushed and hurried tone. It wasn't hard to convince Richard Alvarez that she was scared.

Then Quinn interrupted, playing his part. "Hey!" he bellowed. "What the fuck?" He reached over the table and unplugged the phone.

"All right then," he said.

"That's it?" Teresa asked.

"For now. We got a few minutes, then we're gonna take a little walk."

Quinn got up and started his ritual of wiping fingerprints off anything he may have touched. He started with the knife that still stuck straight out of Sofia's chest and worked his way backward though the apartment.

He didn't bother worrying about Teresa's prints, so he skipped the bathroom. Then, with a paper towel, he took Sofia's cell phone out of her purse and slipped it into his jacket pocket.

While he worked, Teresa sat still at the table trying to figure out what Quinn was planning. There had to be a chance for her to escape, she only had to wait for the opportunity.

The last thing he did was pick up his gun from the kitchen counter. "You ready, kid?" Before she got up, he set a twenty-dollar bill in front of her. "We're going to need this in a minute. We need cigarettes and you're buying."

She nodded, stood, and did her best not to look into the bedroom where Sofia's body lay as she and Quinn went out the front door and back into the afternoon daylight.

Once they were on the stairs, Quinn took Teresa again by the base of her elbow and steered her toward a corner store on 24th Street. His bag was still unzipped, he reminded her. It would only take a second to pull the gun and shoot her in the back if she tried to flee.

"It won't change my overall plan much," he said. "Not really. It'd be better if you lived, I mean, I'd like it if you lived, but as far as the plan goes, it can go either way."

Saying these things into her ear as they made their way down the block.

"Pace yourself," he said. "We still have a few minutes."

Quinn stopped suddenly and told Teresa to reach into his jacket pocket and pull out the cell phone, explaining what she needed to do. "You're gonna call nine-one-one. You tell 'em: 'The guy you're looking for just murdered another person, a woman. He's still there, inside. The address is one-one-six-nine Alabama.' That's it. They're gonna want more, but you hang up and drop the phone on the sidewalk. Okay?"

She said okay and did exactly as she was told. The 9-1-1 operator pressed for more information, but Teresa dropped the cell onto the ground and Quinn crushed it with the heel of his boot.

Once they were in the store, Quinn positioned them near the window where they could watch the front door of Sofia's house. And then, they waited. They pretended to browse a little but never changed their spot. After about ten minutes they saw a car pull up and park in the driveway next to the house. A nice new Mercedes Benz. A small wiry man hopped out and dashed up the stairs.

"See that there? That's Guillermo Gutiérrez. One of your father's right-hand men. He's a smart little fucker, pretty handy too. I wonder why Pops sent him?"

Teresa said, coolly and quietly, "I know who he is."

They watched as Gutiérrez stopped at the front door, listened, and then, without knocking, tried the knob. Quinn had left it unlocked and he now watched Gutiérrez creep right inside.

A few more minutes went by and they heard sirens. Quinn said into Teresa's ear, "Time to get those cigarettes." He moved them toward the counter where an annoyed clerk had been eyeing them. The clerk didn't speak, didn't smile, he sat frozen beside the register with a look of suspicion still painted on his face.

"A pack of Marlboro red and whatever she's smoking," Quinn said as he flashed a wide, white smile.

By the time they were back on the sidewalk, there were three squad cars outside Sofia's house with more arriving every second. Crown Vics, an unmarked Ford Taurus or two. Policemen ran up the stairs, taking them two at a time, with guns drawn. More stood at the bottom of the stairs giving hard looks up and down the block.

Quinn said, "Look at that. Two Asian cops. There goes two more. Two black ones. What's that guy, a Mexican? Jesus, it's been so long since I seen 'em swarm like this. Things really have changed."

Two dark sedans pulled up with pairs of plainclothes cops in both.

"There they are. The white ones. Detectives. Homicide. The white fuckers still hanging on to the best jobs."

They watched from their vantage point down the block as the serious and slow detectives asked a few questions to the officers in front before they sauntered up the stoop.

"Perfect," Quinn purred. "One down, three to go."

Manuel Herrera waited patiently atop the grassy hill that gave him a full view of the intersection at Anza and Blake. It was a steep green slope that bordered the back of the University of San Francisco's Lone Mountain campus. Too steep for buildings or paths for citizens to be walking on. Manuel was a loyal dog and, of the many things Alvarez had asked him to do over the years, this was an easy task. Beat them there and make sure they didn't alert the police, Alvarez had said. That and keep him informed. Alvarez always wanted to be kept up to date. A lot of guys in his position liked to keep a little distance between them and the dirty work. Not Alvarez. He was hands-on. It was how he kept control.

Manuel's spot was high up off the street and obscured by trees. Alvarez had chosen the corner because of this spot. They'd used it before. It was almost impossible for someone on the street to notice him up there and it was quiet enough that whoever needed watching wouldn't get mixed up in any crowds or traffic.

He eyed the old cop and the young man sitting on the corner in their bland green Acura. Just sitting there, waiting, hoping their friend would show up. Fools, thought Manuel. He's *never* going to show up—anywhere. He took down the license plate number, did his best to judge the year and make of the car. What were they doing down there, though? They sat talking, clearly having some kind of serious conversation. What would an old man be doing with a kid like that? Maybe he's a faggot, thought Manuel. Wouldn't be the first old cop to have a sweet tooth.

Then he saw something else. Another car up the block. One full block back on the corner of Collins and Anza. He recognized it. A fucking Ford Focus. He knew that car.

Tremblay.

What the fuck was that piece of shit doing here? Wasn't he supposed to be back at the restaurant waiting for Alvarez, waiting for orders?

He pulled out his cell and started scrolling for Alvarez's number.

Then the old cop's car started up, began to move.

Manuel hopped down the hill taking long double strides. He'd be in his car before they got two blocks.

He reached his Dodge Charger prepared, key in hand. He jumped in and started the engine. When he looked back, he saw Tremblay's car was already gone. He pulled his car out and started after Carl and his young friend. They'd gone up to Masonic and taken a right and were heading toward the Panhandle. As soon as Manuel made the turn he saw them less than a block ahead. If the lights played in his favor, he'd have no trouble tailing them.

There it was, Tremblay's car, about three car lengths ahead of him and one lane over. No question who was driving. He was staring at the back of Tremblay's fat head. Tremblay was following the Acura, too. This was going to make it all easier. Tremblay was doing half the work for him.

Carl and Steven had been sitting and waiting. Carl's eyes darted from the windshield to the mirrors. His guts told him this was a ruse, but he wasn't ready to give up on his friend yet. The seconds ticked by. Carl tried to keep his mind away from the worst-case scenario by absent-mindedly asking Steven questions. What he and Quinn had for lunch. What did he say his plans were in the city? They'd just gotten round to talking about Teresa when the phone rang.

It was Panzer saying there was another victim. This

time a female. That was all he knew. He was en route to the scene.

Carl pressed Panzer. How'd he know it was the same killer? What was the cause of death? Panzer said he had no more information, but he'd happily meet Carl at the scene.

Carl must have mentioned it was a female victim out loud, because he looked at Steven and saw the boy's eyes welling up. He asked Panzer for more particulars, an age, a physical description, anything. Panzer repeated he knew nothing. Carl asked Panzer the address and turned over the engine.

As they pulled into the street, he asked the boy if he was familiar with the address. 1169 Alabama. The kid said he had no idea where that was.

"Well, make yourself useful and punch it into my phone and tell me how the hell we get there." Carl was having trouble hiding the apprehension in his voice.

While Carl stayed focused on the traffic, Steven played navigator with the phone. He pulled and stretched the map with his fingers and directed Carl through streets he'd never traveled.

Neither had time to notice the two cars weaving through traffic behind them.

Steven wasn't used to using this kind of phone, this kind of map, or giving directions. Although a panicked sense of urgency ran through them, it didn't part the traffic ahead, or flatten out the city's steep terrain. Steven made mistakes more than once and had to allow the phone's GPS to correct itself before telling Carl which way to turn next. His stomach contracted when he thought about Teresa and he couldn't concentrate on the map or the road.

They worked their way through the Lower Haight and pushed through the Castro District. More than once Carl asked, "Are you sure you put the right address in there? Are you sure you spelled it right?"

They'd reached Dolores Park when the phone went off in Steven's hand causing the map to disappear.

"It says Panzer."

Carl frowned and reached for the cell. He thumbed the yes button and said hello.

"I'm here," Panzer said. "Where are you?"

"On the way. You looking at the victim?"

"Oh yeah. Fuckin' knife right in the heart. Just like the others. Looks like our guy all right."

"What's she look like?"

Steven sat paralyzed while Carl listened to the answer. The sick feeling spread from his stomach to his whole body, causing his skin to rise up in cold goose bumps.

Carl slowed the car. "I'll be there in a few more minutes," he told the man on the phone before hitting the end button and passing it back to Steven.

Steven wanted to ask, but couldn't.

Carl said, "It's not her."

"Are you sure? How can they know for sure?"

"It's a woman, probably in her late forties. They're guessing it's the leaseholder of the house where they found her. Sound like Teresa?"

Steven shook his head. He was relieved she wasn't dead, but the sick feeling didn't dissipate. She was still out there somewhere. In danger. With Quinn.

CHAPTER TWENTY-THREE

"What now?" Steven asked.

Carl said, "Enough with this cowboy stuff. We're gonna head over there and see what's going on. I'm going to have to talk to my friend on the force face to face and they'll take it from there."

Steven sighed and looked out at the hilly sides of Dolores Park. Its grassy slopes forming a green bowl, lined with people tanning, lunching, and walking their dogs. All of them seeming relaxed and enjoying life in a way Steven never could. Regular life. It was right outside the car window and somehow unreachable.

If they were going to talk to the police, the chances of him finding Teresa had just shrunk away. Would they hold him? What would happen to him if he put his fate in the hands of the police?

"I'm sorry, kid. I've been putting this off, but I can't anymore. My partner's missing, your friend is gone, there's a killer out there who's probably got her. This is no time for heroics. We've got to do the right thing. I may be retired, but I'm still a lawman."

Steven brought his gaze back into the car. "You're retired?"

"Yeah. I didn't mention that? Like you, I'm just a regular citizen in way over his head."

"Is your friend retired, too?"

"Ha, no. But I'm afraid he'll be retired against his will if we don't do something about finding out where he is."

Steven began thinking about Teresa again.

"Don't worry, we're going to find her, too," Carl said. "This is the real deal though, no movie or TV show. These guys are for real and they play for keeps."

"I know that. Don't you think I know that by now? I was with him. I saw what he did with that fork. I saw what else he did when we came back." The words came out in a torrent of emotion. "That's why I'm scared. He wants to kill me. He wants to kill Teresa, if he hasn't already. He's out there with his big fucking shiny gun and he's got her and he's looking for me."

"Shiny?" Carl asked.

"What's going to happen if we go to the cops—even if he is your friend? If Quinn finds out, he'll kill her. Just like that. I know it. He doesn't care. He acts nice, but he just...just..."

"I know, son, I know," Carl said. But he didn't know. He didn't know what to tell the kid. He didn't know what drove a man like Quinn. He had no idea why Quinn grabbed the girl or what he intended to do.

"Steven," Carl said. "*Steven.*"

Steven's focus was once again pulled back to the present.

"I still need you to help me find this place. We're at Twenty-second and, let's see," Carl looked up to find a street sign, "Guerrero, it looks like. Which way do I turn?"

"Left," Steven said. The streets had once again become an understandable grid, the blue dot on the GPS catching up to their position. "Follow Twenty-second all the way down and we should eventually hit Alabama Street."

They turned and had gone less than one block when Steven said, "Stop the car."

"What do you mean, stop? I thought you said we keep going—"

"That was *them*. Stop the car."

"Who? That was who? Where?"

"*Teresa and Quinn*. I just saw them. They were on that street we just passed."

"You sure?" Carl found it hard to believe. The kid must have been traumatized, maybe slipping in to shock.

Steven shouted, "*Turn*."

Carl took a hard right on Valencia Street. Tires squealed and people in the crosswalk jumped back. Steven grabbed at the padded door handle and missed it. The inertia of the turn threw him across the seat toward Carl.

Carl said, "A man doesn't spend thirty years on the police force without learning some tactical driving skills." He raced to the end of the block and yanked the wheel over for another hard right. A half-block up was a side street, San Jose Avenue, an alley by San Francisco standards, but wide enough for two lanes of traffic. Carl took another right onto the alley and slowed. They saw no one. No moving cars. No pedestrians. Carl sped up the block, looking for anywhere the two may be hiding, but the street was empty. Just as he reached 22nd Street, the same spot where Steven thought he'd seen Quinn and Teresa, Carl saw something he did recognize. Tremblay's

Ford drove right in front of them on 22nd, in the same direction they had just gone.

"Well, I'll be damned," Carl said.

Manuel lost sight of the car containing Carl and his young friend when they turned left on 22nd Street, but he was still only a few car-lengths behind Tremblay and Tremblay was sticking close to Carl. He made the left as the light turned yellow and stuck close, too. Tremblay had slowed down in front of him. He looked ahead and didn't see the Acura.

Tremblay braked, then took a hard right on the corner of Valencia. Manuel started to follow, but before he could get half-way down the block, Carl's Acura darted across the side street behind him. Manuel barely caught the flash of green in his rearview. There was no way to tell if the old man had seen him. Manuel was left with the decision to stay on Tremblay, or stick with the old man.

He performed a quick three-point U-turn and pulled right onto the side street and followed Carl and the boy.

The side street, though, was void of traffic. There were no other cars at all, only his and Carl's. He was made. No way had he gone unnoticed. He'd practically rammed up against the other vehicle's back bumper. Carl's car tripled in speed and barely stopped at the next stop sign.

"Shit," whispered Manuel to himself.

He checked his rearview and saw Tremblay's car racing up behind him.

Manuel said, "Motherfucker."

* * *

Quinn had Teresa tucked into a doorway on San Jose Avenue right before 22nd Street. He saw the way her eyes lit up when the Acura passed them. He knew it was trouble. Now, still in the doorway with his body pressed up against hers, keeping her still and hidden, he whispered, "Who was that in that car? I saw the way you looked at them. Who is it?"

"I don't know what you're talking about," she said in a voice loud and defiant. Too loud.

Quinn's lips peeled into a snarl. He bared his teeth. The straight white lines parting just enough to promise a nasty bite.

Teresa flashed back to the head-butt he'd delivered to Sofia. Her face was only a few inches from his. She was sure Quinn would chew a hole right through her cheek. He looked animal, inhuman. She didn't say anything more.

With his one free hand, he dug his index and middle fingers up under her sternum and pushed.

"Who was in the car?"

"You're hurting me."

"I know."

Quinn heard a short squeal of tires somewhere on the block and turned his head to see the car. A green Acura passed in front of them. An old man drove and in the passenger seat he saw, he was sure of it, Steven.

"Fuck me," he said.

The tire squeal, though, had come from too far away for it to be this car. He stayed pressed against the door, squeezing the air out of Teresa. Seconds later, another car drove by.

A blue Ford Focus. Tremblay. My old friend Tremblay.

He was in the same car that he'd chased Quinn in earlier that day. Tremblay was speeding, staring straight ahead, focused on something else. The other car. Tremblay was following Steven.

Pinching Teresa in the neck right above the collar bone, Quinn leaned out from the doorway and looked down San Jose Avenue. Both the first car and Tremblay's were driving away on the next block. But a third car had wedged in between them and was racing up on the first.

"Fuckin' idiots."

Teresa repeated, "You're hurting me."

In the intensity of the moment, Quinn didn't notice how hard he was pinching her neck. He let go and quickly grabbed her again at the elbow. "Sorry, but it's the best you're gonna get from me."

He dragged her back into the street now. She was stumbling, probably hoping to stall long enough so her friends would come back around and see them.

"Let's go," Quinn said. "It's time for us to hitch a ride."

Carl's phone went off. Steven held it in his hand. Carl said, "What's it say."

"Caller name withheld."

"Lemme see that."

Carl took the phone and hit answer as he made another right to round the block. Tremblay.

"You know you got a tail?"

"Where are you?" Carl said.

"Right fucking behind you, you dumbfuck. You got one of Alvarez's boys riding your ass."

Carl checked his rearview and saw the Charger drawing up close behind.

"Who is that?"

"You don't recognize him? He was at the restaurant. I'm right behind him."

"No, I don't recognize him. I'm trying to keep from running anybody over. Did you see them?"

"See who?"

"Quinn and the girl. They were right there."

"Where?"

"You really back there?"

"Where did you see them?"

"The boy saw them. Two blocks back. I'm going round for another look."

Tremblay had already hung up the phone.

Quinn pulled Teresa by the arm all the way down to the corner of 22nd and Guerrero. There was a four-way stoplight and he walked up to the first car he saw, a late-model Subaru station wagon. All four windows were partially rolled down. Without hesitation he threw his bag into the backseat and reached in and unlocked the door. He got in first, dragging Teresa behind him.

The driver, a meek bespectacled man in his thirties cried out, "Hey! What the hell do you think you're doing?"

"Police business," Quinn said. "When the light turns, drive straight ahead."

"Police business? You can't just jump in my car. I've got—"

By then Quinn had his .45 out of his bag and was pressing it to the back of the man's head. Hard, just below his right ear.

"Drive straight and listen to my instructions."

CHAPTER TWENTY-FOUR

Teresa started to say something. She didn't even get out the first syllable. Quinn gave her an icy stare that froze her and left her mouth hanging open.

"Not a good time, Teresa."

The driver was moving forward, waiting for further instructions. He was scared out of his mind, but had enough instinctual self-preservation to control the car. Quinn knew that wouldn't last, though. Within a few blocks this candy-ass would run a light or get in a fender-bender that would draw the heat or immobilize them.

"You got a phone?"

The man nodded.

"Let's have it. Throw it to the girl."

The man picked up an iPhone from the front seat and tossed it back toward Teresa.

"Take what you want," he said.

"I intend to," Quinn said.

They reached 19th Street and traffic was slowing down, backing up from other cars waiting to make left-hand turns.

"Get in the right lane. Take a right."

The man made the right.

"See the second left, that little street? Pull in there."

"Please don't hurt me."

"Stop being a pussy." Quinn looked at Teresa, a smirk on his face, but she was drawn, white, and as fearful as the man in the driver's seat.

The man made the turn and half-way up the block Quinn told him to stop. He cowered over the wheel, awaiting his fate.

Quinn said, "Gimme the keys and get out." Then he turned to Teresa, the gun pointed at her face. "You sit still, don't move a muscle."

Quinn hopped out of the back and opened the driver's door for the terrified man.

"C'mon, c'mon. Let's go."

The man got out and he and Quinn stood face to face on the sidewalk. Quinn held out his left hand and the man gave him the keys to the Subaru.

Quinn pushed the barrel of the gun deep into the man's stomach. He smiled.

Teresa cried out, "Please don't. Please."

Quinn was ready to pull the trigger, drop the man and buy them a few more minutes, but something about Teresa's plea stopped him. He glanced at her. She was leaning over in the back seat, eyes wide and wet.

"Lucky day, Mr. Subaru. The girl took a shine to ya."

Quinn got into the driver's seat and fired up the car. He told Teresa to climb over into the front seat and put on her seatbelt as they pulled away.

Peters hung his head down. His whole upper body was leaning forward. His hands were zip-tied to the back of the chair, anchoring him so he could lean no farther. He watched drops of blood spatter on the floor between his feet. His nose was broken, he was sure of it. Probably a couple of ribs, too. There was a loud ringing in his right ear and he probably had a concussion or worse.

He stared at his feet. The wicked smaller man had smashed each of his pinky toes with the ballpeen hammer. The damage was concealed by his shoes, but the pain was excruciating. He felt the swelling toes push against the canvas along with the warm, wet blood in his shoe.

Alvarez's voice came back into focus. He squatted in front of Peters with the hammer raised in his hand. "Why would you come here looking for her if you didn't know who she was?"

Peters was afraid to answer. For over twenty minutes now Alvarez had been asking him about a girl. Some young girl named Teresa. He had no idea who they were talking about. Each time he answered, professing his ignorance, he was delivered another blow. He'd tried to explain why they were there, why he and Carl felt the need to come to San Francisco. It sounded ridiculous even to him now—taking time off, going out of your jurisdiction on your own dime, to try to find a man who may or may not know something about a homicide. It shouldn't have even been his case to begin with. Homicides were investigated by the Sheriff's Department. They were right; he was only a patrolman, why would he do this?

Alvarez's questions took a turn. "What about the reporter? Hmmn? You know who I am talking about, don't you?"

"Reporter?" croaked Peters. "What are you—"

Crack. The ballpeen came down again on his toe. The same spot. The same crushed pinky. The pain connected immediately with his brain, white and hot. He winced and tried to suck in air through his nose, but his nasal passages were caked with dried blood. They must have him confused with someone else. This must be a case of mistaken identity.

"Friedlander. From the *Chronicle*? Are you saying you've never been in contact with him? We're going to find out everything eventually. You may as well tell us now and save yourself some pain."

The cell went off in Alvarez's pocket and he dug the phone from his jacket. The screen read *Home.*

His tone turned tender as he answered. "Teresa? Sweetheart?"

Quinn laughed on the other end. "Sweetheart? You kidding me? I'm pretty sure she's not gonna buy that act and I know I *definitely* don't."

"You...you..." Alvarez was at a loss for words. "What do you want? Where is my daughter?"

"She's right beside me. Careful with that word, I don't want her to hear you. You'll spoil my surprise. Yeah, she's all right, too. In case you were going to ask."

Alvarez held his breath, waiting for Quinn to make his move, his demands.

"You sound as chipper as ever, Ricardo. I bet you didn't think you'd be hearing my voice anytime soon."

"How much?"

"How much? How much for what? What do you think I'm doing? Kidnapping her? I don't think so. You should be asking when. When am I going to show up at your door. When is the other boot gonna drop. When is your façade going to crumble."

"I know about the reporter. Tremblay is picking him up right now."

Quinn laughed. "Bullshit. I just saw Tremblay. He's down here in the Mission chasing my ass around. He might as well be chasing his own tail because he'd have better luck. Shit, Ricardo, you got a whole wagon train on my ass down here. Whatever happened to being discreet? These yahoos should've had parade banners on."

Alvarez wasn't sure if this was a bluff or not. He hadn't heard a report from Manuel, and Tremblay wouldn't answer his phone.

"I just wanted to touch base" Quinn said. "Let you know I'm doing good and I'm right on track with fucking your shit up. Tell you what though, the cell battery is running low so I'm gonna—*we're* gonna—have to call you back."

Alvarez, not wanting Quinn to hang up, said, "Do you actually have her? Let me speak to her."

To Teresa, Quinn said, "Hey girl, say hello to this punk who calls himself your father."

The way Quinn said father, the almost sarcastic tone, threw Teresa off. All she could think to say was, "Hello?"

Quinn punched the end button and dropped the phone on the seat.

"What do you think of this car? You think we look like one of those well-to-do lesbian couples in one of these things? I hear they love the Subaru station wagons. Is that true?"

Teresa slumped down in her seat. She didn't laugh. It looked to Quinn as though she were about to throw up.

"C'mon now. You're not gonna go into one of those drug convulsions are you? You already getting sick for a fix? You just had some a while back."

"No, I'm not getting sick. You're the one that's sick. This whole thing, what you're doing, is sick."

Quinn laughed. "Sweetheart, you don't know the half of it."

Carl and Steven pulled over. The Charger whizzed past them, the driver keeping his eyes straight ahead. Carl saw in his rearview that Tremblay was pulling up behind them and stopping. The cell started ringing again.

"It's that Panzer guy again," Steven said.

"Don't answer it."

Tremblay got out of his car and walked toward them. Carl told Steven to stay in the car. Steven was glad to do so.

"You sure you saw 'em?"

"The kid did. That's good enough for me."

Tremblay eyed the back of Steven's head through the rear window.

"You never told me the deal about the kid. Who is he?"

"Quinn found him on the roadside up north. Brought him along to try to lure the girl. Almost worked too, until the boy got wise and took off with her."

Tremblay's gaze hadn't broken.

"That's it," Carl said. "He doesn't know anything more than what I've told you. Now it's time for you to enlighten me a little further."

Tremblay's phone went off inside his pants pocket.

He pulled the cell, looked at it, holding a finger up to Carl.

"This should be interesting."

He hit the answer button and immediately Alvarez's voice blasted through the tiny speaker. "Where the hell have you been?"

"Hello to you too, Richard." He turned away from Carl so the conversation could not be overheard. "What's up?"

"I'm in the middle of a *pinche* crisis here and you're flitting off to hide and do your cocaine, that's what. I need you to draw on your resources and find someone for me."

"Resources?"

"I need you to find a reporter. Seth Friedlander. Are you writing this down? He works for the *Chronicle*. You think you can do that one small thing without fucking up and fucking off?"

"Sounds like a job for Gutiérrez."

Alvarez's voice jumped an octave. "Gutiérrez is gone. He went to get the girl. Fucking Manuel is out chasing that old cop. I'm sitting here alone babysitting the useless cop."

"What cop?"

"The ones that were at the restaurant. I got the young one here in front of me."

"Where are you?"

"I want to hear from you in thirty minutes. *Comprende*?"

"Sure. Seth Wheelender."

Now Alvarez's voice doubled in volume, making the tiny speaker crackle.

"Seth Friedlander. *Mierda*, can you fucking pay attention? Stop drinking and doing blow for five fucking minutes and find this piece of shit before we all end up in prison. Half an hour." He hung up. The call was over.

Tremblay took a few short steps back to Carl who was leaning on the door of his car.

"Looks like your friend is still alive."

Carl expelled a long breath that felt as though it'd been trapped in his chest for the last several hours. "How do you know?"

"Alvarez's got him."

"Where's Alvarez? At his restaurant? Let's go get him."

"Slow down there, pops. We need to think about this a minute. I seriously doubt he's at the restaurant. Ol' Richard is smarter than that. I know that greasy fuck, how he deals with trouble. If he gets spooked he'll off your friend and make him disappear."

"What do you mean disappear? He's a cop. You can't go around killing cops."

"You can if you're Ricardo Alvarez," Tremblay said. "We just need a bit of a plan."

"Plan? I'll tell you a plan. I make a phone call and bring in the goddamn cavalry. I must be out of my mind chasing around this town without back-up. Now you're telling me I've jeopardized my partner's life?"

"Just hold off for a minute. Let's think this thing through."

"A kidnapped police officer? A string of dead bodies? There's nothing to think about. We're going to have the SFPD raid and ransack every conceivable place where this character could be and we're going to find Peters."

"I'm telling you, don't do it. Alvarez has been up against this kind of shit before. He's prepared and he don't cave easily. He's got friends *everywhere.* You start shaking the bushes and your friend will be gone forever. Alvarez is as close to untouchable as they come."

Carl stood in front of him, chest out, breathing hard. He was trying to read what was behind Tremblay's eyes. What was this guy's real motive? Everything about him was no good. Christ, Carl thought, he *works* for the man who kidnapped your partner.

Carl opened the driver's side door and asked Steven to hand him the cell. He went straight to missed calls and hit the first one.

CHAPTER TWENTY-FIVE

"Where the fuck are you, Bradley?"

Carl started to tell him, but Panzer cut him off.

"I've been calling you for the last hour steady. You said you were going to meet me here at the scene. What the fuck is going on? What would possess you to fuck with me and my department?"

Carl said, "Peters is missing."

"What?"

"Missing. Actually, not missing. He's being held hostage."

"What the fuck are you talking about?"

"Richard Alvarez has him."

"Who the fuck is Richard Alvarez?"

"Richard *Allen*. C'mon, Panzer. You're the one that told me about him."

"Why would he grab your partner? You're not making any sense."

"He took him at his restaurant on Geary Street. While I was on my way down to the first scene."

"Jesus fucking Christ, Carl. What the hell aren't you telling me? You better get your ass over here and straighten this shit out. If Alvarez has anything to do with the whereabouts of your friend, we'll find out. But first, you better get your ass over here. In fact, fuck that.

I'll come to you. Where are you—*exactly*?"

Carl looked up and saw Tremblay getting into his car.

Panzer went on, "I'm gonna remind you of something, Carl. You are *not* a cop, not anymore. This is a murder investigation. You've been afforded every courtesy by this department, but enough is enough. At this point you're obstructing, probably tampering, and who the fuck knows what else. If you don't haul it in here quick, I can't promise you won't be arrested."

"Arrested?" Carl was watching Tremblay sit behind the wheel of the Ford Focus. "If that's the case, then how do I know I won't be arrested when I come in?"

Panzer made a sound that was half sigh, half growl. "Honestly, I can't promise you that either."

Tremblay started his car and pulled around Carl and Steven. Carl held up his palm, signaling for Tremblay to hold on. But Tremblay wasn't looking at Carl; he was taking a last glance at Steven.

Steven looked back at Tremblay as he drove by. Although it was through two car windows, it was the closest Steven had been to Maurice Tremblay. Tremblay's face was forced into a pathetic excuse for a grin, but Steven wasn't looking at his expression, he was looking at his eyes. Dark and buried behind purple bags and a heavy brow, the eyes frightened Steven. It was only for a quick passing second, but those eyes told Steven everything he needed to know about the man. He was evil.

Carl told Panzer, "I'll call you right back."

Tremblay now had the name. He recognized it, but didn't know Seth Friedlander. Maybe he'd seen in it the paper's bylines over the years, maybe he knew it from somewhere else. A reporter. Quinn was finally playing his ace card. He called Pino on his cell and told him to meet him again at the All Star Donuts on 5th Street.

"Good," Pino said. "I got some shit to tell you, too."

No way was Tremblay going to sit around while Carl Bradley talked with his detective friend from the SFPD. That would be like sticking the cuffs on himself. It was a mistake to talk to the police; he knew this from personal experience. This thing was unraveling faster than he expected. He rolled down the windows and let some of the cool afternoon air in the car. Night was on its way and the wind was picking up. He decided he had enough time to pull over for a quick blast before meeting Pino.

This time a parking spot would suffice. He found one on Folsom near 10th Street and pulled over. He rolled up the windows and dug out his bag of coke. He took the keys out of the ignition and stuck one straight into the bag, digging down near the bottom where the powder would be finest. Two keys into each nostril and then a hit from the Maker's Mark. Instantly he felt better. But not quite enough. He took a credit card from his wallet and crushed a rock of solid cocaine on the back of a CD case. He used the card to chop it up into two fat lines. He carefully sat the CD case on the seat beside him while he searched his jacket for a piece of paper to roll into a tube so he could snort the lines. He found one, a numbered receipt from a recent fast food order. He rolled it up, took another long pull from the whiskey, and then picked up the CD case and sucked in the lines.

* * *

238

Seth Friedlander lived under the freeway in an under-developed, underused part of Oakland. His neighbors were mostly warehouses and industrial shops. That and vacant businesses. The freeway above him had collapsed in the 1989 earthquake and most of the residents never came back. The structure over his place was sound and secure, but after the quake, the idea of living under a freeway had lost its appeal. What appeal it ever had.

Seth had always considered himself an outlaw journalist. His heroes were the Hunter S. Thompsons and the Tom Wolfes of the world. He considered himself kin to the innovators of the New Journalism, a natural heir, especially to Thompson, who'd also written for a San Francisco paper during the eighties. But, really, the only thing he shared with Thompson was an insatiable appetite for drugs. First it was weed and acid as he tried to glean some sort of glow from the embers of the sixties, then came cocaine and heroin. Somewhere along the line he'd learned to smoke his cocaine and that's when his life really began to unravel. He lost a wife, a house, his car, and most of his possessions, but somehow managed to hang on to the one thing that gave him his identity—his job.

He decided to reel in his life, getting off the rock. It wasn't that hard, he used a unique detox method: he began smoking crystal meth. As the twenty-first century rolled in he was also able to make the switch from cheap Mexican heroin to prescribed opiates. Vicodin, then Percocet, then, for a while, Oxycontin. Nowadays he got by on the hydrocodone from a narco script his doctor reluctantly kept filling. He wasn't above smoking a little black tar heroin when things got rough, but from where he stood, he was miles away from the pathetic man he'd been. He had his life together, manageable at least, and he was poised for a comeback. And Quinn McFetridge was going to make it happen.

When he hit bottom in the late nineties he'd spent a short period of time in state prison. He was sentenced to eighteen months, but he hoped to be out in less than half the time. The newspaper gave him a leave of absence, treating it as though he were in an extended-stay rehab. It wasn't tough for them to do; the *Chronicle* was shrinking and they were happy to lighten the payroll. Although the experience wasn't dramatic enough to force him to change his ways, there was one great caveat: He met Quinn.

They weren't cellies, but they managed to spend some time together at meals, the yard, and eventually at a job they both held making mattresses in the PIA. It was only for a few months and Quinn lost his job before Friedlander was released, but the bond they formed was forever. Gossiping by the industrial sewing machines, Seth found Quinn to be as funny and charismatic as anyone he'd met. He was fascinated by Quinn's stories of the criminal underworld.

As soon as Quinn learned Friedlander was a disgraced journalist, he began cultivating his new friend. First he encouraged him to stick to his guns and become the man he always wanted to be, the man other newspaper men hate with a jealous passion. Success is the best revenge, he told him. All it takes is one great story.

"Look at that guy who broke the CIA crack connection for the *San Jose Mercury*. What was his name?"

"Gary Webb," Seth said.

"Yeah, that dude has it made. One good story. The kind of stuff that people crave. They love to hate their government. They love finding out they've been had. I don't understand it, but I don't need to. It's a fact. Look at Watergate or any other story that they stick 'gate' on the end of."

"What the hell can I do from behind here? I'm all fucked up, man. I probably won't even have a job when I get out."

"You get out and hang on to the job. Any decent reporter job. Then, I can help you."

"Help me what?"

"Help you with that one great story."

To Seth, it sounded like a con. He chuckled. "What do you wanna do? Make probation and become a cub reporter? Is that something you've always dreamed of doing?"

"No," Quinn had told him. "I already have the story. All you need to do is tell it."

After Seth was released, Quinn began to call him collect once or twice a month. He only told Seth parts of his story, bits of the puzzle, but it was enough that Seth became convinced it was the one thing that would punch his ticket to immortality. He began to see himself not as a Hunter S. Thompson knock-off, but the next Bob Woodward. When this piece broke, he'd be a household name in the Bay Area and beyond. He'd be able to work for any news organization in the country. He only had to keep getting Quinn to filter out the tale.

Their phone conversations morphed from teaser interviews into Quinn instructing Seth to run errands. Seth knew he was helping Quinn build a case for his release, but he didn't examine it further than that. He set aside his journalistic curiosity at Quinn's request and kept his eyes on the prize, the big story. Soon he was meeting with a young lawyer Quinn had working on his case. Seth ran evidence and envelopes all over the city with the cloak-and-dagger secrecy of a spy.

Now the fruits of his work, and his patience, were about to pay off.

He knew Quinn was out and had been for almost two weeks. After a couple of cryptic phone calls, he decided to hole-up and wait. No sense in worrying; all he could do was prepare. He sketched out the parts of the story he already knew, did some qualifying research on the people whose lives he was about to disrupt, and stayed good and high.

The knock sounded as upbeat and joyful as Quinn himself. Shave and a haircut, two bits. Seth leapt off the couch and swung open the front door. There was Quinn, looking more tired than he ever did in prison, and a pale young girl at his side. The girl looked half-dead. Quinn was smiling. The girl wasn't.

"Come in, come in, come in," Seth said. He swung his arm toward the interior of the house and ushered them inside. As soon as the girl stepped over the threshold, he saw that Quinn had a large and shiny automatic pistol pointed at the small of her back.

Quinn watched Seth's facial expression change when he saw the gun. He reassured him with a wink. "Just a precaution. Everything is fine, just fine."

When Quinn and Teresa were seated on the couch, side by side, Seth asked if anyone wanted a drink. "Soda? Beer? Water?"

"I'm okay. How about you, sweetheart?"

"I'm not feeling too well," Teresa said. She looked at their host. He was small, skinny. He wore greasy sweatpants and a dirty sweatshirt. His eyeglasses were taped together in the corner and looked opaque with fingerprints.

"Well, our friend here is no stranger to drugs or needles, so there's no need to go hiding in the bathroom. You can set up shop right here. Isn't that right, Seth?"

"Sure, sure. Whatever you need."

"Thanks," Teresa said, bitter and sarcastic. "I think I'll hold off for now."

Quinn said, "Suit yourself. Time is a murderous bitch, as they say. Maybe we should get started. Seth, tell us what you need. Blood, urine, what?"

"Pretty simple really. It's just a cotton swab in the inside of your cheek."

Teresa made a face. "Cotton swab? What the fuck for?"

"DNA," Seth said.

Quinn leaned in toward their host. "Here's the beauty of the thing, Seth. Teresa here doesn't know the whole story. She'll be learning it as this thing unfolds. That could be an angle for your article, right? Talk about your human interest."

"Yeah, yeah, yeah," agreed Seth. His eyes were already lit up with ideas for the piece that'd not yet been written. "Totally. It'll flesh it out, give people a hero and a victim."

"What the fuck is he talking about?" Teresa asked.

"You're sure your boy can get these results back quick? I'm always reading in the newspaper this shit takes weeks, even on the big-time cases."

"Aah, newspapers. You can't believe everything you read."

At this, Quinn and Seth broke out laughing.

It was Tremblay's intention to go into the donut shop and grab a quick bite, but the coke and whiskey had quelled his appetite, so when he pulled into the parking lot and saw Pino sitting at a table near a window, he just bleated his horn.

Pino frowned at him and got up and hurried outside to the car.

"C'mon," he said, signaling Tremblay to follow him.

Tremblay rolled down his window. "Get in."

Pino shook his head. "Fuck no. That car is hot, let's use mine. And hurry up before someone sees us."

Tremblay's first impression was Pino must be dipping into the evidence room for his own personal use. He powered up the window, grabbed the bottle of Maker's, and got out of his car. By the time he reached Pino's car, an unmarked Ford Taurus, Pino was already in the front seat looking over his shoulder. Tremblay got in on the passenger side and unscrewed the Maker's for another pull.

"Let's take a drive," Pino said.

With the burn of whiskey still in his throat, Tremblay

rasped, "Sure. Where we going?"

"Anywhere but here."

Tremblay didn't waste any time. "I need a favor. There's a guy—a reporter—I need you to run. I've got to find this asshole double-time. His name is Seth Friedlander. Ever hear of him?"

"Shit, Tremblay, what're you in, a cloud? You're a wanted man. Don't you know this? Panzer over in homicide has the whole fucking force looking for you."

There was that name again, thought Tremblay. "Me? What for?"

"He's got an all-points out for you. Your car is on the hot sheet. You're a wanted man in a big way."

"You better not be driving me in, Pino. You and I have a history."

"Don't worry, I'm not bringing you in, but I definitely don't want to be seen with you. If I were you, I wouldn't get back in your car, either. It's a magnet right now. Slouch down in the seat a little and put that fucking bottle away."

Tremblay took another hit and screwed the cap back on the bottle.

"What the fuck is going on?" Pino continued. "There's a string of murders in town and suddenly you're on the most wanted. You *and* these two wannabe cops from Calistoga. The two that reached out to me? What're you guys now, friends or enemies?"

"You sure about that? The two cops? Are they still wanted? Can you check?"

"Yeah, I'm sure. I don't need to check. Persons of interest. This shit is coming over the radio every five minutes. You want to explain why I'm risking my ass talking to you?"

"I'm about to clear my name, but I need you to run this guy Friedlander. Can you do it or not?"

Pino wheeled the car into the center of a parking lot under the freeway that led to the Bay Bridge. He stopped in the middle and turned off the engine.

"Yeah, I can run him, but that's it. No more favors. This is putting more than my job at risk; you're putting my freedom in jeopardy."

"It's all I ask."

Tremblay spelled out Seth Friedlander's name for Pino and waited as he ran it though the computer attached to the dash. The length of the arrest record that came back surprised Tremblay.

"This guy is supposed to be a reporter? You sure this is the right Seth Friedlander?"

"He's the only one that pops. Take it or leave it."

Tremblay copied down the most recent addresses beside the name. The last known was an address in Oakland, downtown, near Jack London Square.

"One last thing," Tremblay said.

"No. No more favors. This was the last thing." Pino pointed at the screen.

"I need a ride to Oakland."

"Fuck. Are you kidding me? It's rush hour, the bridge'll be packed. No way."

Tremblay sat there, not moving, a blank expression on his face.

After about a minute, Pino said, "Oh, all right. Let's go. I'd be happy to dump you in someone else's jurisdiction."

CHAPTER TWENTY-SIX

Carl crisscrossed through the Mission. Every few blocks he would dial Peters' number, but it sounded like the phone had been turned off. He was acutely aware of the fact the police were now looking for him. He was sure Panzer had remembered the make and model of the car from the other night. It was dusk now and soon it would be night, every minute that crawled by announced to him he'd never see Peters again.

Steven sat across from him, patient and silent. He'd completely given over to the sensation that his fate was out of his hands. He felt like an old Styrofoam cup bobbing up and down in a turbulent ocean. Playing over in his mind regrets of ever taking the weed and heading out for the city, he went through each detail as though he could have changed his fate. I never should have said I'd move the smoke. I never should have taken Greyhound. I never, ever should have gotten in the truck with Quinn. He remembered thinking at first that Quinn was a cop. He wished he were a cop. He'd be safe in a holding cell in Willits. He was no cop, that's for sure. He was a monster.

Carl broke the tension. "Well, son...I don't think I can stall this thing much longer. I'm going to have to go into the Hall of Justice and have a talk with Detective

Panzer. My friend's life is apparently in jeopardy. I knew this, I guess, I was just hoping against hope."

"If that's the case, why are you stalling?"

Carl reached for his mints, but they weren't in their usual pocket. "To be honest, I'm getting a bad feeling about Panzer. I've known the man for years, but, really, he's only been an acquaintance. In this business, you have to rely on your instincts. My gut tells me that my partner is still alive and that my friend on the force may be no friend at all."

"I should have listened to my gut and stayed where I was. If I never got on that bus, maybe none of this would have happened."

"Ha! No, it would have happened. It just would have happened without you. But you got to look at it from the other side. If you weren't here, maybe Teresa wouldn't still be alive. Maybe you're her only hope, the wild card that puts Quinn's plan into a tailspin."

"But he's got her. We don't even know if she's alive, we don't know if your friend is alive either. We're just driving in circles."

"That's the trick to positive thinking, son, it takes a little effort sometimes. You have to forgive yourself for the situation you're in and have faith in your ability to do what's right. You have to look at what's before you, and deal with it the best you can."

Steven let that hang for a moment before asking, "Why didn't you tell your police friend about me? I heard you on the phone; you didn't mention my name once."

Carl sighed as he turned another corner. "I don't know. I figure there'll be time to sort all this out later.

No need to throw another log on the fire."

"Log on the fire?"

"Sorry, it's the best I could come up with. Keep an eye out for that Ford now."

The ride across the Bay Bridge was slow. It was rush hour and it seemed the city's entire population was funneling onto the bridge. Tremblay kept taking small sips from his bottle of Maker's. When traffic came to a standstill before Yerba Buena Island, he suggested Pino hit his lights and sirens. Pino told him he was getting drunk and to lay off the whiskey.

Tremblay responded by keying into his bag of coke once more.

"What are you doing, man? This is a police vehicle. What if somebody sees you?"

"If they see it's a police vehicle, they'll know to mind their own fucking business."

"You're a fucking liability, Tremblay. No wonder they gave you the boot."

Traffic began to break up slightly as they traversed the tunnel in the middle of the Bay Bridge.

Pino asked, "What the fuck do you think you're gonna do over there, anyway?"

"I'm meeting an old friend."

"At a junkie reporter's house?"

"It's the only place I know where he'll be."

"Who's the friend?"

Tremblay smiled. "Some son of a bitch from the old days. Before your time, youngster."

"This have something to do with what's going on with you in the city?"

Tremblay snickered, a dry hollow sound like an emphysema cough. "Oh yeah. This has everything to do with that." He patted his jacket for his cigarettes.

"Why you wanna go poking your nose further in the shit? Why the fuck don't you just leave town and hide, like you usually do?"

"Because this guy owes me. Big time. I'm gonna settle this shit once and for all. I'm gonna fix it so I'm outta hock to Richard and sink this fucker at the same time."

"Richard? You mean Alvarez? How's that work? He involved with these killings?"

They were on the Oakland side now, coming off the bridge. "You don't know the half of it."

"I don't know nothing 'bout it. Why don't you enlighten me?"

Tremblay sensed he'd said too much. Fucking whiskey. He looked at Pino and tried to read him. Cops were curious by nature and loved to gossip as much as gangsters, but...

"Take the first exit here, over on the right." Tremblay pointed toward the 880 Alameda off ramp.

"I know where I'm going," Pino said.

They got off the freeway and started to move through the streets toward the address Pino had looked up on the computer.

Tremblay told him to stop.

"We're not there yet."

"This is fine. I wanna walk, get some air."

Pino pulled the car to the curb. Before Tremblay could open the door, he told him, "Look, man, as a friend, I'm telling you: Richard Alvarez is a powerful man. He's got tentacles on shit you never expected. Forget the police department, he's got friends all the way up the ladder. The big chair at City Hall and upward. We're talking mayors, senators, you name it. If what you're about to do is gonna fuck him up, I seriously suggest you rethink your plan."

"As a friend? *As a friend?* You and me ain't friends, Pino. We're associates at best. You're just another bottom-feedin' fuck like me. Guys like Alvarez have the power because they got lucky. They got no bigger balls than us, they're not supermen. Fuck Alvarez and, thanks for the ride, but fuck you too."

Tremblay got out and slammed the car door.

Pino watched him walk away. He waited until Tremblay was one full block away, then he picked up his cell phone and dialed Bill Panzer.

Tremblay didn't notice that Pino stayed parked, he was making his own phone call.

"Carl?"

Carl's voice sounded far away. Tremblay heard the traffic in the background. This was good; Carl was still in his car and not with the police.

"I hear you haven't talked to the cops yet."

"How would you know that?"

"I told you, I'm not without my resources."

Tremblay pinched the cell between his cheek and shoulder while he stopped and lit a cigarette.

"I got some new information for you. You ready to copy an address?"

"Where are you?" asked Carl.

"I'm in Oakland, near Jack London. I'm on my way to a reporter's house. His name is Seth Friedlander. He's the guy Quinn's gonna use to bring down the old man."

"Alvarez?"

"Yeah, who d'you think? I'm close and I figure if Quinn and that little girl aren't already here, then they're gonna be soon. How long 'til you can get here?"

"What's this got to do with my partner? I want to know that he's safe. You have any word there?"

"Yeah, I got word," Tremblay lied. "I spoke to Alvarez. He still has him. He says he's holding him 'til Quinn is secured, then he says he's gonna release him to you if you two will fuck off outta town."

"He knows we can't do that. What is he, nuts? There're bodies piling up. This whole thing will be under scrutiny by a long and thorough investigation. Everything we're doing is going to come out. Doesn't he know that?"

"Of course he does, he's just trying to play you. Get you to come to him. He wants Quinn back in jail, he wants you and your friend dead, and—most of all—he wants the girl."

"Why? What does he need the girl for?"

"The girl is the key to his secret. He'll probably kill her too, but he can't afford to have her die at the hands of someone else. He doesn't want to leave any evidence around."

"Evidence?"

"The girl. She's the evidence he needs to hide. Shit, you really don't know what's going on, do you? Once he has her on ice, he can move forward."

"You're not making any sense."

"It'll all make sense to you soon. Get your ass over here."

"I want to know where my partner is," Carl said.

"I know where they're keeping him. I promise I'll help you get him out, but you need to come here first. If you go to the cops now, Alvarez is gonna know, believe me. He's already in touch with his friends on the force. Then he will kill him, stick him in the trash heap, no one will find even a hair on his head. This is what he does; he's an expert at making people disappear. He's been doing it for years. Trust me, I'm your only connection to Alvarez. We can do this, you and me. You get your killer, and you get your partner back. It's the only way."

"What do you get?"

"After we settle up with Quinn and your boy, Alvarez's world is going to crumble. That's it, that's what I get. I get out from under one of the biggest assholes in the history of assholes and I get to start living my life again. I get my freedom."

As soon as Tremblay said he was in Oakland, Carl had turned the car toward the Bay Bridge. Now he was at 9th and Bryant. Two blocks from the Hall of Justice; one block from the East Bay onramp. He had to make a decision. He tried to feel his gut, what it was saying, but his mind was racing, rational thoughts and emotions were colliding.

When he passed the light at 8th Street, he swung the car to the left and got onto the freeway.

"I'm on the way. What's the address?"

* * *

Alvarez was pacing, quietly cursing to himself in Spanish. He'd replaced the rice sack over Peters' head. Peters sat, slumped forward, with only his zip-tied arms behind the chair keeping him from completely collapsing. In fact, with the sack on his head, Alvarez had no idea if the man was even still alive. He'd worn himself out torturing the poor man, and was now convinced the young cop had no other information to offer.

Alvarez was debating brewing a pot of coffee or opening a bottle of wine when Manuel walked in and gave him the news. Tremblay was there with Carl and some kid, on Anza and Blake. He must have already been tailing them, said Manuel. They both followed Carl and the kid to the Mission. Then something happened to make them stop, either they spotted Manuel or maybe they got word about Quinn. When he circled the block, he saw them outside on the sidewalk talking to each other. They'd both been on the trail of Quinn and Teresa, he figured. If he didn't know better, Manuel said, he could have sworn they were working together.

"You don't know better, you stupid fuck. Of course they're working together. That shitheel Tremblay isn't picking up his phone. Fucking Gutiérrez has fallen off the face of the earth. You don't bother with calling—you wait until now to tell me this shit? What the fuck is going on?"

Manuel only shrugged. He knew better than to say anything at a time like this.

Alvarez's phone rang. The caller ID was coded, but he knew exactly who it was: Bill Panzer from the SFPD.

"*What?*"

"Hello to you too," Panzer said. "First off, I thought

you'd like to know we got your boy, Gutiérrez, down here at 850 Bryant."

"What for?"

"Right now? Murder. He was found at the scene of a homicide on Alabama Street about an hour-and-a-half ago."

"Homicide? Who's fucking dead? Tell me it's Quinn."

"No such luck. A woman was stabbed to death. Can't figure out what he was doing there, but he clammed up until he's lawyered up so we're gonna have to wait to find out."

"Shit."

"That's not all."

Alvarez didn't like Panzer's tone. The detective always sounded smug when he spoke to him. He'd like to squeeze that smugness out of him one day. Not today, he needed him today. But...one day.

"What is it?"

"I just got a call from a colleague of mine. He says he just dropped Tremblay off in downtown Oakland."

"You're kidding. Why didn't he arrest him?"

"On what charges? Being a prick?"

"Do you know where he left him?"

"I know exactly where. Before he dropped him, Tremblay had him run a name and address. The name was Seth Friedlander. My boy said he's a reporter at the *Chronicle*. Mean anything to you?"

Alvarez's throat tightened. "What was the address?"

Manuel stood at attention while Alvarez talked on the phone, stoically awaiting his next orders.

Alvarez walked into the back office and came out with his PPK .380. His favorite gun. He pointed it at the still rice sack over Peters' head and said, "I believe everything you've told me. You are useless to me now."

He fired once.

Peters' head recoiled, flipped up inside the sack. His head now hung at an unnatural angle, his obscured face pointing up at the overhead lights behind him. There was an exit hole in the back of the sack, but all the blood and brain matter was held inside. He was still.

"What now?" Manuel said.

"I need you to get over to this reporter's house in Oakland. But first, help me get him into the incinerator. I can't carry him by myself. Let's hurry, before he starts dripping."

CHAPTER TWENTY-SEVEN

"So that's it? I thought for sure there'd be a blood test or something. Shit, I could have done that myself," Quinn said.

"They didn't swab you in the joint?"

"Sure, but for some reason I thought this'd be different." Quinn was relaxed now, sitting between Seth and Teresa on the couch, leaning back with his arms stretched around both of them. "What's next?"

"Next I wanna ask Teresa some questions. That all right with you, Teresa?"

She didn't answer.

"Good," Seth said, without taking a breath. "I got some stuff worked up. Just to build some emotion. You know, how your life's been affected. What you're doing now to get by. I hear things have been rough on you."

She still wasn't speaking, but her brow became knotted. It was clear she had no idea what Seth was talking about.

Seth suddenly jumped up from the couch. "So...who wants a drink first? I got some beers just for the occasion. Quinn?"

"Sure, I never say no to a nice cold one. Or a warm one for that matter."

Seth disappeared through the doorway to the kitchen

and busied himself with the fridge and glasses.

Teresa finally spoke. "What the hell is he talking about?"

"Your story, baby. You're gonna be famous."

"What story?"

"I guess it's time to shine a little light here." Quinn took his arms from the back of the couch and leaned in. His face and tone became serious. "You're not who you think you are. That is to say, of course you're *you*. And everything about you is all you, but there's some shit about your past you don't know."

Teresa's expression said get on with it. She was tired of Quinn beating around the bush.

"Let's start with this. Your father, that controlling prick you've come to know as your father, is not really your dad."

"Excuse me?"

"Years ago, when your father—well, not your father—Ricardo Alvarez first came to this country, he was trying to build an empire. He was knee-deep in the drug business and he needed to have a place or two that could make him respectable. He needed legit businesses, not only to wash dirty cash and all that other shit, but because he wanted that respectability. He craved it; he just didn't know how to go about making it happen. The way he is, he did it the only way he knew how. It's his nature."

Quinn paused as Seth came back into the room and handed him a beer in a frosty pint glass. "Beautiful," Quinn said and took a grateful slug.

Seth set a glass down before Teresa too, but she didn't pick it up.

"Anyway," Quinn continued, "first it was the nightclub. You remember the club? Big disco place out in the Dogpatch on Indiana Street. You probably don't remember. There was nothing out in the Dogpatch then. It's all built up now, but back then, it was a shithole. He had this big ol' joint ready to start jumping, but the city was hanging him up. Zoning, permits, whatever. He needed someone at City Hall to grease the wheels. That's when he got close to one of the city supervisors. This guy, the supervisor, made the deal happen. Once he had the club going, he wanted to branch out. San Francisco is a goldmine for money laundering. An expensive city like this? Easy to move cash around. Some of his friends from south of the border wanted in. Next thing you know, Ricardo wants to open a few restaurants. Again the city hangs him up. Get in line kinda thing. So Richard has this supervisor introduce him to someone else on the board. A Chinese guy, his district was the Richmond."

"What's this got to do with me?" asked Teresa.

"I'm getting' to it. Hang on. So this new guy, the guy in the Richmond, he was already a crooked fuck. In with the triads or tongs or whatever you call 'em. He and Richard understood each other and they started a partnership."

Quinn stopped and lit a smoke and offered Teresa one. She took it and let him light it for her. Then he went on, "The Richmond guy, he had a wife, white girl—hot piece of ass. He didn't know it, but she was fucking around behind his back. Richard was fucking her, I was fucking her. Who knows who else. So the wife, she gets pregnant—not by her husband, the supervisor. She tells the guy that Richard is the real father. This is all real hush-hush. This guy is a powerful man, all ego, you know. He don't want nobody to know, figures it'll be too damaging to recover from—politically speaking. He thinks the baby is gonna come out half Mexican, not half Chinese. So Richard helps her hide out and have the baby. I have a hand in that, too, and while she's hiding out—gestation hibernation, I called it—she tells me, guess what? *Boom*—I'm the real father. This shit blows me away. I'm trying to figure out what to do. 'Cause when the baby comes out, the truth is gonna come out, too."

Teresa's eyes are welling up. She knows where this is going.

"When the kid is born, Richard gets all hot under the collar. He can't stand I fucked her, even though she's somebody else's wife. He knows what's up and he has the mother taken care of."

Quietly, Teresa asks, "Taken care of?"

Quinn puts his index finger to his temple and pantomimes pulling a trigger.

"Yeah, taken care of. The chick is history. The poor politician has to scramble to find a way to explain why his wife disappeared. Nobody ever found out; it's *still* a cold case file."

Teresa felt a pang in her stomach, a sickness welling up. The story she'd been told about her mother had been a lie. It'd all been a lie. The idea she'd clung to, no matter how far-fetched, was now crushed. Her mother was not out there somewhere lost in a bag of dope. Any hope of a distant reconciliation was now gone. The terrible feeling in her gut was the punch of truth.

Quinn continued, the shock blanching Teresa's face not slowing him down. "Anyway, while he's doing this, the first guy I told you about, the first guy from the Dogpatch, he figures it out. Soon he's holding it over his fellow supervisor. It's like he's got two votes on every-thing because the Chinese guy has to do whatever he says."

"I'm that girl?"

"You got it, kiddo."

"And…he had my mother…killed?"

"Yep."

She looked at him a moment. Looking at his blue eyes, his white skin.

"And you're…" She let it hang.

"Yes, again. I'm the guy. I'm your real father."

Teresa looked as though she'd be ill. Her face became more blanched than it already was.

Seth said, "Take a sip of your beer. It'll be all right, just hang on."

"Hang on?" Teresa said. Then to Quinn, "Hang on to what? You're telling me that you're my father. After all the shit you dragged me through today, the shit I saw you do? I'm supposed to be happy about this?" She finally broke down and started sobbing.

"Sssh, it's all right. Let 'er out." Quinn tried to com-fort her by patting her on the back but she pushed his hand away.

"Why? Why now? Why are you telling me all this?"

His voice grew more stern. "Because your father—Richard—is a prick. I fucking hate him and it's time for him to pay. He kept me from you. He stuck me in a hole. He wanted me to die in prison. Fuck him, that's what I say. Look what he did to you. Did he ever treat you like his daughter? Like flesh and blood?"

Teresa silently shook her head.

"I didn't think so. When this comes out, it's going to bring him down. He'll be finished."

"Why would anyone care now?"

"Tell her," Seth said.

Quinn stubbed out his smoke and took a long slow pull off the pint glass.

"Because, that wasn't the end of it. This supe in the Dogpatch, he knew the score, and he held it over the other supervisor's head. This went on for years. About nine years ago, this Chinese guy has finally had enough. He wants out from under this guy. So he goes to Richard, wants it taken care of. So this prick that calls himself your dad has me and another one of his lackeys take out this politician. It was a big deal when this guy went missing. The story went on for months. Fingers were pointing every which way. What was never suspected, was that the guy that put the hit on him, made him disappear, was another supervisor."

Teresa looked confused.

"That guy, the guy who was married to your mom *and* helped cover up her murder, the guy who had his fellow supervisor whacked and reaped the benefits, the guy who's been in bed with the bad guys since he was in short pants, his name is Ronald Woo."

It took a second for the name to register with Teresa.

"The mayor?"

Quinn sat smiling. No teeth, just a tight upturned smile. "One and the same."

* * *

It wasn't hard for Carl to find Tremblay. He was the only one out on the deserted streets of the rundown neighborhood. Tremblay stood on a corner a half-block up from the house. He was smoking a cigarette and had something in his hand. At first Carl thought it was a weapon, but as he pulled up he saw that it was an odd-shaped bottle. Tremblay took a short sip off the neck as Carl pulled to the curb.

Tremblay flicked his butt into the street and leaned into the driver side window. "Hey, how're you doin'? I see you still got the kid with you. Hey, kid."

Steven didn't say anything back. He could smell the alcohol on Tremblay's breath from where he sat. The booze didn't make him seem any less evil. More so.

"What's the deal?" Carl said. "They in there?"

"Not sure," Tremblay said. "There's only one way to find out."

"What's going to happen? Do you think we can just walk up and knock on the door and say, we're not cops and we don't have warrants, come with us?"

"I was thinking something a bit more, ah, proactive."

"I think it's time we called the police in. *Past* time."

"Too late for that. We go in like cops, arrest Quinn and hold him for your murder up in Calistoga. Shit, he'll get hung up on any of the stiffs he's left around the last few days. While we're waiting, we free the girl." Tremblay noticed Steven's eyes perk up. "Yeah, she's in there too. She's at risk, time's a wastin'."

"What about the reporter?" Carl said. "What's he got to do with this?"

"That's a little more complicated. We need to make sure he stays alive. He's the one that's got the goods on Alvarez."

"Stay alive?" Carl was wondering what Tremblay was really planning. "What goods?"

"Look, we don't have time to go into all this now. You brought a weapon, didn't you? You got cuffs and shit in the trunk? How about a badge? Tell me you got a badge."

"What are these *goods*? What the hell're you dragging me into here?"

Carl was getting annoyed, Tremblay could feel it. He decided to give Carl a little more of the story. "Open up and let me in."

Tremblay got into the back seat and asked, "Mind if I smoke?"

Ever since he quit, Carl hated to be in close proximity to tobacco smoke. He said, "I'd prefer it if you didn't."

But Tremblay was already lighting up.

"This all started years ago," began Tremblay. Tremblay told the story from his perspective, leaving out the details implicating him in any crimes. To him, the equation was simple. Go in, get Quinn, free Teresa, save the reporter and the story. Once they'd secured Quinn and the story, they'd call Alvarez and get him to release Peters. If the cops got there first and arrested Quinn, the story would surely come out, but Peters' fate would be in question. At least this is what he told Carl.

Carl was having trouble believing it: the story about the San Francisco mayor, the motivations of his new *de facto* partner, and, if any of it were true, that they could pull it off.

Steven sat in awe of the two men. Most of what Tremblay told them happened when he was a baby and then a child. He had no idea what a supervisor did or what money laundering was. It seemed that Tremblay spoke partially in code and partially in the jargon of old black and white movies. And yet, the man seemed completely comfortable divulging these secrets in front of him. Steven felt an odd sense of fraternity. He was being treated as an equal in the car, a part of the machine, the plan.

When Tremblay's story was done, Carl asked him, "Why didn't you tell me who Oulilette really was?"

"We weren't sure if he had a copy of the tape."

"What tape?"

"The evidence. The thing Alvarez had him keep outta the trial. It was a time-stamped security tape that had Quinn at the restaurant at the time of the crime. Airtight alibi. Quinn woulda walked."

"And for that you get a vineyard up in wine country?"

"It was an important piece of evidence. If Quinn got off then Alvarez was going down. But it wasn't just that. There was a lot of other shit, too. Julian had been in Alvarez's pocket for a long time. He helped quash a bunch of cases. You can't do what Alvarez does without having friends on both sides of the fence."

Tremblay paused to let his words sink in. He took one last pull from his bottle of Maker's and said, "Gentlemen, let's fuckin' do this while we still have the choice."

Steven wasn't sure what that meant.

Carl wanted to say something more, too. He wanted more information, more details. He wasn't ready to commit himself to such an obviously rogue plan. But before he could say anything, Tremblay opened the door and got out of the car.

He leaned back in through the open door and handed Steven the nearly empty bottle of Maker's. "Here, kid. Hang on to this. I'll be back in a few minutes."

Tremblay stood up straight and slammed the car door harder than he intended. He started down the block toward the house.

Steven looked at Carl, who watched Tremblay barrel down the sidewalk.

"Damn it," Carl said. He got out of the car, too. He went back to the trunk and got out his revolver and cuffs and whatever else he could find in the few seconds he had. He shut the trunk, but before chasing after Tremblay, he came round to the passenger window and leaned in.

"Stay here," he told Steven. "Don't move a muscle. We're going to be back in a few minutes. It may seem like longer, but I'll make it as fast as I can. Hopefully I'll be coming back with your girlfriend, so..." Carl felt the urge to tell the kid that he loved him, that somebody loved him. He didn't know why, he only wanted the kid to know that he was a good kid, that all this wasn't his fault. "Just stay put."

The old man looked scared. It scared Steven too, but there was something about the way he called Teresa his girlfriend that made him feel warm and okay. Steven nodded and smiled.

"Don't worry, I'll be here."

CHAPTER TWENTY-EIGHT

Tremblay was already at the broken wooden gate that separated the house's sidewalk from the city's. It hung off its hinges, pushed inward. It looked as though it'd creak if it were touched, so Tremblay slipped around it, squeezing his bulk though the open space without much finesse.

It gave Carl time to catch up. "Tremblay, what in the hell? Slow down. What are you doing?" Carl slipped past the gate with much more ease.

Tremblay turned and held up an index finger to his smiling lips. He waved for Carl to follow him. Before climbing the two short cement steps that led to the front door, Tremblay reached to his right side and pulled the police-issue 9mm Glock he had tucked into a belt holster. He held it behind his back.

"Wait," Carl said. He tossed him one of the pairs of cuffs he'd taken from the trunk of his car. "If you're going to do it, do it right."

Tremblay took them and tucked the cuffs into the side pocket of his suit jacket. He whispered to Carl, "You ready? You got your piece?"

Carl reached into his own pocket and drew the .38 revolver that had served him so well during the past thirty years.

Then Tremblay knocked. He didn't use the heavy police knock; he tapped lightly with his left hand. Carl guessed he wanted it to sound like it might be friends at the door.

Teresa had asked Seth for some privacy—and a glass of water. Seth looked at Quinn to see if that was okay. Quinn nodded and said, "Sure. I guess it's been a while."

Teresa asked where the bathroom was and Seth pointed down the hall.

"Anyway out from there?" asked Quinn.

"Not unless she's as small as a rat."

Quinn called after Teresa. "Leave the door open."

When she was out of the room, Seth asked Quinn, "She fixin'?"

"You judgin' or jonesin'?"

Seth looked embarrassed.

Then came a knock at the front door.

"Who's that?" Quinn said.

"Shit, I dunno. Maybe it's my friend Paulo. Let me get rid of him."

"Make sure you do. What the fuck you got friends coming over for at a time like this?"

Seth held his hands out, palms up, gesturing for Quinn to stay calm and stay seated. "Okay, okay, okay. It's all right. I'll take care of it."

Seth walked toward the front door as Quinn fixed an eye down the hall where the bathroom was. Before he reached the door, Seth heard another light tapping.

He cracked the door just a little and said, "Paulo? Now's not a good time."

* * *

As soon as he saw the doorknob turn, Carl watched Tremblay point and ready his weapon. When light from inside fell through the crack, Tremblay shoved the door with his shoulder and fired low, at the knee or thigh of whoever was behind the door.

The bullet traveled through the wood and hit pay-dirt; they heard a painful howl from the entrance to the house. Tremblay shoved the door harder and knocked the injured man to the floor. He stepped inside over Seth's feet.

Seth was writhing on the floor with both hands squeezing his wound, a nasty hot hole above his knee.

"Cover him, Carl."

Tremblay didn't point the gun down or even look at Seth. He held the 9mm up at eye level and kept moving inside. He was searching for Quinn.

He moved up the short wall that separated the entrance from the living room. He turned the corner slowly, poking the barrel of the 9mm out first. He could see the couch now—empty. There were three beer glasses on the coffee table and a pack of Marlboro Reds. The glow of a silent TV flickered and shifted onto the couch cushions. He listened. Nothing but the sound of the skinny little fuck groaning in the foyer. Tremblay saw a staircase behind the couch that led upstairs. There had to be a kitchen to the left, but he couldn't see it without exposing himself.

With the barrel of his gun going first, he nosed around the wall into the living room. From there he could see the kitchen. Stove, fridge. No shadows, no movement.

Carl entered the house now and saw the man rolling on the floor with a pool of blood gathering below him. Thigh wound. Artery maybe.

"Ssh. It's going to be all right. Sit tight, there'll be help on the way. You're going to be okay."

But help wasn't on the way. Although he'd probably heard the shot, Steven had no cell to call 9-1-1 and Carl didn't want to chance lowering his weapon to make the call either. He stayed behind Tremblay, nearly straddling the injured man, but still covered behind the wall separating them from the main room. He watched Tremblay take another step forward.

He heard one word. A joyful—*Maurice!* A friendly greeting. A warm white flag.

Then a booming gunshot. Heavy caliber. Bigger than a .38. A .44 or a .45 at least.

He saw Tremblay fold in front of him. Gut shot. Instinct forced Carl back against the wall, although a wall like this was no protection from a gun like that. Somewhere in the rear of the house, a door slammed. For a moment, he thought Quinn had fled, that he was safe.

Then he heard Quinn's voice say, "Goddamnit."

And another boom accompanied by a bullet tearing through the wall inches from Carl's head. It shattered a small window beside the front door. Carl squatted down, out of breath with fear. The injured man was grabbing at his leg, pleading for help.

"Is your name Seth?"

"God, please. Help me."

"Keep squeezing your leg above the wound, Seth. Use both hands, that's it. I'm going to go get help. You just sit tight and stay awake. Can you do that?"

Seth nodded yes, but made a sound like a whimpering dog.

Carl rolled over and peeked around the entrance wall once again. Tremblay was still heaped on the floor. The room was empty. He heard footsteps going up the stairs, heard them clomping on the second floor. A couple of doors opening and closing, then the footsteps came bounding back.

"Seth? Seth?"

It was Quinn's voice. Carl glared at Seth. He didn't want him to make a sound, but that was impossible for a man in that much pain. He pointed his revolver at him and put an index finger over his lips.

Quinn said, "Maurice, you ol' son of a bitch. You still alive? I coulda sworn it'd be a heart attack that took you out."

Another loud shot. Quinn had executed Tremblay.

The living room behind Carl was silent again. Quinn had heard Seth's whimpers, Carl was sure of it. He could feel his presence. He heard the creak of the floorboards as Quinn stepped closer.

Carl made his move; he rolled out and took aim. In the same moment, Quinn was aiming at the wall, correctly assuming it was where Carl was leaning. A fresh bullet tore through the wall right at the spot Carl had been resting his head. The sound of Quinn's cannon threw off Carl's aim and his shot went wide. He saw it hit the ceiling above Quinn's head.

From his position on the floor, Quinn towered over

him. It was the first time he'd seen him. The man was smiling.

Carl was taken aback. He froze for just one moment before trying to fire again. But in that moment, Quinn turned and fled down the back hallway. There was another sound of a door slamming.

He was gone.

The pool of blood underneath Seth was now enormous. The man was talking, but it was in bits of delirium. Carl tried to make out what he was saying.

"Go on, son. What is it?"

Something about a story, a flash drive. Firelight. Make sure he got it in. Pictures for the layout. Needed to ask the girl...Seth's voice drifted into a light, almost melodious mumble.

Seth fell unconscious.

Carefully, Carl got up. He moved to check Tremblay. No chance. There was a bullet hole right through his temple. It was sunburst with the burn marks of a close-range shot. Carl reached around to Tremblay's jacket pocket to grab his cell. He touched a plastic baggie, he pulled it out partway, saw it contained white power, and stuffed it back in. He tried another pocket and found the cell. He stood up, surveyed the room. Right there on the coffee table between the abandoned beer glasses was a flash drive. Carl pocketed that, too.

He pulled his own cell and began to dial. Nine— one—He remembered the boy waiting up the street. He ran to the front door and started toward the car. From his vantage point the car looked empty. So did the street. He kept moving, hearing the air whistle through his lungs. Maybe Steven was hiding down on the floorboards, he thought. He hoped. He reached the car and it was empty.

He climbed into the Acura, started the engine, and again took out his cell.

The back window exploded in a storm of glass. There was a bullet hole in the windshield in front of his face. He shoved his body down on the seat. He reached up and slapped the rearview mirror so he could see what was behind him. There was a car with the front door open and someone taking aim. They were using the front door for cover, just as he was trained to do. Carl could tell immediately it wasn't Quinn. It was the lunkhead bodyguard from the restaurant.

Carl, still trying to stay low in the seat, put the car in drive and pulled out. Another shot came through the broken-out back window. This one ripped through the driver's seat and through Carl's left shoulder. It was like a hard punch. He hit the gas. He'd only gone a few yards when the burn started. He pushed the accelerator down. Nothing he could do but drive. The pain was excruciating. He didn't even look back to see if the bodyguard was following. He took a hard right and raced down the block. The light was red, so he made another right. Where is the boy? he thought. Where is the girl?

Manuel didn't follow Carl. He got back in his Charger and pulled up to the address Alvarez had given him. He got out and ran to the door. It was blocked. He pushed his way in and saw it was obstructed by a man on the floor bathed in his own blood. The man's skin was whiter than white; he looked dead. He moved, gun drawn, to the living room. There, Tremblay lay on the floor. Brains blown out. Tremblay's Glock a few inches from his dead hand. Manuel squatted down and checked his pockets. A fat bag of blow, nothing else. He took the bag and Tremblay's gun and moved on through the rest of the house.

Alvarez had told him to find anything with the possibility of a story. Computers, flash drives, folders, anything. He knew time was running out. The police would probably arrive any minute. Manuel went upstairs and checked the rooms there. Nothing. There was a small PC in one room, he yanked its tower from the cords and took it downstairs and set it by the couch. In the kitchen, he spotted a laptop sitting on the table. He tossed it on the couch by the PC.

Steven had watched the two men go up to the door. Only seconds later he heard a gunshot. He sat terrified, ears peeled for more reports. Then he saw her. She was running out the mouth of the alley to his left. Legs pumping, arms flailing. She was alone and moving as fast as her body would carry her.

He scrambled from the car and shouted, "Hey." She didn't slow, she was at the end of the block now. Steven started running after her. It was all he could do. He pushed his body as hard as he could. She darted across the street and started up the next block. He followed. She was slowing down. He was gaining.

"Teresa," he called. And then tried, "It's me."

She kept moving, her heavy boots beating down on the cement. More gunshots now, sounding more distant.

Her head kept turning from side to side as she looked for a new direction to dart.

Steven kept up his sprint. His lungs began to burn. Finally, almost four full blocks from where they'd started, he yelled, "Please, wait. It's me, Steven."

She stopped and turned. As soon as she saw him her eyes welled up. She doubled over, wheezing and panting as he trotted and closed the last few feet between them.

Both of them now, facing each other, hands on their hips, gasping for breath. They looked into one another's eyes with amazement.

"You're okay," Steven said.

"What the fuck are you doing here?"

"I'm looking for you."

She rolled her eyes, grabbed him by the hand and pulled. "Let's go. We've got to keep moving."

CHAPTER TWENTY-NINE

Quinn ran to where the alley met the street. He saw no sign of the girl. No sign of anyone. He ventured across the street into the next alleyway. Still nothing. He tried to think like a nineteen-year-old junkie girl, but that wasn't working for him either. He slowed his pace, listening hard for footsteps, bushes rustling, anything.

Then came the sound of a gunshot. Then another. A high rev of an engine.

Weighing his options, he decided. The girl was alive. That's what he wanted. She'd have to fend for herself for the time being. Now he needed to keep the story alive. He turned and retraced his steps back to Seth's house.

When he reached the back door, he could tell there was movement inside. No lights or sirens, so it wasn't the OPD, not yet anyway. He drew the .45 from where it was lodged in the small of his back and stepped lightly toward the backdoor.

That old fuckin' cop is looking for the story, thought Quinn.

He crept up to the back entrance off the kitchen. There was no mistaking Manuel in the living room. Big, lumbering Manuel. A laptop pinched under one arm and his two hands clasped around a PC tower. Quinn could tell Manuel thought he was alone, but also in a hurry.

Smart fucker, he's taking all the evidence.

Manuel passed through the front door and Quinn came right into the main room behind him. Tremblay was still on the floor; Seth had bled-out in the foyer. No body of the old cop.

He stayed behind the wall that he'd shot at moments before and watched Manuel load the Charger. Both computers went into the trunk. Manuel slammed the trunk and returned to the house. Quinn drew back into the kitchen.

Once inside, Manuel pulled out his cell and dialed. One touch. Last call made.

"Hey, it's me. No Quinn, he's gone…I saw the old man pull away, but he was alone, I'm pretty sure…I don't know, I took everything I found…I don't even know how to begin to burn down a house…all right, all right. I'll call you back when I'm on the way."

Manuel hit the end call button and said "Fuck."

Quinn came from the kitchen, .45 extended before him, and fired once. Head shot. Manuel dropped, all his weight thumping onto the floor. Eyes wide and dead. Quinn leaned over him, picked up the cell from the floor, and went through his pockets.

In Manuel's pants he found keys, and cash folded and wrapped with a rubber band. He felt around to the small of his back and found his PPK. In his jacket he found two extra clips and something else.

"What's this now?" Quinn said. He yanked out the baggie of blow. "Manuel, you been getting high on your own supply?" Quinn stood, pocketed the coke and the phone, slipped the PPK into his waistband, and went outside to the Charger with Manuel's keys in one hand and the .45 in the other.

He stood for a moment before he got into Manuel's car. He listened for sirens. There were none. Nice town, Oakland.

He drove slowly through the surrounding streets, still hoping to spot the girl. After a few blocks he gave up and started looking for a freeway onramp.

Carl pulled over. The pain from the bullet-hole through his shoulder was almost too much to bear. He took out his phone and dialed 9-1-1. First he told the operator the address of Seth's house and said there had been a homicide. There was a seriously injured man in the doorway of the house. No, he was not on the premises. No, he could not return. No, he would not give his name. Not yet. The usual barrage of questions followed. Carl said he'd have to call back, he promised. Then he hung up. He held the phone in his hand for a moment and turned it off.

He tossed it on the passenger seat beside Tremblay's phone. He wondered if he should have called from Tremblay's number, but decided he wanted that line live. It was a hotline to Alvarez.

He was lost now, driving in circles, trying to find the kids. That's what they were, kids. Mixing them up with this psychopath and hurling bullets over their heads didn't change what they were—children.

He wouldn't be able to drive much longer. He knew he should go to a hospital—if he knew where one was. But as soon as he entered an emergency room, it would be all over. Peters, Steven, even Teresa; there'd be nothing he could do for them. So he kept driving and looking and trying to find his bearings.

He'd wandered too many blocks from the scene of the crime, and was sure he'd lost them forever. Then he spotted two figures, barely shadows, disappearing around a corner at 2nd and Franklin. He U-turned.

As he turned, he saw them duck down between two parked cars. He powered down the windows and pulled up slow, shouting Steven's name.

It was Steven's head that popped up first. Then it slipped back out of sight.

"I see you, Steven. It's me, Carl."

Steven's head popped back up, then Teresa's. Carl winced a sigh of relief.

"Both of you, quickly, get in the car."

Steven sprang up and reached for the door handle, but Teresa stayed crouched.

"C'mon. Let's go," Steven said.

She didn't move.

"What's wrong?"

Teresa was looking past Steven at Carl. She was scared, but wore a defensive mask. She looked as though she was ready to fight.

"It's all right," Steven said. "I know him. He can help us."

Carl cut in, "I'm not kidding, you two. We have to move. As far as I know that maniac is right behind me. It wasn't too hard for me to find you and it won't be for him, either."

Teresa pursed her lips and crawled into the backseat.

The moment Carl turned the wheel, Steven saw that he was injured.

"Holy fuck. What happened to you? You're bleeding. Did you get shot?"

"It's nothing. Went right through."

Steven leaned forward and saw the whole front of Carl's shirt had been stained red. "Man, I dunno. It doesn't look like nothing. You sure you can drive?"

"Yeah, I'm sure."

"Maybe we should get you to a hospital?"

"No. Not yet. I have a plan. Just help me find a darn freeway onramp."

Alvarez made coffee while he waited for Peters' body to finish cremating. It was a solid two hours before a corpse was completely done. Making a pot of coffee had become something of a ritual to pass this time. He was alone in the crematorium. Gutiérrez was apparently in custody and Manuel wasn't answering his fucking phone, but he felt safe in the bunker of his funeral home. He always had. It was locked up, windowless, and underground. The silence down there soothed him. He started a throaty hum to a tune he knew from somewhere in his past. He couldn't remember where he'd heard it or what it was, it just always seemed to creep up at times like these.

The coffee was done long before the body and he poured himself a deep mug. He sat down in the same chair where he'd executed Peters and patted his shirt pocket for one of his favorite cigarillos. He drew one out and unwrapped it. The sweet rich smell helped quell the array of unpleasant odors in the mortuary.

He'd just lit it when his cell went off.

He looked at the screen. *T.* Code for Tremblay. He hit answer.

"Where the fuck are you? You better have some good news for me, you shit."

Carl said, "Things didn't go as planned."

"Who is this?"

"I'd like to speak to my partner."

"Aah, Mr... I've already forgotten your name. Carl, is it?"

"I just want to know that he's okay. Then we can talk."

"Oh, he's okay. He's fine. Tell you what, you can talk to him when you pick him up. I understand you borrowed his car."

"I have Teresa with me."

Alvarez fell silent. It was a curveball.

"Where are you, Carl?"

"Never mind where I am. Tell me where I can pick up my partner."

"Sure. C'mon over. Who are you with? I'd like to know if I need to set up a cheese plate."

"I'm alone. Just me and the girl. Where is Peters?"

"You expect me to believe that you haven't enlisted the help of the police? Are you playing Batman, Carl?"

Carl didn't like the way his name sounded when Alvarez said it, as though it curdled in the back of his throat like sour venom.

"Believe what you want. I told you who I'm with. I'd like to come and get my partner now."

"And you'll bring the girl?"

Carl was crossing the Bay Bridge while he talked to Alvarez, the skyline of San Francisco rising up on his right. He looked into his rearview at Teresa sitting in the backseat. She had her head against the window and was staring out at the bay. He was sure she was listening to everything he said.

"Yes."

"Call me back from this number when you're at, oh I don't know, say Geary and Arguello and I'll give you the address. I'll make sure your friend is ready. I don't want to spend a lot of time chit-chatting."

Alvarez was about to ask about Tremblay's fate, but Carl had already hung up. He sat back down with the cell in his lap and picked up the coffee mug. He loved the smell of the cigarillo when it blended with hot coffee.

He wasn't sure how he was going to deal with the old cop once he arrived. He only knew an opportunity to get the girl in his crematorium was too good to pass up. It'd solve so many problems. The article the reporter had threatened to write could be quashed as slander. His unfortunate death could be blamed on a pattern of misadventure. Tremblay's reputation was so sullied it'd be no problem to spin him into the mix. Two disgraced men on drugs found dead in an Oakland slum? How hard could that be to sell?

But, if he was going to do this right, he was going to need help.

He set down his coffee and dialed Manuel.

Quinn fled Seth's house when he heard sirens approaching. He hoped Manuel had done a thorough job picking up all the fragments that contained the story. The last thing he grabbed on the way out were the two tiny vials that contained the DNA swabs he and Teresa had given.

Now it was time to find Alvarez. He wandered briefly through the streets of Oakland, almost taking a wrong turn into the tunnel to the island of Alameda, before he found a freeway ramp marked San Francisco.

Quinn enjoyed testing the power and speed of Manuel's new Dodge Charger.

As he approached the Bay Bridge toll plaza, he felt around for cash and dug out Manuel's wad of bills. All twenties. He handed a bill to the toll-taker and smiled at her when he received his change. When he got onto the cantilever section of the bridge, he moved over to the right lane so he could enjoy the lights of the city.

Manuel's phone went off. The ringtone sang an unintelligible pop song in Spanish. He let it go for a moment before he saw the caller ID read out the letter *A*.

"*Yello?*" answered Quinn.

"Manuel?"

The voice on the line sounded suspicious, guarded. Quinn recognized it instantly. His old boss, Richard Alvarez.

"*Buenos noches*, Ricardo."

The line went quiet. Quinn could only imagine the look on Alvarez's face.

"You looking for Manuel, Richard? Word on the street is he quit the business. But don't worry, what you sent him to pick up? I got it. It's safe and sound."

It took another moment, but Alvarez said, "I sent him to pick up the girl. And that, you don't have."

"Now, how would you know that?"

"Because I do."

"Impossible. Don't bullshit a bullshitter, Richard. I just left her, she's fine."

"I know she is. She's on the way to see me. She wants to forgive me and put all this behind her. She don't want no stories bringing up the past and making her life more trouble than it already is." Alvarez paused for a moment, then added, "She's afraid of you, Quinn."

Quinn tightened his lips across his teeth. It was too great a risk to call his bluff.

"Fine. Let's meet. You can have your story and let me take Teresa."

Alvarez laughed. "Why? If I have her, I have everything. You have no story. I know what you think in that twisted brain of yours, but she is my daughter. I raised her, Quinn, not you. What are you thinking, you're going to take her away and play daddy? Bring her up right? You and I both know you'll be dead or back in prison by morning."

Quinn hit end-call and dropped the phone between his legs.

CHAPTER THIRTY

Quinn powered the Charger over the bridge, shifting lanes and pushing the car as fast as the law allowed. He didn't want to get pulled over, not now.

He was trying to decide what exit to take, what approach he should use to try to find Alvarez, when he pulled up on the right side of a green Acura. He saw the profile in the Acura's passenger window, and it almost didn't register.

The boy. *Steven.* The kid was looking straight ahead and didn't see Quinn driving beside him. Quinn didn't know if he wanted to kiss him or kill him.

He let his foot off the accelerator and eased back and stayed on the car's right. There was Steven, no doubt about it. Twenty-five feet ahead of him. A head poked up from the backseat, too. He couldn't say for sure, but his gut told him it was Teresa. What he couldn't tell was who was behind the wheel.

The Acura signaled right and took the ramp to the central freeway. Quinn followed. They were heading to Fell Street. Quinn's plan had been made for him. He should have known Alvarez was bluffing.

The freeway ended at Octavia Street and Quinn was now one car-length behind them. Whoever was driving was oblivious to his tail. They started their short convoy up through the timed lights of Fell Street. At the crest of the hill, the car between them made a left. Quinn was now inches from the Acura's bumper. He was sure it was Teresa in the backseat. As they passed under the streetlights, her greasy dyed mop was unmistakable.

Steven asked, "What do you plan to do?"

Carl was honest. "I can't say that I know for sure. The best I can think of is when Peters walks through that door, as soon as he's clear of Alvarez, I shoot the son of a bitch."

"Is that legal?"

"No, but at this point, I don't know how else to end this thing. I have to make sure Peters is safe. If he doesn't come out that door, I don't know what I'll do." He glanced in the rearview at the backseat. "How you doin' back there, young lady?"

"Shitty. I'm sick. I'm tired. And I want to get out of this car."

"It won't be long now. Just hang in there."

Carl put his left hand on the wheel and sucked air loudly through his teeth as the pain in his shoulder burned through him. With his right hand he drew the .38 from his hip and handed it to Steven.

"Son, you know how to load this thing?"

It was the second time in four days that Steven had held a gun. Again, he was surprised at its weight. "No, I don't think so."

Teresa spoke up from the back. "Lemme see it. I'll do it. Where're the shells?"

"Steven, in the glove box there's a box of shells.

Beside it you should see two speed loaders."

"I thought you kept this stuff in the trunk?"

"Just open the damn glove box, Steven."

Steven did. Inside he found two boxes of shells. "Which ones?"

"The ones that say thirty-eight. The others are for a nine. Hand them back to your friend."

Steven passed the gun and the shells over the seat.

"Now the speed loaders."

"What's a speed loader?

"Just what it sounds like. They're little round metal things. Feel around for them."

Teresa went about her work. They kept on, flying through the timed lights on Fell Street. The panhandle was on their left when Teresa said, "Get into your right lane. We're going to make a right at Stanyan up here."

"How close are we to Geary and Arguello?"

"Close," she said.

When Alvarez was finished loading his own gun, his precious PPK, he placed a call to Bill Panzer.

Bill answered with the characteristic gruffness of a homicide cop. "Panzer."

"Bill, it's me. Can you tell me if you've heard from our friend from Calistoga yet?"

"That son of a bitch has gone rogue. He made a semi-anonymous call to the OPD about some killings there about forty minutes ago."

"If it was anonymous, how do you know it was him?"

"I heard the tape. It was him all right. If you hear

from this jackass, you let me know. We'll take care of him. He's stacking up charges like a regular gangster."

"My only concern is finding my daughter."

"Maybe you should've been looking for her last week before the shit hit the fan, eh, Richard?"

Alvarez hung up. He climbed the stairs from the basement to the main floor where there were windows to watch out of.

It was less than two minutes before his phone rang again.

Carl pulled off Fulton onto a side street named Parsons. He didn't want to get too close to the meeting spot in case Alvarez had people on the corner waiting for him. He hit the redial button.

"It's me. I'm here. Let me talk to Peters."

"Let me talk to the girl."

"No."

"I guess we're both going to have to trust each other."

"Tell me where you are."

"Why don't you tell me exactly where you are, and I'll guide you in. If you don't mind, I'd like to stay on the phone with you 'til you get here."

"All right," Carl said.

Alvarez overheard Carl ask someone about their location. Then he heard a girl's voice say Fulton and Arguello. It was Teresa's voice, it had to be. The old man was honest, at least.

"Drive out Fulton. Toward the beach. Tell me each block you're at and I'll tell you where to turn."

Carl held a finger to his lips to ensure the silence of

his passengers and then hit speaker phone. He turned the car around on Parsons, took a right, and started out Fulton, slowly.

"Second Avenue," he said.

"Keep going." Alvarez's voice sounded playful as though he were enjoying a game of warmer and colder with a child.

Carl drove slowly so he could follow Alvarez's instructions. There was only one set of headlights behind him and they slowed as much as he did.

"Fourth Avenue."

"Keep going."

They went on like this until 8th Avenue. Then Alvarez told Carl to make a right on 10th. Carl made a right at the light and crawled up the block.

"Keep coming," Alvarez said. "You're not there yet."

Carl went two more blocks in silence. He watched his rearview. The headlights turned at 10th Avenue, too. They hung back one full block.

"I just passed Anza. You got somebody following me?"

"There's no one following you," Alvarez said dismissively. "When you get to Geary, take a right."

Carl did as he was instructed. When he reached the end of the block, Alvarez told him to make another right.

Alvarez asked, "Who's the guy in the front seat?"

"Is that you behind me?"

"I told you, there's no one—" Alvarez's voice trailed off.

* * *

The McGovern Funeral Home sat on the corner of 10th Avenue and Geary Street. Alvarez had been sitting in the lobby, behind the stained glass, waiting for Carl to turn the corner. He spied the Acura as soon as it approached. He saw Carl behind the wheel, Teresa in back, and a young man in the front seat.

Then he saw Manuel's Charger. He had no doubt who was behind the wheel.

Alvarez's heart actually skipped a beat.

"Go around the block, Carl. I'm at the funeral home on the corner of Tenth and Geary. You just passed me. There's a side entrance on Tenth. Double-park. I'll be at the door."

Alvarez hit *end* and pocketed the cell. He drew his automatic from his waistband and racked the slide.

It took almost a full minute for the Acura to appear on the block again. Alvarez held the gun behind his back with his right hand, took a half-step out, and waved to Carl with his left.

Carl stopped the car in front of McGovern's side entrance and got out. He didn't move away from the car door, he stood in the street with the Acura and another parked car between him and Alvarez. He held the .38 out of sight at his side.

Carl called out, "Where's Peters?"

Alvarez kept his eyes up the block, not on Carl. "He's inside. C'mon in. Bring those two with you."

Carl followed Alvarez's line of sight and looked over his shoulder at the empty block.

"Peters first. Where is he?"

"Listen to me, I was wrong. You've been followed. Quick now, step inside, all three of you."

"No chance. We're staying right here. Send Peters out."

The Charger's headlights came round the corner at Anza. They crept up the block.

"Look, the man who followed you here. He's not one of mine. If he sees the girl, he's going to kill her. Her first and then you. Please, get in here before someone dies."

Carl looked up the block again and saw the Charger. He recognized it, not only from the Mission alley that afternoon, the one that trailed him and Tremblay, but as the vehicle that pulled up behind him in Oakland when he was fired upon. The Charger stopped fifty feet behind the Acura. It sat, idling. Traffic hurled by on Geary, but on 10th Avenue there was only the Charger and Carl's car.

"You set me up," Carl said. "Peters isn't here. I'll be back with the police."

But Alvarez wasn't listening; his eyes were locked on the Charger.

The door of the Charger opened and a man stepped out. The car's headlights were still on so it was tough to make him out, but Carl recognized Quinn instantly. Even at that distance, even at night, Quinn was unmistakable. Movie star good looks.

Quinn called out, "How y'all doin'?"

Without waiting for a response, Quinn lifted his gun above the edge of his open door and fired a shot at Alvarez.

Alvarez pulled back into the doorway when he saw Quinn draw, but not quick enough. The heavy caliber tore through the meat on the outside of his right shoulder.

Carl pointed his .38 at Quinn and took aim, but his wound slowed him and Quinn got off a shot first. Carl took a bullet in the chest. It slammed him back into the Acura's door and he fell to the pavement in a sitting position.

Quinn didn't pause to inspect the damage to Carl. He marched, .45 held out in front of him, from the Charger to the doorway of the funeral parlor.

There was blood, a bullet hole in the wood of the doorway, but no Alvarez. Quinn moved into the darkness inside.

Steven flopped over the driver's seat, tangling himself in the shoulder belt. He pulled himself closer to Carl. The bloodstain on Carl's shirt from the previous injury was now a slick red wetness. Steven couldn't see where Quinn's bullet had pierced him, only that the life was draining from his new friend.

"Are you all right?"

Carl's voice was a dry rasp. "No, I don't think so. Not this time."

"Sit still, I'll call for help. Just don't do anything."

"Do me a favor and feed my dog."

Steven was perplexed. "I don't know where your dog is?"

"Buford's a good judge of character. He's going to love you." Carl's eyes began to roll back into his head. "Peters can show you how to get there. Brenda will tell you where I keep the food."

Steven reached into Carl's jacket, peeling the coat away from the tactile mess of blood. The lining of his coat was also saturated. He pulled the cell and tried to light the screen through the red film covering the phone.

The backdoor slammed.

Steven lifted his head just enough to see Teresa run into the building.

"There she goes," Carl said. "You better go get her."

"I can't leave you."

"Why? I'm not going anywhere. Dial nine-one-one and drop that phone in my lap. Do the right thing, Steven. I'll be fine. Go get her. That's why you're here, isn't it?"

Steven dialed and dropped the phone, but before he pulled himself off the seat, he grabbed Carl's snub nose .38. The grip was sticky with blood.

Steven sat up straight and thumbed the clasp on his seatbelt. As he climbed out of the car, he eyed the side door of the funeral parlor. It was open and dark.

Quinn entered the basement. His senses sharp. Eyes straining for any glint of light, ears tuned for the slightest scratch of sound, nose trained for the scent of blood.

It was Alvarez's turf and he had that advantage in the dark. Quinn held fast as a hunter and waited.

A shot rang out and for a brief second the room lit up with a lightning flash. Quinn's ears echoed with the report.

Quick steps to his right across the linoleum. Footsteps behind him on the stairs. Quinn knew he had to act now.

Alvarez's voice taunted from the darkness. "Does she know, Quinn? Does she know it was you who pulled the trigger? You want to be her daddy now, but does she know it was *you* who killed her mother?"

The footsteps on the stairs stopped.

Quinn stepped silently to his left, squatted down, and took aim into the absolute black.

The voice called out again. "You think you can—"

Quinn fired. Four rounds. The quick blasts deafened the room.

The voice stopped. There was stillness. He could feel it.

A light came on. He swung his .45 around at the doorway to the stairs. Teresa stood there, framed by the doorjamb, one hand curled around to the light switch on the wall.

"It's true?"

Quinn held the sight on her for a few seconds, then lowered the gun to his side.

"It's done. I'm through. Get out of here before the police show. You're going to be all right. The story'll come out. You're a victim, everybody'll love you." He said again, "Everybody'll love you. I did this for you."

Steven stepped around Teresa and fired. Carl's .38 jumped in his hand. The bullet hit Quinn in the chest. He fired again. This one hit home in the stomach. Again he squeezed the trigger. A puff of drywall bloomed far beyond Quinn. Steven kept squeezing. The next shot hit Quinn in the face and drove him backward, his head taking all the inertia, until he lay flat on his back.

Steven pointed the barrel at the prone body, squeezing the trigger over and over, but the hammer slapped metal.

The dry metallic clicks were almost inaudible in their ringing ears.

"Fuck. Enough," Teresa said. She squatted down on her haunches and put her head in her hands. She teetered there a moment then fell flat onto her ass and began to sob, the father she'd always known on one side of the room and the father she'd just gained in front of her.

CHAPTER THIRTY-ONE

Steven wasn't sure if he heard sirens. The blast from the gunshots had deafened him. Then he heard the shouts of police, the authoritarian orders that sound just like they do on television. "Show me your hands...drop your weapon...don't move...get on the floor." Conflicting orders that so confused him, he froze and waited for someone to come from behind him and pluck the gun from his hand.

He felt the cool linoleum pushing against his cheek as a strong hand held his head on the floor while others pulled his arms behind his back, cuffing his wrists. His legs were kicked apart and he was told over and over not to move, not to resist. But he wasn't moving; he had no intention of resisting. He was exhausted, drained. It was finally over.

Black shoes and boots stomped around him. The police spoke in their obtuse language of numbers and codes.

Then came the paramedics, confirming the dead were dead and the living were uninjured. He heard Teresa telling someone at first to take it easy, and then to fuck off.

Steven was rolled over and someone pressed a stethoscope to his chest. He asked the medic, "How's Carl?"

The man said, "Who's Carl?"

Steven tried to tell him but the man told him not to speak before turning him back over onto his chest.

Steven lay quiet, letting the commotion ramp up around him. With his cheek pressed to the floor and his hands cuffed behind his back, he began to lose circulation. It put him in a state of semi-consciousness. The sounds pinged off the walls, far away. The brightness of the fluorescent light took on a hazy, opaque quality. The room continued to fill with people. Soon, instead of only the black shoes and boots, he saw the paper-covered feet of the crime scene unit. The covers looked like the ones surgeons wore while operating.

Then a pair of brown shoes stood in front of him. Close to his face. They were unlike any other shoes in the room. They looked expensive and they were cuffed by a pair of denim jeans.

The man in the jeans squatted down, but Steven still could not see his face.

"Roll him over."

Steven felt two sets of hands pull him again onto his back.

"Who the fuck are you?" the man said.

He leaned in close. So close that Steven smelled an odor of onion, or garlic, fouled in with his aftershave. Steven didn't answer.

"I asked who the fuck are you?" The man was chewing gum, rolling an old dead wad over and over between his molars. Still the stale food odor seeped through.

A disembodied voice answered. "His name is Steven

Mitchell. Twenty years old. He hasn't given a statement yet."

The man's gaze did not break. He said, "Well, Steven. I'm Detective Panzer with the homicide division. You want to tell me what the fuck went on here?"

Steven slowly shook his head. It was as though Panzer were a feral cat and, if Steven flinched, he'd be scratched and bit.

Panzer pointed and asked, "You know that man over there in the corner?"

Steven didn't try to look.

Panzer asked, "How about that one over there? There's two dead men here, young man. Do you know them? Did you shoot them?"

Steven didn't answer. He only asked, "Where's Teresa?"

"Teresa? Is Teresa a friend of yours? You come here with her tonight?"

When Steven didn't answer, Panzer stood up and said, "Give him a GSR swab and take him down to 850. Hold him as a suspect until I can get a statement from him. Oh, and don't let anyone else talk to him. I'm the lead on this one."

Two sets of arms hauled up Steven and led him away. As they brought him through the side door of the funeral parlor, he saw that the night was lit up with the roving strobes of red and blue. Police vehicles and ambulances crowded the street. The whole intersection of 10th Avenue and Geary had been shut down. There was yellow tape, crowd control, and even a satellite-dish-topped news vans on the perimeter.

No sign of Teresa and no sign of Carl.

Steven's cuffs were removed and he was asked to place his hands in front of him. Bags were then placed over his hands before they were re-cuffed. They stuck him in the back of a police cruiser and made him wait. No one else spoke to him. No one else looked at him.

When two officers finally joined him, climbing in the front seat with their radios crackling with activity, Steven asked, "What happened to Carl, the older man that was shot outside?"

The officers ignored him and pulled through crowd control and into the San Francisco night.

At the Hall of Justice, Steven was secured in an interrogation room. A friendly-looking policewoman came in to offer him a glass of water.

"I think I'd like to speak to a lawyer," Steven said.

Her expression turned cold. "You haven't been charged with anything. You don't need one yet."

"I'd like to go to the bathroom."

"That'll have to wait," she said.

He waited alone with the hum of the A/C droning on around him. There was a beehive of activity going on beyond the closed door, but no one came in to speak to him. Other officers came and performed their GSR swab, after which Steven was taken to a different room and fingerprinted.

"Am I under arrest?" he asked the technician.

He was told: "This is for identification purposes."

Then he was put back in the interrogation room.

It was a long time before Detective Panzer appeared in the room.

"Mr. Mitchell," he said as he pulled out the chair opposite Steven. He dropped a heavy manila folder on the table and drummed his fingers on it for a moment. He said a few perfunctory words regarding the date and whom he was speaking with, letting Steven know that the whole proceeding was being recorded. Then he said, "Let's start at the beginning. How'd you come to be at McGovern's Funeral Parlor this evening?"

"I'd like to speak to a lawyer."

"Before you talk to me?"

"Yes."

"Generally that's regarded as a bit suspicious, Steven. But, whatever you say. What's his number? I'll call him for you."

"I don't have a lawyer, I need one. Isn't there someone I can talk to?"

"What, you mean like a public defender? We don't provide those unless you've been charged with a crime. If you'd like to make a statement in regards to your involvement tonight, I could determine whether or not it'd be likely that you'll be charged, then we can get you someone to talk to."

"I was there. I can admit that."

"We know you were there. We were the ones that found you, remember?"

"Is Carl okay? Did he make it?"

Panzer's expression changed. "You know Carl Bradley? How do you know him?"

"Is he okay?"

"No, he's not okay. Carl's in ICU, barely hanging on. He's got a gunshot wound to the chest. Two actually. Did you fire those shots, Steven?"

"I'd like to go to the bathroom."

"Steven, if you don't start talking we're going to

charge you with obstructing a homicide investigation. You don't seem like the type to be involved with this kind of mess, but if you don't start telling us what's going on, this is going to turn very ugly for you real fast."

Steven didn't say anything. He held his eyes with Panzer's. It was a test of will. He thought about what Carl had said about Panzer. He didn't trust him, and now Steven could tell why.

"Have it your way," Panzer said. "Pending further charges, you are hereby being held for obstruction of justice." Panzer picked up the folder, stood up, and walked to the door. Before he opened it, he turned to Steven and said, "I guess you can have your lawyer now."

Steven was left alone again. At one point he yelled to the emptiness that he was going to piss his pants. Five minutes later, a uniformed officer took him to the toilet. The policeman left Steven cuffed while he urinated. Steven didn't complain. He'd waited so long to pee that he almost couldn't go. Almost.

He was returned to the room and cuffed to the table. It was almost two hours before the door opened again. A man walked in and introduced himself as Herman Chu, San Francisco County Public Defender.

"Have you given any statement, Steven?"

Steven said he had not.

"Do you understand the charges that have been brought?"

"Obstruction? I think so. But when the whole story comes out, I think it'll be okay."

Herman Chu looked confused. He opened a folder that he'd been holding under his arm. "Steven, it says here you've been charged with two counts of murder, possessing an illegal firearm, possession of a stolen vehicle, kidnapping, attempted murder, murder in the commission of a felony, and unlawfully discharging a firearm within the city limits."

Steven felt a pit in his stomach as Chu slowly read off the charges. It wasn't until hearing the last one that he decided it was a ruse, an attempt to scare him. "Discharging a firearm within the city limits? Are they serious?"

"Mr. Mitchell, murder in the commission of a felony is a capital offense. They are *very* serious. You could be looking at the death penalty here."

CHAPTER THIRTY-TWO

The case was slow to unravel at first. With the rapid rash of deaths in the city, the police were reluctant to link them all together. But within days it became apparent that they were all linked. Friedlander, the woman in the trunk of her own Mercedes and the junkie in her front seat, Joe-Joe, Sofia, Raja, and the unlucky guitar player, all of them were linked to Quinn and thus to the two murders at the funeral home and the missing, but presumed to be dead, Peters. Last to be linked were the killings of the wealthy vintner in Calistoga, Julian Hyde—also known as Oulilette, and the owner of Quinn's gray truck from Clear Lake. Over a dozen killings in less than a week were enough to keep reporters working double-time for months.

When Panzer's number was discovered on three of the cell phones at the scene at McGovern's, he was first removed from the case, then put on administrative leave. He remained tightlipped about his involvement, preferring a police department lawyer make his denials for him. Charges began to filter down. He would delay his day in court, but it was inevitable. His career-ending disgrace dwarfed even Tremblay's.

The story Friedlander wrote came out early in discovery. What they found on the hard drives of the computers in Manuel's trunk was duplicated on the flash drive in Carl's jacket pocket. It changed everything. It was leaked to the *Chronicle*, its original intended destination, and the entire city was enthralled and repulsed at the inner workings of corruption at city hall. Story after story came out in the fevered hunger for corroboration. The DNA tests Quinn and Teresa took were discovered, validated, and the twisted details of the paternity were revealed. The sordid tale of retired Assistant DA Julian Hyde and his servitude to Alvarez was laid out—how his loyalty was rewarded with a new identity and a vineyard in Calistoga. The media fed all of it to the public in bits and bytes, making the whole saga seem like a real-life soap opera. Then, in an information avalanche, the secret empire of Mayor Ronald Woo was exposed and scrutinized.

The mayor faced charges for conspiracy to commit murder, participating in a murder for hire, accomplice after the fact, and conspiracy to defraud civic government. As the trial was scheduled, more charges stacked up. And although he announced his intention to fight them all, the evidence was too damning. He was finished. The scandal had set in motion a zealous hunt through all his business activities and soon everything he'd touched was tainted. It was only a matter of time before the mayor himself was behind bars.

Gutiérrez was the state's key witness. Being the only surviving member of Alvarez's hierarchy—thanks to his early arrest on Alabama Street—he was quick to put pieces of the puzzle together for the prosecution and keep his own ass out of the fire. He was cleared, barely, of killing Sofia when it was shown that the call Quinn made on Sofia's cell was made outside the house and after her presumed time of death. The jury inferred that the killer might not have stayed on the premises—where Gutiérrez was found. Reasonable doubt. It was through his testimony that Panzer's full involvement came to light. Payoffs, hidden bank accounts, and tampered evidence. Also, Gutiérrez was the only one able to unlock the encrypted mysteries of Alvarez's financial shell games. He was Alvarez's tech wiz and he led investigators wherever they wanted to go. Assets were seized. Accounts were emptied. Soon the doors were padlocked on no less than fifteen restaurants and bars in the Bay Area.

Buried deep within Friedlander's files was Quinn's confession for the murders he committed on behalf of Mayor Woo and Alvarez. Late in coming to the fore, it was the most damning portion of Friedlander's document. The defense team for Ronald Woo said it'd never hold up in court, but it was too late. It detailed Quinn's involvement, gave the specifics of the killings committed years before, and worst of all, a play-by-play description of the murders.

The confession was a love letter from Quinn to his daughter. He begged for forgiveness while stating he was freeing her from the life she'd been shackled to. Toward the end of his confession, he said she could be alone now and that's what God intended. No web of lies holding her to a sadistic and cruel beast like Alvarez. He made his case for the bloodshed being a noble gift. A gift, he knew, he'd never be around to see her appreciate.

As for Carl, his recovery was slow. It took him a few days before he regained consciousness and the first thing he asked about was his dog, Buford. Eventually he was allowed to leave the hospital and the neighbor who'd been looking after Buford ended up looking after Carl too, stopping by daily to check on the retired policeman and his dog and drop off groceries and other household supplies. Carl, for the most part, stayed on his couch, flipping channels and eating eggs and trying not to buckle under the burden of guilt he felt for encouraging his old colleague—his *friend*—Peters to take the wild ride to San Francisco.

It was months before Steven saw Teresa again. It was at a pretrial hearing. They were both only witnesses now. During the endless hearings, depositions, and statements, their paths had come close, but never crossed. It was as though their handlers saw to it they stayed apart. But now, in the cold and crowded halls of the state courthouse, their eyes finally met.

She'd obviously cleaned up. Her eyes were clear and her skin blossomed with color. The two-tone dye job had been redone with a less radical, but still vivacious, red. Steven thought she was the most beautiful girl he'd ever seen. She was dressed up, as she'd been instructed by her lawyer. Gone were the torn jeans and the ragged T-shirt, replaced with a subdued beige skirt and blouse. However, Steven noted her witness stand outfit clashed with a pair of tough-looking, but new, boots.

"So you're clean, I mean, you're off the stuff."

"Shit, that happened in jail. Fuckin' awful. Worst way in the world to kick."

"You look great."

"I know," she said with a smile. "So do you. You look so grown up in a suit."

"It ain't me. I feel ridiculous."

"You kiddin'? When'd you ever think you'd see me in a skirt?"

"To be honest, I didn't think I'd ever see you again. Dress or no dress."

"Technically it's a skirt, not a dress. Speaking of no dress, we still got some unfinished business we started in the park."

Steven blushed. She was so bold, so comfortable in her own skin. He wanted to kiss her right there and then. It must have shown on his face.

"After this thing," she said. "What are you doing? I mean, where are you staying?"

"I'm back home with my parents in Humboldt."

"Living with the hippies, huh?"

"Yeah, sort of. It's not so bad. They let me come and go. I'm not a kid anymore."

Herman Chu waved to Steven from across the hall, letting him know the hearing was about to start. The heavy oak doors opened and people began to file into the courtroom.

"Maybe, if you want, you can come up there. Visit for a bit. My parents won't mind."

"And get outta this town? I thought you'd never ask."

She reached out to touch him, to let him know she was serious, that she'd be waiting for him after the hearing. On her forearm, he noticed a new tattoo. It was a cartoon red devil holding a pitchfork. Stenciled across the devil's chest was the word *Dad.*

ACKNOWLEDGMENTS

There's a lot of people I'd like to thank for this novel, but at the top of the list are my wife Cheryl, my daughter Lula, and my boys Logan and Dane, especially Dane, who had to listen to me yammer on about who was chasing who and who was going to die as I paced around in front of his screen and interrupted his gaming.

And thanks to Eric Beetner, for not only giving me a great cover (again) but putting up with my fickle back and forth while we created it. Great big thanks to Eric and Lance at Down & Out Books for showing me how a press should run. And Clifton Shoemaker for getting me a gun when I really needed it (for the cover, honest!). Thanks to Ro Cuzon, Joe Clifford, Steve Lauden, Bob Pitts, and all the other beta readers who took the ride with me. And of course, Rob Pierce, who can spot a typo at a hundred yards.

And a special thanks to my agent Amy Benson-Moore at Meridian Artists who always encourages me, and never says something can't be done.

Tom Pitts received his education firsthand on the streets of San Francisco. He remains there, writing, working, and trying to survive. He is the author of the novel *Hustle* and two novellas, *Piggyback* and *Knuckleball*. His shorts have been published in the usual spots by the usual suspects. Tom is also an acquisitions editor at Gutter Books and Out of the Gutter Online.

TomPittsAuthor.com

OTHER TITLES FROM DOWN AND OUT BOOKS

See www.DownAndOutBooks.com for complete list

By J.L. Abramo
Chasing Charlie Chan
Circling the Runway
Brooklyn Justice
Coney Island Avenue

By Trey R. Barker
Exit Blood
Death is Not Forever
No Harder Prison

By Eric Beetner (editor)
Unloaded

By Eric Beetner
and Frank Zafiro
The Backlist
The Shortlist

By G.J. Brown
Falling

By Angel Luis Colón
No Happy Endings
Meat City on Fire (*)

By Shawn Corridan
and Gary Waid
Gitmo (*)

By Frank De Blase
Pine Box for a Pin-Up
Busted Valentines
A Cougar's Kiss

By Les Edgerton
The Genuine, Imitation,
Plastic Kidnapping
Lagniappe
Just Like That (*)

By Danny Gardner
A Negro and an Ofay (*)

By Jack Getze
Big Mojo
Big Shoes
Colonel Maggie & the Black Kachina

By Richard Godwin
Wrong Crowd
Buffalo and Sour Mash
Crystal on Electric Acetate (*)

By Jeffery Hess
Beachhead
Cold War Canoe Club (*)

By Matt Hilton
No Going Back
Rules of Honor
The Lawless Kind
The Devil's Anvil
No Safe Place

By Lawrence Kelter
and Frank Zafiro
The Last Collar

By Lawrence Kelter
Back to Brooklyn

(*)—Coming Soon

OTHER TITLES FROM DOWN AND OUT BOOKS

See www.DownAndOutBooks.com for complete list

By Jerry Kennealy
Screen Test
Polo's Long Shot (*)

By Dana King
Worst Enemies
Grind Joint
Resurrection Mall

By Ross Klavan, Tim O'Mara
and Charles Salzberg
Triple Shot

By S.W. Lauden
Crosswise
Crossed Bones

By Paul D. Marks and
Andrew McAleer (editor)
Coast to Coast vol. 1
Coast to Coast vol. 2

By Gerald O'Connor
The Origins of Benjamin Hackett

By Gary Phillips
The Perpetrators
Scoundrels (Editor)
Treacherous
3 the Hard Way

By Thomas Pluck
Bad Boy Boogie (*)

By Tom Pitts
Hustle
American Static

By Robert J. Randisi
Upon My Soul
Souls of the Dead
Envy the Dead

By Charles Salzberg
Devil in the Hole
Swann's Last Song
Swann Dives In
Swann's Way Out

By Scott Loring Sanders
Shooting Creek and Other Stories

By Ryan Sayles
The Subtle Art of Brutality
Warpath
Let Me Put My Stories In You

By John Shepphird
The Shill
Kill the Shill
Beware the Shill

By James R. Tuck (editor)
Mama Tried vol. 1
Mama Tried vol. 2 (*)

By Lono Waiwaiole
Wiley's Lament
Wiley's Shuffle
Wiley's Refrain
Dark Paradise
Leon's Legacy

By Nathan Walpow
The Logan Triad

(*)—Coming Soon

CPSIA information can be obtained
at www.ICGtesting.com
Printed in the USA
LVOW12s0401220717

542222LV00002B/474/P